Holding up the sky

Holding up the sky

REBECCA ALASDAIR

SOUTHSCRIPT PRESS

CONTENT WARNING

 This book contains content that may be distressing to some readers. A full list of potential triggers is available on the author's website, which can be accessed by scanning the QR code at left: rebeccaalasdair.com.

for Nanna

this first one was always going to be yours

Shadow

I can't forget the last words my brother said to me.

You know I'll always be here for you, right?

They bounce around in my skull like an echo off the walls of a steel drum, only the sound never fades. Never. It's like he's trapped in there, screaming, and I'm the only one who hears.

No matter what happens next year, I'll be here.

But Miles didn't see the next year.

I always knew he would leave me one day, just not like that. Never like that. The universe couldn't be so cruel to someone like my brother.

I'll always be here for you. I promise.

It was the first time he'd ever lied to me. It was the last time he ever had the chance. He and Dad walked out the door, and they never came home again.

I remember it was raining that day. Spring flowers were in bloom, and fuzzy green growth sprouted from the trees like hair on a newborn child, but still, the sky wept. It cried for Miles, and for my father.

It isn't raining now. Not even with what I'm about to do. But I don't expect it to rain. The sky won't cry for me.

In the world beyond the frosted glass, the sun is setting, turning its back on me like everyone does in the end. It casts an eerie scarlet glow across the horizon—the colour of blood.

My grip on the edge tightens as I look into the mirror. I don't recognise the person who stares back. All I see in my reflection is a shell. A shell filled with so much weakness, so many lies.

How did I become this person? How did I stray so far and get so lost?

I turn away from my shame.

My eyes burn, but my cheeks remain dry. I taste salt on my face—the memory of all the tears I've shed—but now there are no more tears. The time for tears has passed.

I pick up my phone, and for the first time in a long time, my hands don't shake as I tap out the words in my heart.

I'm sorry. I love you.

It's not enough. It's never enough. But it's all I have left to give.

The sun disappears. There are no stars tonight. No light, no hope. There is nothing but darkness here for me.

A shadow winds itself around my heart. It runs through my veins and fills my lungs, cutting off my air. I am trapped in a prison of my own making, and now there is only one way out.

I cut through the tethers binding me, and I set myself free.

Silence

one

One day when I was five, I thought the sky was falling.

It was late autumn, and Miles and I were walking home from school. The frosty Melbournian air carried with it the chill of the coming winter, fogging our breath and turning our bare fingers numb and pale. I looked up at the steel-grey sky and swallowed nervously, wondering if we would make it home before the heavens split wide open.

My brother didn't seem to share my worry. He strolled along the cracked footpath beside me, a skip in his stride as he told me about his day. But I couldn't focus on his stories, so great was my fear of the oncoming storm. I might have jumped out of my own skin if it wasn't for Miles' hand on mine.

We were a few blocks from the safety of our house when thunder rolled overhead. The swollen clouds released their burden with a near-audible groan, and suddenly, I was struck by a thousand pinpricks of shocking, biting cold.

I screamed and tore my hand from my brother's, sprinting away on my skinny little legs as if I could outrun the assault from above.

"Carter!" Miles yelled. "Carter, come back here!"

But I was too petrified to stop, let alone turn around. There was only one explanation for what was happening: the sky was falling. The sky was falling, and I had to get to the house before I was crushed beneath its almighty weight.

Miles barked a word that would've earned him an earful from Mum before he took off after me. Being five years older and considerably taller, he caught up before I got too far. He grabbed my shoulders, jerking me to a halt in the middle of the now-slick path. "What the hell, little bro?" he demanded. "Why did you run like that?"

"We have to get home, Miles. The sky is falling!" Struggling in his grasp, I tried to shield myself from the celestial shards that stung my skin like needles, but it was useless. I was trapped.

"The sky…" Miles glanced up with a frown, but after a moment the confusion cleared from his face. "The sky isn't falling. It's just hailing."

My bottom lip was quivering, so I bit it. I tasted blood. "H-hailing?"

"Yeah." Pulling an umbrella from his schoolbag, Miles opened it over our heads and pointed at the footpath. "See? It's just ice. It's so cold that the rain has frozen solid into hail."

I peered down, and sure enough, scattered across the concrete were tiny spheres of hard white ice. Not pieces of broken sky.

Just hail.

"Oh," I mumbled. My cheeks grew warm.

"Besides," my brother added, "even if the sky *was* falling, you wouldn't need to be scared. You have me, little bro, and I'll protect you." He squeezed my shoulder and smiled, and everything was right with the world once more.

We ran the rest of the way home hand-in-hand.

Miles teased me about that day for years. My embarrassment over the incident faded with time, but I never forgot that feeling of overwhelming panic, the paralysing helplessness I felt when I thought the sky was collapsing.

That was how I felt right now.

I was chatting with Tiffany Johnston about her summer when *he* sashayed into the classroom. There was no other way to describe his rolling gait as he followed our teacher in. With a confident flourish, he set a pile of school diaries on the front desk and turned to survey the thirty-odd faces before him.

I stared, the words I'd been about to say caught in the back of my throat.

The boy looked like a punk rocker playing dress-up in school clothes. His hair was a riot of colours so garish it hurt my eyes. It was impossible to determine its natural shade beneath the gelled spikes of lime green, electric blue, hot pink, and fluoro yellow streaked through with black and purple. A number of silver facial piercings, clearly against regulations, glittered with defiance against his pale skin. Even his uniform was a disgrace. It was several sizes too small and hugged his slender frame obscenely.

Anger simmered in my gut, laced with that memorable dread. Who was this guy to think he could flounce in here like he owned the place and break every dress code the school had? Beneath the table, I clenched my fists until my knuckles ached.

And yet, I couldn't bring myself to tear my eyes away.

"Morning, ladies," he drawled to the girls in the front row.

They broke down in a fit of giggles.

I took a deep breath and reminded myself that the heavens weren't going to implode because some insolent new kid had disrupted the flow of my carefully ordered life.

The boy glanced up, and from across the room, his blue-grey eyes met mine. An icy finger ran down the length of my spine. Why was he singling *me* out from the crowd? I was hardly the only guy gawking at him, but the boy held my gaze for an eternity.

His eyelashes were long and dark in a way that bespoke cosmetic enhancement, and they brushed against the elegant sweep of his cheekbones when he blinked—no, winked. Oh God. Why was he *winking* at me?

"Psst! Carter!"

I flinched at the loud hiss in my ear and managed to wrench my gaze from the walking disaster at the front of the room to glare at my best friend. "What?"

"That kid," Jake whispered. "He's pretty camp. Has to be gay, right?"

"And?"

"And nothing." Jake leaned closer. "Kennedy is going to make life hell for him, though. I can tell you that right now."

I winced. Jonah Kennedy and his gang of small-minded thugs were barely tolerated by anyone outside the footy field in winter, but that never discouraged them from harassing their chosen victims. And Jake was right—the new kid may as well have painted a target on the back of his too-snug shirt.

I could already sense the disgusted glower that Kennedy, slouched against the rear wall between a pair of sagging bookcases, was casting in his direction.

But that wasn't my problem. I might have had a reputation for helping out the new kids and standing up for the down-and-outers, but this boy was a train-wreck just waiting to happen. He was barrelling full speed ahead towards the edge of a cliff, and it was too late to slam on the brakes. Far too late.

He was more trouble than he was worth.

"Good morning, everyone, and welcome to your first day of year twelve!" the teacher's chirpy voice cut through my less than gracious thoughts. "I trust you all had a nice summer break and are now ready to buckle down and study." The statement was met by a chorus of groans. "It's only one more year, guys," she laughed. "It'll be over before you know it."

Jake scoffed. "Yeah, right."

"For those of you who don't know me, my name is Ms Osbourne," she continued. "I'm your homeroom teacher, so if you need anything throughout the year, please don't be afraid to come and see me. Mr Fielding, the head of year twelve, is also available for those who'd prefer to speak to a male member of staff."

At last, she gestured to the boy. "We have a new student starting with us this year. Obviously, he hasn't read our dress code yet."

"My apologies, ma'am," he said with a shrug. "I wasn't aware there was one."

His audacity made the hairs on the back of my neck stand upright.

Ms Osbourne gave him an admonishing look. "You have until Monday to comply with the rules set out in the school diary. That gives you five days to fix your hair."

The boy's eyes narrowed.

"Understood?"

For a second, I thought he was going to protest, but then he pouted. "Fine."

"Good. Now, why don't you tell the class a bit about yourself?"

He heaved out a put-upon sigh, as if she'd asked him to scrub the floor of the boys' toilets with a toothbrush. "Well, folks, the name's Remy Montrose. I'm eighteen years old, but don't ask me to buy you beer because the answer will be no." His lips curved upwards in a sardonic grin. "I moved here from a sunny little town near Byron Bay with my parents and my sisters. My maman is French and cooks a mean soufflé."

He placed a hand over his heart, that grin stretching wider. "As for moi, I like long walks on the beach, sipping mojitos while watching the sun set, and sharing romantic candlelit dinners with gorgeous men."

Jake snorted. He wasn't the only one.

"Fucking fag," Kennedy growled.

I tensed, but the boy—Remy—either didn't hear him or chose to ignore the insult. All he did was slide his eyes across to Ms Osbourne and raise one slender brow. "Too much information?"

"I think that will do, thank you." The faint flush on her cheeks was the only sign of her displeasure. "I expect everyone to make Remy feel welcome. Do I have a volunteer to show him around and help him settle in?"

A hush fell over the room. The ticking of the ancient clock above the whiteboard resonated like a bassline in the sudden absence of sound. Moments passed, and the silence grew longer, louder. If I hadn't been watching Remy, I never would have noticed the way his expression went taut.

I was hardly surprised by the reticence of my peers. They may have snickered at his grandiose self-introduction or admired his blatant flaunting of the rules, but no one wanted to be seen associating with someone who was so obviously…different. None were prepared to single themselves out from the pack, not for his sake, so they left him to stand there on his own, slowly suffocating in the stillness.

I remembered how that felt. I remembered it all too well.

Remy bit his lip, and something inside my chest gave way.

Damn it.

I raised my hand.

Ms Osbourne blew out a short breath. "Thank you, Carter."

My heart pounded and my palms were slick with sweat, but no one batted an eye. This was the type of thing I did, after all, and despite my misgivings, I couldn't leave Remy to the tender mercies of Kennedy and his mates. I wasn't that cruel.

Kennedy's hateful gaze drilled a hole between my shoulder blades, but I thrust all thoughts of him from my mind as Remy sauntered down the aisle towards us.

He slid into the empty chair on my other side and flashed me a smile so brilliant, I was momentarily blinded by it. "Thank you, mon chou."

"No worries," I ground out, tamping down irritation that he presumed to give me a pet name. Sure, I'd offered to help him, but we weren't friends. I didn't know him, and he certainly didn't know me.

Ms Osbourne got to work passing around our diaries and class timetables, and chatter soon smothered the lingering echo of silence. Remy propped his chin in one hand and zeroed in on me. "You're the school captain, right?"

"Um…yeah." I ducked my head so my hair flopped over my face, concealing my discomfort. I was proud of my new position, especially since I'd been elected to it, but the extra attention would take some getting used to. Forcing a smile, I offered him my hand. "I'm Carter Cantwell."

Remy's palm slid into mine, cool against my clammy skin. His fingers were long and nimble, like a guitarist's or a painter's, but his knuckles were rough with callus. Surprised—I'd expected his hands to be as smooth as the rest of him—it took me a moment to notice when the pad of his thumb brushed over my wrist.

I jerked my hand away, the tips of my ears burning.

"That speech you and your counterpart made at the assembly this morning was amazing," Remy mused. "*Seriously* entertaining. I almost wet myself when you—"

"It was all right."

Remy didn't need to know that all the witty lines, even mine, had been written by my co-captain. Humour wasn't my thing, and I was just relieved I got through the damn speech without stumbling.

Jake jabbed my shoulder. "Don't be so modest, mate. You and Katie *killed* it." He leaned across me so he, too, could shake Remy's hand. "I'm Jake Brenner, best friend to the fearless leader of our glorious institution. You're in good hands with this one."

"Hmm, I can see that." Remy chewed on his lip ring and peered at me through his thick lashes. Up close, it was obvious that he was indeed wearing makeup. It was understated, just a dash of colour on his lips and liner around his eyes, but it suited him. Quite well.

I was staring again.

Annoyed, I turned my attention to the timetable Ms Osbourne had just tossed onto the table before me. That was what I needed to be focusing on. School. Classes. Learning things that would get me through the year with flying colours.

Transposing the schedule into my new school diary absorbed me for a time, and then I busied myself by writing a list of the tasks I needed to complete over the next few days. I wrinkled my nose at the list—it was already alarmingly long.

When the bell rang for the start of recess, Jake shoved his chair back and raced out the door as if the hounds of hell were nipping at his heels...leaving me all alone with Remy. Mentally cursing my best friend, who had the patience of a six-year-old on Christmas morning, I rose with a little more decorum and ushered Remy from the room.

"Thanks for offering to show me round," he said.

"Don't mention it."

"No, seriously. Nobody wanted anything to do with me. I could tell." He sighed, shoulders lifting in a sheepish shrug. "I know I'm a bit much. I just can't seem to help it. I thought for sure I'd be left to fend for myself—again—but then in you swooped to save the day."

Heat crept up my neck. "Everyone deserves a chance."

Remy blinked. "Carter Cantwell, you are my new hero. My undying gratitude is yours."

Great. His undying gratitude was the last thing I needed.

"You're welcome," I said. It sounded like I had a rock lodged in my throat.

We entered a dimly-lit breezeway. One wall was crammed full of old lockers, their deep blue paint chipped and peeling, exposing the tired, rust-flecked metal beneath. Remy pressed closer to my side in the confined space and I fought back a shiver. Having him so close was unnerving; I could feel the heat radiating from his body, spreading goose bumps along my arms.

For a moment, I couldn't breathe, but then the corridor ended, and we emerged onto one of the school's two football ovals. My lungs expanded again. I spied my friends in the distance, already sitting in our usual spot beneath the giant gum tree at the edge of the field. The summer hadn't been kind to the old eucalypt; its bark was sloughing off everywhere, and several small branches dangled precariously from its trunk.

I needed to speak to someone about that.

"Oh my God, Jake, you're so tanned!" Paige exclaimed as Remy and I approached. She grabbed Jake's forearm and lined it up against hers, gaping at the way his sun-darkened skin contrasted with her porcelain complexion.

"I take it you enjoyed Vanuatu," said Katie.

"It was hot and wet," Jake quipped. "I don't know why my parents had to take us there in the middle of cyclone season. We got put on lockdown in the resort during a storm not once, but *twice*."

"Sounds like a real hardship."

Jake scowled. "Lauren made me sit with her while she had her hair put in those little braid thingies. It took bloody *ages*. Can you believe I had to hold my fifteen-year-old sister's hand like a primary schooler?"

"*My* baby sister is still a primary schooler," Remy announced. "I hope you don't hold that against her."

All eyes snapped to him.

"Everyone," I said weakly, "this is Remy Montrose."

"Hello!" Remy waggled his fingers in the most ridiculous imitation of a wave I'd ever seen.

Stifling a grimace, I nodded at the long-legged, blonde-haired beauty who also happened to be my co-captain. "Remy, this is Katie McKinley, and the guy she's sitting on is Spencer Douglas."

Spencer smiled shyly. He and Katie had been together for almost two years now. Sometimes it still surprised me how well they fit even though they couldn't be more different. Katie was larger than life, bubbly, confident, a sun around which the rest of us lowly planets had no choice but to orbit. Spencer was the complete opposite, gangly and awkward, quiet, the still, dark space between the stars.

I gestured to the last member of our group, but Paige was never one to let others speak on her behalf. "I'm Paige Wu," she said, grinning in a way that might have been charming if she didn't show quite so many teeth. In a decade of friendship, she hadn't changed all that much. She was still tiny, still a firecracker, and her main goal in life was to confine her overbearing parents to a pit of endless torment, just as it always had been.

Remy gave the angel-faced devil an extravagant bow. "How do you do, Paige Wu?"

Paige's jaw dropped.

So did mine.

"I—"

A football shot through the centre of our circle, cutting short whatever Paige had been about to say. It bounced hard off Spencer's knee and rolled to a stop not far from Remy. As he bent to pick it up, I turned, searching the field for its owner. My spine went tense when I saw who was jogging our way.

Jonah Kennedy.

Kennedy screeched to a halt when he noticed Remy cradling the ball and glared at him with thinly veiled revulsion.

"Here you go, man," Remy said before *throwing* it back towards Kennedy.

I almost groaned, even before it fell short and landed at Kennedy's feet with a pathetic *thump*. Kennedy's lip curled. "Are you kidding me?" he demanded, sounding honestly offended.

"He's from up north," Jake was quick to interject. "You know, where they think *rugby* is real football."

Remy crossed his arms. "Excuse me? Rugby is the *only* real type of football."

"That would be AFL, mate." The look Jake turned on Kennedy was pained. "See what I mean? The poor guy has probably never heard of a handball in his life. Cut him some slack."

Kennedy spat on the ground. "He's a fucking fag."

I cringed. There was no ignoring the insult this time, not when it was said right to Remy's face. My insides twisted as I grasped for something appropriate to say, but Remy's tongue was faster.

"Well, you know what they say. It takes one to know one." His tone was casual, pleasant even, but his smile was sharp as a blade. "I'm sorry to break it to you, mon chéri, but you"—he pointed a finger—"are not my type."

Kennedy's face darkened to a disturbing shade of puce. If he were a cartoon character, I wouldn't have been surprised to see steam billow from his ears. He puffed up, preparing to say something that was no doubt as spiteful and tasteless as ever.

Things would only go downhill from there.

"Jonah, that's enough," I said. I couldn't let any more of that poison spill from his vile mouth. "Take your football and go."

He stared daggers at me. My skin crawled, but I stood my ground. I knew he wanted to avoid a repeat of our last trip to the principal's office just as much as I did. He was on thin ice after being suspended twice last year, and the last thing he needed was to cause a stir on the first day back.

Kennedy spat another large glob of sputum onto the grass. I braced myself, but he scooped up the ball and stormed off without another glance in Remy's direction.

"Oh man, that was *priceless*!" Jake crowed. "Did you see the look on his face?"

I swallowed and put my hands in my lap so nobody saw how badly they were shaking.

"I saw," said Remy.

Jake draped an arm around his shoulders. "Don't let him get to you. He's just a dickhead bully with absolutely nothing going for him."

A smug quirk sprung to Remy's lips. "Yeah, I've met the type: alpha male with daddy issues who's so deep in the closet, he'll never see the light of day."

"You think Kennedy's gay?" Spencer gasped. "No way!"

"He must be compensating for *something* with that attitude."

"Okay, that's enough," I said again.

Jake rolled his eyes. "Fine. You always have to do the right thing, don't you, Carter? Even defending the likes of *that* waste of oxygen."

If only it was that simple.

Kennedy's attitude left something to be desired, yes, but none of them knew what I knew. None of them had seen the bruises down Kennedy's back like I did last year—right before he exploded at me and got himself suspended the second time. Things were always more complicated than they seemed.

"Moving on…are *you* really gay?" Paige asked Remy.

"Yes. Problem?"

She shook her head. "Not at all. There just aren't many people who are out at this school. I mean, in our year, there's only Jamie

Ray, but he's an antisocial jerk who spends most of his time in the music building playing his cello."

I thought it wise not to remind her we depended on Jamie and his cello for our string quartet, where Paige and I played the violin.

"It's not really that surprising," Katie said. "There are still plenty of bigots stuck in the Dark Ages out there."

I took a bite out of the apple I'd kept stuffed in my pocket, wishing they'd change the subject. It wasn't that I had a problem with gay people—I got along just fine with Jamie Ray and couldn't care less about his sexuality. But the thought of what my mother would say if she overheard this conversation made my stomach squirm.

"Hey!" Remy's excited shout snapped me back out of my head. "We're having a housewarming party on Saturday. You guys should totally come along. If it's hot, we can swim in the pool."

"You had me at 'party,'" said Jake.

"You had me at 'pool,'" said Katie.

"A chance to escape Mr and Mrs Wu?" said Paige. "Count me in."

Spencer murmured his agreement.

"Carter?"

I met Remy's questioning gaze. That was a mistake. Those big, blue-grey eyes looked right through me, probing my tranquil surface to tease at the maelstrom beneath.

They were *all* watching me now, faces expectant, pleading. My heart beat faster and sweat beaded under my arms. "Uh, sure," I said. I wanted to tug at my collar, but I kept my hands in my lap. "I'm working on Saturday morning, but I guess I could come over later in the afternoon."

"Excellent!" Remy beamed.

The vice around my chest loosened. My friends went back to speaking with Remy, laughing at his clever jokes and complimenting him on his outrageous hair. Paige asked him what other body parts he had pierced, and his only response was an impish grin.

I closed my eyes and took a deep, steadying breath.

Remy Montrose had walked into my life less than two hours ago, and despite my intention to keep my distance, it appeared he was here to stay. I'd tried to pull on the brakes, to stave off disaster, but I still saw his train nosediving straight off the edge of a cliff.

Only now I was stuck onboard with him.

two

"Son of a—"

The keys landed on the doorstep with jingling *splat*.

"Damn it!" I wiped my slippery palms on my shorts before bending to retrieve them. As I straightened, my head gave an unpleasant throb, and a pearl of moisture slithered down the back of my neck.

I jammed the key into the keyhole and twisted, slumping in relief when the handle turned, but when I crossed the threshold, I found it was just as stifling within the house as it was outside. Stomping into the kitchen, I dropped my schoolbag unceremoniously to the floor and poured myself a glass of ice-cold water which I drained in a few long gulps.

As far as I was concerned, autumn could not come soon enough. We couldn't afford air conditioning—a fact I cursed almost daily this time of year. The only way to make things remotely bearable in the summer months was to get some air flowing through the house.

After peeling off my sodden uniform shirt, I pried open the

kitchen window. The breeze that rushed in was hot and stale, but it was better than the muggy stagnation indoors. Shuffling wearily from room to room, I repeated the process in the living area, the bathroom, and my bedroom. I paused at the closed door opposite mine, fingers already halfway to the handle before I caught myself.

Swallowing, I let my arm fall back to my side and moved on.

There was an empty wine bottle lying on the floor in Mum's bedroom. I took it outside to put straight into the recycling bin. I threw it in without looking and a sudden, shrill noise rent the afternoon air. Biting my lip, I inched forwards and peered into the bin. My stomach sank at the sight of the half-dozen bottles littering the bottom.

How long had it been since the rubbish was last collected? A week? Six days?

I slammed the lid shut and moved back into the kitchen, a chill crawling down my limbs despite the heat.

Mum wouldn't be home until six tonight. She'd texted me about it at lunchtime along with a request to prepare dinner. A quick inspection of the island bench and the fridge revealed that she hadn't taken any meat out of the freezer this morning.

"Vegetarian it is."

I scrounged together the ingredients for a pesto pasta salad for two. I would have preferred something a bit more substantial, but the recipe was quick and easy, and trying to defrost meat now seemed like too much effort.

Once dinner was ready in the fridge and the kitchen was spotless, I sat down at the bench to do my homework. There wasn't much since it was only the first day back, but it was going to be a busy year, and I needed to be on top of things right from the start.

The sun was sinking listlessly towards the horizon when Mum arrived. Her eyes were bloodshot, and wisps of auburn hair had escaped her chignon to curl around her chin. I refrained from asking about her day—she didn't like talking to me about her work.

I watched in silence as she entered the kitchen and headed straight for the wine rack in the corner. She filled up a glass to just below the brim and took a lengthy sip. As she lowered it back to the stone benchtop, mouth stained a deep ruby, she stilled. "What are you doing?"

I glanced down at my exercise book. "My chemistry homework."

"Don't be smart. What are you doing *here*?"

"What do you mean?" I asked, puzzled.

"It's Wednesday. You're supposed to be helping Anna at the soup van."

"Oh." My confusion ebbed. Anna was a woman Mum had known for years, since before I was born. She worked with a charity, and I volunteered my Wednesday nights to join her in providing soup and sandwiches to the city's homeless. "She's picking me up at seven, Mum. We start later during the summer, remember?"

Mum pursed her lips. "Good. Volunteering is important for you this year. Are you still serious about becoming a doctor like your dad?"

"Of course!"

"Getting into a medical degree requires an interview," she reminded me as if I could ever forget. "Taking part in a range of activities, especially volunteering, not only looks good on a résumé but teaches you important skills for the selection process."

A queasy feeling roiled in my belly. The prospect of going through a competitive interview process to get into my dream university course was not a pleasant one. "I *am* taking part in a range of activities," I said. "I'm doing heaps of stuff through school, and I have a part-time job."

"Good." Mum swallowed another mouthful of wine and pushed away from the bench, cradling the bowl of the glass in one hand. "I'll let you get back to your homework, then. You need top marks as well."

"Yes, Mum." She wasn't telling me anything I didn't already know, but the doubt in her voice stung. She doubted I could do it. She doubted *me*.

I picked up my pen and looked back down at my books with renewed determination. I'd show her. I'd show her she could depend on me. I would make Mum proud.

I *had* to.

I chained my bike in the carpark behind the shelter on Saturday morning and tugged my tee-shirt away from my sticky skin. Typical of late January in Melbourne, it was already pushing thirty degrees, and it wasn't even nine o'clock. I headed for the building's rear entrance, and as I stepped inside, I was struck by a blast of frigid air.

My boss' head popped out from behind the closest doorway. "Good morning, Carter!"

"Morning, Megs. Why is it like the Arctic in here?"

"It's going to be a scorcher today, so I'm preparing early. You should be thanking me. You're sweating like a blonde at a spelling bee."

"That's offensive," I scolded, but I was unable to keep from smiling.

Megs shrugged. "You'll live. Go get cleaned up and then walk the dogs. I want them exercised before it gets hot. Well," she amended, giving me a brief once-over, "hotter than it already is."

"Yes, ma'am."

She tried to swat me as I passed her, but I dodged the swing and manoeuvred out of reach, chuckling to myself.

I loved working with Megs, though it had taken a bit to get used to. *She* had taken a bit to get used to, even with our unspoken history. Megs was nothing if not passionate when it came to caring for abused and abandoned animals. She'd been a permanent fixture at the shelter since she was in high school, and she took over as manager after finishing her degree last year.

I didn't bother cleaning up too much, given I was heading straight back outside. If entering the shelter had been like stepping into an industrial-sized refrigerator, exiting was like stepping into a sauna. Max, the old yellow lab up first for his walk, grunted as the oppressive heat enveloped the two of us, his long pink tongue lolling sideways over his jaw.

Walking the dogs gave me time to think. Sometimes I enjoyed the solitude, relished the knowledge that no one was watching me, waiting for me to put a toe out of line. At other times, like today, I loathed the silence. It allowed frenzied thoughts to crowd my head, jostling for position at the forefront of my mind.

Stress did that to me, and a murky haze of stress had settled around my shoulders the past few days. Between homework, orchestra and string quartet, cricket tryouts, my new responsibilities as school captain, work, and volunteering, I'd barely had time to breathe since I donned my uniform on Wednesday morning.

The phone in my pocket vibrated. Tightening my grip on Max's lead, I glanced over my shoulder before pulling it out. Megs would hang me up by my ears if she caught me on my phone during work hours, but I hadn't spoken to Mum yet today, and I didn't know if she might need something from me.

I swiped my fingers across the screen.

REMY: Hope you're having fun

A bubbling sensation fluttered beneath my diaphragm. I rubbed at it, unsure whether I was pleased he remembered I was working or annoyed that he texted me anyway.

ME: Nothing I'd rather do on a Saturday morning :P

I hit SEND, then immediately grimaced. What was wrong with me? I knew better than to encourage him. Now he was going to—

My phone buzzed with another message.

REMY: Can't wait to see you in your togs...

Warmth flooded my cheeks. I stared at the screen, hands quivering and mouth as dry as old parchment. What was I supposed to say to that? How to navigate a fledgling friendship with someone who was openly gay—and a shameless flirt—was not something they taught us at school, and every time Remy opened his mouth, he managed to catch me off guard. I *hated* being caught off guard.

REMY: Just teasing! See you later xoxo

My brain stalled on the 'xoxo'—what the hell was *that* supposed to mean?—then I let out a breath and stuffed the phone angrily back in my pocket. I shouldn't have humoured him, not even for a moment. I should never have picked up the damn phone while I was at work.

"Come on, Max." I pulled at the lead to get the dog moving again, but he stumbled over. Max whined, looking up at me with hurt in his eyes. I gritted my teeth against a wave of guilt and crouched to rub his ear. "I'm sorry, boy. Are you all right?"

Max thumped his tail on the pavement and heaved himself back onto all-fours.

I tried to put Remy out of my mind as we turned back towards the shelter—a near impossible feat given he was the leading cause of my disgruntlement. The kid had been texting me at all hours, even during class, and he had no concept of personal space. His stupid grin and that stupid swaggering way he moved made me want to slam my head into a brick wall.

In three days, he'd burrowed himself so far under my skin, I feared I'd never dig him out.

By the time I got to his house later that afternoon, I'd worked myself into a bit of a state. My pulse was quick and thready, and sweat dotted my brow from agitation as much as the heat. I felt too worn out to deal with any of this, but I'd promised to come to the housewarming party. So here I was.

The bell echoed down the hall. Loud voices, laughter, and the unmistakable patter of approaching footsteps drifted through the fly-wire door. A shadow took form beyond it before the door swung open, revealing a girl a few years younger than me. Her dripping white-blonde hair was draped over her shoulders and concealed the straps of her royal blue bikini. "Carter, right?"

"That's me."

She smiled. "I'm Monique Montrose."

"Nice to meet you, Monique." I waited, but she didn't move aside to let me in.

Instead, her gaze ran from the crown of my head to the tips of my toes, amiable grin morphing into something far more lupine. I hitched up my backpack and coughed, resisting the urge to turn and flee. "Uh…"

"Monique, stop it." I never thought I'd be glad to hear that now-familiar drawl. "You're embarrassing him."

Monique sighed. "You're such a spoilsport, Remy. It's a cute guy!"

My face flamed.

Remy peeked past his sister, storm-coloured eyes sparkling with mirth. "It's a *very* cute guy," he agreed. "But this one is my friend, so keep your filthy paws off."

"Fine." Monique shot him a sullen look, but it melted away when she glanced back at me. "It was a *pleasure*, Carter," she purred.

I didn't know what expression was on my face as she flounced off down the hallway, but it made Remy laugh. "Don't worry about her, mon chou. She's just starting to experiment with her womanly wiles. She's all bark and no bite."

"Right." I raked an unsteady hand through my hair. Once Monique was safely out of sight, I turned my attention to Remy and did a double take.

I'd noticed him when he appeared behind his sister, but I hadn't really *seen* him. His hair had been dyed platinum blond sometime since yesterday afternoon. Water softened the gelled spikes, making them droop like fern fronds. His skin was so ghostly pale, it shimmered in the afternoon sun. Every. Bare. Inch. of it.

29

Blood roared through my veins. I was vaguely aware I was staring, but I couldn't have taken my eyes off him if a spaceship landed on his front lawn. All Remy wore was a pair of fitted blue-and-orange swimming trunks that left little to the imagination. He was a lot more toned than I expected, the muscle prominent in his arms and all down his torso. A droplet of water rolled across the hollow of his collarbone, leaving a shiny trail down his chest until its progress was halted by the silver piercing in his—

My eyes snapped up.

"You like this, huh?" His voice was husky as he tweaked the nipple ring with the tip of one long finger.

A choking noise, more animal than human, wrangled itself from my throat. I prayed the ground would open up and swallow me whole.

God damn him. God *damn* Remy Montrose.

"Oh, calm down!" he huffed. "There's no reason to freak out. Jake and Spencer stared too. You straight boys are *so* predictable." He rolled his eyes. "Come on, then. Come inside." He grabbed my arm as if to drag me through the door.

I jerked away before I could stop myself.

Remy paused, eyebrows climbing, and the heat spread from my face down my neck. I opened my mouth to apologise, but the words wouldn't form. Remy didn't seem bothered, though; he tilted his head and stepped graciously aside so I could enter the house unaided.

I still felt the touch of his hand on my arm like a brand.

I followed Remy down the short hallway, which ended in a magnificent open-plan room. The right half was taken up by a dining table, a set of sleek black-leather couches, and an enormous plasma screen TV. Glass bi-folding doors framed by lacquered timber stood open against the far wall, leading onto a shaded deck and, beyond that, the pool.

Remy led me into the kitchen to our left, where a woman was assembling a cheese platter while a man chopped up fruit. "Mum, Dad, this is Carter. He's our other school captain and the guy who so bravely offered to help me settle in."

"Bonjour, Carter," said Remy's mother. Her accent caught me by surprise, even though Remy had mentioned she was French. "I am delighted to meet the young man Remy cannot keep his mouth shut about."

Remy scowled. "Merci bien, Maman."

"Remy mentioned you were at work this morning, Carter," Mr Montrose said.

I cleared my throat. "Yes, sir. I'm an attendant at a no-kill dog shelter."

His knife stilled. "Do I look old enough to be called 'sir'?"

"Well, there *are* some grey hairs on your head," Remy snickered.

Mr Montrose's eyes widened. "What? Where? *Ami...*"

"Ignore them." Remy's mum gave me a long-suffering look. "They both have a penchant for drama. Please, call me Ami, and this *enfant*"—she gestured to her husband—"is Rob. Now, tell me about this job. Do you want to work with animals when you finish school?"

I rolled my shoulders, trying to dissipate the strange tightness in my chest. It was bittersweet to watch Remy and his parents, to witness the ease and fondness that coloured their every interaction. "I want to be a doctor, actually."

"Remy wants to be a psychologist, like his mother," Rob said with a shake of his head. "I don't know how I'll survive with *two* of them in the house."

Ami made a face. "Hopefully we will boot him out before it gets to that. But I think being a doctor is a noble calling, Carter. Your parents must be proud of you."

"Oh, it's just my mum and me." The words were out before I could stop them, and as their smiles twisted in silent sympathy, I wished I could take the words back.

They felt like a lie.

Remy recovered first. "Well, we should probably get out to the pool. The others will be waiting for us."

Grateful for the reprieve, I said goodbye to his parents and followed him across the living room and out the open doors. Jake was the first to notice me. He was lounging back on his elbows, feet dangling in the water and his favourite pair of Aviators perched on the bridge of his nose. "You made it!" he cried. "I was starting to think you weren't coming."

I frowned. "I said I would."

"Yeah, well…" Jake's tone was thick with feigned doubt. "How was I to know that today wasn't the day your canine captives made their break for freedom or something?"

Rolling my eyes, I set my backpack down and hung my towel over the edge of the fence. I adjusted the cord on the waist of my knee-length board shorts before slipping out of my tee-shirt and shoes and stuffing them into the bag.

Behind me, Remy sucked in a breath. I peered back and found him staring at me with such open appraisal, it was all I could do not to squirm. I felt stripped bare—and far more vulnerable under the weight of his gaze than I had Monique's. Turning away again, the space between my shoulder blades prickled with unwelcome awareness.

I took a running leap and threw myself into the pool, tucking my knees to my chest as I hit the water. Cold instantly surrounded me, the shock of it robbing my lungs of air. I let myself sink, let the silence embrace me, but when I struck the bottom, the fleeting peace shattered, and I kicked off hard. My head broke the surface in a cascade of glittering droplets. The first thing I saw was my best friend, gaping down at his now-drenched body.

Jake's eyes narrowed.

"Uh oh!" Paige sang.

Jake handed her his precious sunglasses, outwardly calm, and launched himself in after me. With a questionably masculine shriek, I raced for the shallow end of the pool. I wasn't a bad swimmer, but my pursuer was better, and I'd barely made it halfway before I was dragged underwater by a sharp tug on my leg.

We tussled until black spots danced before our eyes. My sinuses stung something fierce as we resurfaced, but that didn't stop me from grinning at Jake, laughing between each ragged breath.

"Glad you could make it, mate," Jake said.

"Me too," I murmured as we paddled back over to the others.

After slathering on some sunscreen, I made myself comfortable in the spa connected to the deep end of the pool. My friends urged me to join in their game of Marco Polo, but I was content to sit quietly and watch. Exhaustion hung about me like a shroud, and with a mostly-naked Remy nearby, the anxious knot in my stomach had coiled unbearably tight.

The truth was, I'd always been shy. If it were up to me, I would spend most of my time alone reading books or playing my violin.

33

But the world didn't work like that. Social interaction was expected of everyone, even those for whom it was a cause of anguish. Even if it made them feel like a deer caught in the headlights with nowhere left to run.

I'd learned that the hard way. I didn't realise how much my brother had sheltered me from those who sought to take advantage of my introversion until that shelter was gone. It was a cruel awakening for a twelve-year-old whose world had just been torn asunder.

To survive, I knew I had to be more like Miles. Strong. Confident. Outgoing. For the most part, I'd succeeded in becoming a completely different person from the boy I was before. That boy had been weak, naïve. Now, others looked at me and saw someone resilient and dependable. Someone capable. And if my hands still sometimes trembled or panic clawed its way up my throat…well, no one knew about it but me.

I'd gotten good at pretending.

Remy's eyes were on me again. I could *feel* it, an itch beneath my skin that I couldn't quite scratch, but every time I turned my head to catch him in the act, his gaze darted away to focus on something else.

I didn't like it. I didn't understand why he kept looking at me, didn't know what it was he saw in me that no one else could see. There was nothing about me that could interest a guy like Remy.

And I wasn't gay.

"He's kind of hot, right?" said Jake, startling me as he slid into the spa. He waved a hand in Remy's direction.

If my cheeks got any warmer, I thought they might burst into flame. "Um…"

"I mean, look at him," Jake continued. "He's so…vivacious. Full

34

of beans. That's attractive. And he clearly takes good care of his body. If he was a girl, or I was into dudes, I'd totally ask him out."

I sat there speechless. I thought I was past the point where my best friend could surprise me. Apparently, I was wrong.

Jake snorted. "You should see the look on your face. Relax, mate. I'm secure enough in my heterosexuality to acknowledge a good-looking guy, and you've got to admit I'm right."

I had to admit no such thing.

I looked back over at Remy, at the other end of the pool. Katie and Paige were fawning all over him, tickling him until he screeched bloody murder.

He *was* full of life, though. I could admit that much. He was confident and sassy and *infuriating*. He'd charmed my friends from day one, and it had been effortless. It had taken me years—years of struggling and doubt—to achieve a fraction of what he did so naturally.

A part of me hated him for it. A part of me wanted to *be* him.

Remy shrieked and flailed as Paige dug her fingers into his sides.

I did not find Remy Montrose attractive. I didn't.

Maybe if I said it often enough, I'd start to believe it.

three

At lunchtime the following Thursday, Jake threw himself to the ground in our usual spot and tore his sandwich in half with his bare hands. He glared at the two pieces, eyebrows pinched together and the corners of his mouth turned down, before tossing them both over his shoulder.

"Wow," said Remy. "What did that sandwich do to you?"

"Nothing."

Katie blinked at the venomous tone. "Then what crawled up your arse and died?"

"*Nothing.*"

Jake had my full attention now. It took a lot to genuinely piss him off, and it had been a long time since I saw him this riled up.

Realising we were all staring, Jake growled, "Kennedy was running his mouth in the boys' toilets." He ripped up a fistful of grass, showering his shoes with dirt. He didn't seem to notice. "About Tim Halloran. Did you guys hear what happened?"

Silence.

I felt it like a fist to the gut.

"Who's Tim Halloran?" Remy asked.

"A good kid," Jake said. "He went to primary school with Carter and Paige and me. And Kennedy," he added reluctantly. "His parents sent him to one of those fancy private schools when we started year seven."

Remy frowned. "And what, exactly, has happened to him?"

Jake twisted the brittle grass between his hands and raised his eyes to mine. The air went tense between us, pulling taut like a bowstring about to snap. "Carter would know more about it than I do. I only just found out myself."

"Carter?"

Coherent thought came sluggishly through the white noise that flooded my head. I glanced down at my watch, swallowing past the sudden lump in my throat. "I have to go."

"Hey, hang on just a—"

"Jake," Paige said quietly. "Leave it."

"But—"

It didn't matter. I was already on my feet, turning my back, and walking away. My best friend's disgruntled protests fell upon deaf ears.

A hot flush of shame swept through me as I fled from my friends, the taste of the lie still coating my mouth like bile. I didn't really have to go, but I couldn't stay either. I didn't want to talk about Tim Halloran. I couldn't.

I was furious that Kennedy had dared to even utter his name.

I released a slow, shaky breath as I entered the music building. Cream-coloured walls soared around me, draped with fabric panels that absorbed the worst of the noise. The timber floor underfoot was scratched and worn from decades of use and emanated a faint astringent scent from the fresh layer of varnish laid down over the summer.

Since the day I started high school, the music building had been my safe place. My haven. A balm to my troubled soul.

After fetching my violin from a storage locker, I found an unoccupied practice room and sank heavily into the single chair. For a moment, I just sat there, staring blankly into space, before flipping the battered case open.

My hands steadied the moment they closed around the violin, one on the neck, the other on the lower bout. I positioned it between my chin and shoulder in one fluid, practiced move and plucked tentatively at the strings…drifting into a choppy *pizzicato* that mirrored the frantic rhythm of my heart.

I was a different person when I had my violin in my grasp. Worry and doubt sloughed from my bones like a snake in full moult, even when I stood centre stage with the lights shining bright in my face. It was the only time I could bare such scrutiny without feeling like a laboratory specimen, my every move observed, recorded, dissected.

With my violin, I was like a boy with a stutter who found his smooth voice the moment he started to sing. The violin was a part of me, as I was a part of it.

Who's Tim Halloran? Remy asked.

My fingers faltered.

Did you guys hear what happened? There'd been hurt on Jake's face above all else. *Carter would know more about it than I do.*

I lowered the violin to my lap and pressed a palm against my stinging eyes.

I was four years old the first time I met Tim Halloran. I could still remember the small boy in navy overalls playing in the sand. He hadn't looked directly at me when I knelt down at his side, hadn't offered me a smile. What he did offer me was a spade, and together, we built a sandcastle, lost in our own little world.

Not a single word passed between us that day. Very few words ever did.

Tim and I were never close, but things were easy between us. Simple. Safe. It was nice being around someone who didn't fill every silence with talk, having someone to sit with on Sundays in the years we went to the same church.

Those memories hurt now.

Because two days before last Christmas, Tim cut open his wrists with a cheap razor he bought at the supermarket. His mother found him bleeding out on the bathroom floor, cold and alone, and by then, it was too late to save him.

Mum took me to his funeral. I sat in our usual pew, feeling his absence beside me like the tingling ache of a phantom limb. Dry-eyed, I watched his mother weep, stared at his father's ashen face as he mumbled that the blood wouldn't wash out of the grout between the bathroom tiles. He never looked away from his hands as if transfixed by rust-coloured stains that only he could see.

He was their only child, and now Tim Halloran was gone.

A hesitant knock jolted me from my doleful reverie. Before I had a chance to respond, the door inched open, and a pale head poked inside. My shoulders tensed. "Remy," I said flatly.

"Hey, Carter." His expression was somewhat sheepish as he pushed the door wide. "Paige said I might find you here."

Remy looked very punk today, even without his piercings in.

39

His white-blond hair was gelled up into a tall Mohawk, and his lashes were rimmed in kohl. The harsh black lines drew a stark contrast to the concern softening his eyes. "I just came to make sure you're okay."

"I'm fine." I should have been flattered he cared, but I wasn't. I didn't want him here, hadn't asked for him to come here. I didn't want him to see me like this.

Rising to my feet, I shuffled over to the open case and placed my violin back inside, hoping Remy would take the hint and leave.

"I'm sorry about your friend."

I shut my eyes and wrestled down a scream. The topic of Tim Halloran was like a Band-Aid on a wound—every time I thought it was starting to heal, someone ripped it off too soon, only for it to start bleeding again.

"Jake said Kennedy said that Tim was…gay."

I slammed the violin case closed, my fists clenching tight. Somehow, I doubted that was the word Kennedy had used. "What?" I bit out. "Just because a guy is soft-spoken and shy and gentle, that means he's gay?"

"Of course not." Remy edged half a step closer, coming across the threshold and into the suddenly too-small room.

My chest constricted. "We weren't that close. I wouldn't know if…"

There was something sombre about the way Remy tilted his head. "But he was still your friend," he said gently.

Grief roiled in the pit of my stomach—grief…and guilt. I turned away from him.

"I don't see what difference any of it makes now."

"Maybe none." A pause. "Or maybe it makes all the difference in the world. People aren't kind to those who are different. And not all of us can hide it."

"What, like you?" I snapped.

Wait...

Had I really just said that?

I whirled around. "I'm sorry," I croaked, almost tripping over the words in my hurry to get them out. "That was uncalled for. I'm sorry."

"You're not wrong, Carter." He waved a hand, delicate wrist bending and flexing as he gestured to himself. "I've never been able to hide my sexuality, but that's okay." Colour suffused his cheeks and his eyes flashed, voice rising with passion. "This is just how I was born, and I'll be *damned* if anyone tries to make me feel ashamed of who I am!"

My pulse hammered in my throat. Jake was right, I realised, with a sick twist low in my belly: Remy Montrose was attractive. The world hadn't yet broken him down and sucked away all that light shining out from inside of him.

It felt dangerous, being so close to him. Like, if I stayed too long, my flickering inner light would be drowned out by his roaring flame.

"Sorry," I repeated.

Remy sighed. "Don't worry about it. This sort of thing just pisses me off."

"What sort of thing?" said a new voice.

I almost leapt out of my shoes, and Remy spun with a startled curse. So entranced had I been by his tirade that I didn't notice we were no longer alone.

Remy's chin lifted, the challenge clear. "Youth suicide," he answered with his typical bluntness. "Especially by those who don't fit within the box that our heteronormative society tries to shove us all into."

I blinked. *What?*

The newcomer's brows crept towards his hairline. Propping a gleaming cello case against one hip, he raked dark eyes down Remy's body. The hint of a smirk curved his lips. "You must be Remy."

"You've heard of me?" Remy sounded oddly pleased.

"You could say that." He whipped out a hand. "Jamie Ray."

I saw the recognition spark on Remy's face. *There just aren't many people who are out at this school,* Paige had told him. *I mean, in our year there's only Jamie Ray...*

Remy stepped forwards. "Enchanté," he purred.

Their palms slid together and held.

Paige had called Jamie an antisocial jerk who spent most of his time in the music building playing his cello, and she wasn't too far off the mark. I'd never met anyone as focused, as coolly intense, as Jamie Ray. He was tall, imposing, and aloof with a veil of contempt drawn almost permanently across his face. Sometimes, he reminded me of a Victorian nobleman with his slicked-back hair, patrician features, suave manner...self-possession that bordered on arrogance.

He and Remy couldn't be more different. Jamie was the dark to Remy's light, the ice to Remy's fire, the *freddo* to Remy's *allegro*.

But they were both gay.

I was abruptly reminded of that fact as they studied each other, fingers still entwined, heedless of the discomfort now prickling across my skin.

Jamie's coming out had been quite the scandal back in year ten when a teacher caught him and a year twelve boy making out in a supply cupboard. He'd dragged them both from the closet—

literally and figuratively—and proceeded to lecture them about inappropriate schoolyard behaviour. Right in front of everyone walking past.

The year twelve boy didn't return the next day.

Jamie released Remy's hand. "So," he said, hefting his cello, "who killed themselves?"

"*Excuse me?*"

Jamie shot me an impatient look. "Your friend here said he was pissed off about youth suicide. What non-heteronormative kid killed themself this time?"

Rage struck me, boiling the blood in my veins. How dare Jamie be so flippant about someone's life? "His name was *Tim*," I snarled as I yanked my violin case off the ground so violently, it slammed against my knee.

"I'm sorry, mon chou," Remy said again.

"Stop *calling* me that!"

He flinched, shoulders curling in towards his chest. The brightness about him dimmed, dampened, like I'd just cast a shadow over the sun. "I…" He swallowed. "I'm going to…" The smile he flashed Jamie was more grimace than smile. "It was nice meeting you."

"Likewise," said Jamie.

Remy nodded, then turned and slipped back through the door. I could almost see the storm clouds dancing over his head.

Only when he was gone did I realise I was trembling.

"Smooth, Cantwell. That was real smooth." Jamie put his cello down and drummed his fingers on the back of the chair. He glanced at the door, then at me, a speculative gleam in his eyes that I didn't like at all. "I'm sorry for your loss," he offered.

43

I choked back a hysterical laugh. *I'm sorry for your loss.* What a useless expression. As if he were personally at fault. As if an apology would make it all better, make the pain go away.

As if 'I'm sorry' could adequately convey the tragedy of a premature death.

I'd heard enough 'I'm sorrys' to last me a lifetime.

"Thank you," I said.

Jamie sat and started fiddling with the buckles on his instrument case. After a moment, he cleared his throat. "I have this room booked now, you know."

"Oh. Right." I didn't know why his lack of compassion surprised me. In the five years I'd known him, I'd only ever seen Jamie truly care about two things: his music and himself.

"You'll be at quartet rehearsal after school, won't you?"

"When am I ever not there, Jamie?" I was unable to keep the bitterness out of my voice.

Jamie either didn't notice or didn't care. He turned back to his cello with a grunt. "Just making sure. We have a recital on Saturday."

I didn't bother saying goodbye.

I stowed my violin back in its storage locker and briefly pressed my forehead to the smooth timber door, slightly warm from the sunrays filtering in through the skylight. I felt stretched thin and wrung out, like a damp cloth hanging heavy from a washing line.

This wasn't how I'd intended to spend my Thursday lunchtime, hiding from my friends in the music building, battling unpleasant memories dredged up to the surface without warning.

Sighing, I thumped my head against the locker. "Get a grip, Carter," I muttered. "You can't hide out here forever."

The thought was tempting, though.

The afternoon light stabbed into my eyes as I left the building. I scrubbed a hand viciously over my face, blinking away the glare—and froze.

Remy sat on one of the granite boulders framing the entranceway. The rock was so large, his toes barely brushed the ground, and he swung his legs absently, calves connecting with the stone on every downward swing.

An unfamiliar feeling shivered through me at the sight of him sitting there, waiting.

I wanted to turn and run.

Coward.

My shadow fell over him as I approached. Remy glanced up, and I slid my eyes away, scuffing my shoe along the ground as I tried to find the right words. "I didn't mean to shout at you," I finally said.

"And I didn't mean to upset you more," he replied. "I really did come to see if you were all right."

I dragged my gaze up to his face. His open, honest face, fringed by that pale gold hair, robbed of its luminous sheen now that I was blocking his sun. "Why?" The question came out on a near-inaudible breath.

But Remy still heard it. "What do you mean *why*?" he said, taken aback. "You're my friend, and I was worried about you. Isn't that reason enough?"

I didn't point out that none of the others had come. Not even Jake.

Now that we were out of that suffocating practice room, now that my irritation with Jamie had chased away the worst of my melancholy, I was oddly…touched that Remy was here. That he had stayed and was pushing me for answers. No one pushed me like that anymore.

He was studying me like a puzzle he couldn't solve. "You're an enigma, Carter Cantwell."

"O...kay."

"You're so friendly with people," Remy went on. "You say hi to everyone, and I've watched you greet them all by name, even the kids in other year levels. You always make time to help others with their problems, even when you're so busy yourself."

A frown crept across his face. "But you're quiet when no one is looking. Sometimes you go almost a whole hour at lunchtime without saying a word, and I've never heard you ask a question in class. You seem remarkably wary of the limelight for the most well-known guy at this school."

Remy saw all that? His perceptiveness was unnerving. He'd noticed in little more than a week what my friends hadn't noticed in *years*.

But there was still so much he didn't know.

"You like to keep your troubles to yourself, huh?"

I licked my lips, shifted my weight from one foot to the other. Back again. I didn't know what to say. What did he want me to say?

What do you want me to say, Remy?

The thoughtful hum that came from him immediately set me on edge. Remy slithered off the rock, rubber soles crunching on the gravel of the garden bed where he landed...

Bringing him chest to chest with me where I stood mere inches away on the path.

I sucked in a breath, leaning back, but Remy's arms snaked out and wound around my waist. Pulled me close.

I stilled, the surface of my skin running hot, then cold, buzzing with the murmur of a hundred thousand ants.

Then he stepped away, and his Mohawk scraped my chin. The faint strawberry scent of his hair gel lingered in my nose. "Sorry," Remy said, cheeks pink and glowing with earnestness. "You looked like you needed a hug."

I swallowed. It felt like I was swallowing glass. When was the last time anyone had hugged me? I couldn't...

My gaze dropped to the concrete beneath my feet as I remembered a day of thunder and hail and rain. The sun was out today, the expanse above my head whole and clear, but it felt as if the sky was falling on me all over again with no way to hold it up.

Miles wasn't here to protect me anymore.

He hadn't been for a long time.

four

"You look nice."

The unexpected compliment halted me midstride. "Thanks, Mum." My beige chinos and short-sleeved white collared shirt were nothing to write home about, really. Though if she liked them enough to comment...

I turned, but Mum was already looking back down at the magazine in her lap. A bottle of red sat beside her, half empty. I couldn't see an accompanying wine glass, but it was probably hidden behind the stack of Dad's old medical journals that took up permanent residence on the coffee table. "Can I get you anything before I go?"

"Hmm?" She rubbed absently at her chin. "Oh. No. I'm fine."

"Okay. See you tomorrow, then."

"Don't stay out too late. We're helping set up the morning tea before church tomorrow."

"I remember. Love you." I hovered there a moment longer, waiting for her to reciprocate, to look up at me. Something. *Anything*.

Nothing.

Forcing away the ache in my chest, I slipped outside and found Jake waiting for me.

"Finally," he said, sliding his phone into his pocket. "I was about to send you another message. You ready to go?"

I pasted on a smile. "Yeah, I'm ready."

And just in time, too. I'd been up since dawn for school cricket, after which I raced off to the shelter on my bike for an afternoon shift. I made it back home again with twenty minutes to spare—barely enough time to grab a quick snack and jump in the shower. The ends of my hair were still damp.

I stifled a yawn. Tonight was Piper Guido's eighteenth birthday party, and though my bed was beckoning, I knew that crawling straight into it wasn't an option. Piper was the first new friend I'd made at high school. We met during orchestra auditions on the second day, bonding over our love of string instruments, and now she played the viola in our quartet with Jamie and Paige.

My presence at her party was mandatory. Expected.

"How's the belly going?" Jake asked.

I threw him a dry look. "About as well as you'd expect." I pulled up my shirt to show him the ball-shaped blue-and-yellow bruise blooming just beneath my ribcage.

Jake whistled.

"Oh my God! What happened?"

My eyes jerked up, to where Remy and Paige stood gaping with fascinated horror. I smoothed the shirt back down over my exposed flesh.

"He took a ball to the stomach at cricket this morning," said Jake, laughter in his voice. "Point blank range. Man, when he went

49

down, I thought for sure he wouldn't get back up, but this one's tougher than a pair of old boots." He elbowed me none-too-gently in the side, right where I was tender, but I barely felt the jab.

My attention had been snared by something else.

Some*one* else.

Remy's dark jeans were so tight they looked as if they'd been painted on. A black Queen singlet top hung loosely from his slender shoulders, baring far too much of that fine, pale skin. His feet were stuffed into a pair of Converse high tops covered in purple sequins, and matching violet streaks had been painted through the gelled spikes in his hair.

And the piercings were back: two small hoops in his right ear and a bar through his left eyebrow, almost blending in with the thick silver eyeshadow that glimmered under the glow of the setting sun.

I was flat on my back in the grass again, stunned, the wind knocked right out of me.

Remy crossed his arms. "You can close your mouth now, Carter. Didn't your mum teach you it's rude to stare?"

I shut my mouth with a snap.

"You straight boys," he drawled, "are *so* predictable."

Paige giggled and looped her arm through his. "It's just because you look hot."

"And you're too sweet." Remy pecked her on the cheek.

Something twisted in my stomach—something sharp. Studiously ignoring the warmth in my face, I shoved my hands into my pockets as deep as they would go. "Come on. We'll be late for the party."

Jake snorted. "Right."

I pinched my thigh through the fabric of my pants. Piper's house was in our neighbourhood, which was why we'd all chosen to walk, and it wasn't as if a few minutes here or there would matter. It was a party, not an exam.

I needed to chill the hell out.

Paige tugged Remy down the footpath, past the row of ornamental pear trees whose leaves were starting to change with the first touch of autumn. Her gait was unsteady in her tall ruby heels, and she leaned into Remy for support. "Piper's cousin will be there tonight," she told him. "He's gay, too. I suspect that someone's trying to play matchmaker."

"Great," Remy groaned.

Jake shot a quizzical look at his back. "What's wrong with that?"

"Just because two guys are gay doesn't guarantee they'll have anything remotely in common."

"Except, you know, liking other guys," Jake pointed out.

Remy glared over his shoulder. "That's like saying you and... and Jonah Kennedy should be best mates just because you both like girls." His brow creased. "Although I suppose liking girls is debatable on Kennedy's part. He sure seems to have a hard-on for me."

Jake clapped his hands over his eyes. "TMI, Remy!" he cried. "T. M. I. Now I'm *never* going to get that image out of my—"

"But you never know, I suppose," Remy went on. "Maybe Piper's cousin will be fun to dance with. Or make out with."

The sharp thing in my stomach twisted harder.

My best friend dropped his arms, still grimacing. "No offense, mate, but I am *far* more interested in the free alcohol than watching you get your freak on." He patted his front pocket. "Got my note from my parents and everything."

"I can't believe we need a permission slip to drink alcohol," Paige

51

muttered. "Which old, balding politician came up with that stupid law?"

"It's only a few more months until you turn eighteen," Jake reminded her. "Besides, when have you ever let *that stupid law* get in your way? I know just how good you've gotten at forging your dad's signature, Paige Wu."

Paige's lips twitched. "I don't know what you're talking about."

Remy laughed. "Ah, it's good to be a legal adult." His bright gaze flicked my way. "How about you, Carter? Did your mum write you a note?"

"I don't drink," I said too fast, an edge to my voice I hadn't intended to put there.

"At all?"

Jake slung an arm around my shoulders. "It's cool. All the more for the rest of us."

Remy watched us for a moment, then shrugged. "Fair enough," he said, turning back to Paige when she stumbled on a crack in the path.

I met Jake's eyes, hoping he saw the gratitude on my face and that he understood what I couldn't put into words. Hoping he knew how much he meant to me, even when he drove me nuts or spoke before he thought.

Jake squeezed me and let go.

I wished he hadn't. I wished he'd kept the arm there, chased away the chill now crawling down my spine.

A part of me did wonder whether Mum would write me a note if I asked. I doubted it. She'd hated when Dad let Miles take beer to parties, and I couldn't imagine her being any more amenable to the idea now than she had been then.

Not after everything that happened.

Not that it even mattered since I would never ask.

The party was in full swing by the time we got to Piper's house, if the music rocking its foundation was any indication. Her two older brothers stood guard at the front door, checking names off a list taped to the back of a music stand. They collected Jake's authentic note and Paige's forged one, brushed a brief glance over Remy's ID, and handed the three of them fluoro pink wristbands—*for the bar*, one brother grunted—before ushering us all inside.

They hadn't even read the notes.

Paige's scepticism about the underage drinking laws was understandable. Surely whoever came up with the idea knew that teenagers would find a way around it, knew they'd get their hands on alcohol if they wanted it, regardless of what their parents—or the law—had to say.

I knew that better than anyone.

A sonic wave struck me square in the face as I crossed the threshold, accompanied by a whirlwind of flashing coloured lights. The air was thick with smoke that had a sticky-sweet flavour as it coated the back of my throat. Cringing slightly, I peered through the pinkish fog.

The house had been transformed almost beyond recognition. All the couches and tables were shoved back against the walls to make room for a dancefloor, and the trinkets that usually decorated the long mantelpiece had wisely been cleared away.

The birthday girl was nowhere to be seen, but I spied Katie and Spencer lounging on one of the couches near the door. Spencer kept adjusting his glasses, his tongue darting out to wet his lips as he glanced around the room.

"Here, drink this," Katie told her boyfriend, pressing a red cup into his hands.

He took a sip without asking what it was. A second later, his face puckered in revulsion, and he spat the mouthful back into the cup.

"Damn, Katie," I said as I approached. "I hope you're not trying to poison him."

Katie laughed and rubbed Spencer's leg, her blue eyes sparkling with affection. "It's just a little liquid courage. We're going to tear up the dancefloor later, aren't we, Spence?"

"I haven't agreed to that yet," Spencer mumbled, brown skin darkening as he eyeballed his cup with distaste.

Katie's smile broadened. "You will." She looked up at me, then past me. "Wow, is that Remy? He looks *hot*!"

"What? Where?" said Spencer.

"Over there, with Piper."

Spencer frowned, bewildered. "Should I be jealous?"

"No, sweetie," Katie replied with endless patience. "He's gay, remember?"

"Oh. Yeah."

I craned my neck to see what they were looking at. Across the room, Mr Guido was controlling the flow of alcohol through a makeshift bar running out of the laundry. Piper stood on the opposite side of the table to her father, both her hands clutched tightly in Remy's.

I cleared my throat. "I should go and say hi to Piper. I'll see you guys later."

The house had continued to fill even in the short time since my friends and I arrived. A tight press of bodies shifted and swayed with the throbbing pulse of the music, bumping up against me as I weaved my way between them. My skin prickled with every unwelcome brush of skin, and I fought to hold back a shudder.

"Carter!" Piper's face lit up when she spotted me. She lunged forwards with typical enthusiasm, but in her haste, she overbalanced, and I caught her just as she went flying past my shoulder. The momentum made me stagger, and when Piper twisted in my grasp, her heavy mass of straight black hair smacked me right in the eyes.

"Oh, shit!" Piper broke down in a fit of breathless giggles.

I set her back on her feet and rubbed my smarting eyes. "Happy birthday, Piper," I rasped.

"I am *so* sorry!" She straightened, still chuckling, a bright blush suffusing her cheeks. "I'm so clumsy when I wear these heels! Are you all right?"

My bruised ribs protested the sudden wrenching movement, and my sight was still a bit blurred, but I wasn't going to say so. "I'll live."

Piper sagged. "Well, thank God. I was just about to introduce Remy to my cousin. Want to join us?"

Remy. How could I have forgotten *Remy*? Now I felt the weight of his gaze upon me, felt the pleading look he sent my way. "No," I said, "it's fine. I just wanted to say hi."

"Well, thanks for coming," Piper replied easily. "And sorry again for almost knocking you on your arse. We'll talk later, okay?" She grabbed Remy's arm. "Come on. Let's go find Matteo."

As Piper dragged him off, Remy glared at me…and stuck out his tongue. The shock of it ran through me like a live wire, frazzling every one my nerves. What would Piper think if she knew that *she* wasn't the one who almost knocked me on my—

No.

Don't go there.

I gave myself an angry shake and braced for the wearisome task of mingling with my peers.

From there, the night progressed just as I expected it to. Despite Mr Guido's best attempts to limit the alcohol consumption, it wasn't long before many of the guests were drunk. Girls with made-up faces tottered in their high-heeled shoes, hanging onto each other for support, while a number of guys dashed out to the front yard and emptied their stomachs in the garden bed.

After Piper cut her cake and the customary eighteenth birthday speeches were made, someone ratcheted up the music, and everybody hit the dancefloor. Well, almost everybody.

Spencer and I sat at the outskirts of the packed room, nursing cans of Sprite as we watched the seething mass of bodies. The thrumming bassline was so loud, it vibrated the metal between my hands and plucked at the sliver-thin membrane of my eardrums like a violin bow about to fray. I clutched the can harder to stop myself from clapping my hands to my ears. No doubt they'd be ringing by the time I left. Probably still would be when I got up for church in the morning.

I rolled my shoulders, trying to ease the tension building there.

As one song transitioned into the next, Katie came shimmying out of the crowd. Without a word, she plucked the can from Spencer's hand, drained it, and set it down on the table by my side. Then her fingers latched onto his, and she hauled him to his feet.

The pure terror that splashed itself across Spencer's face as his girlfriend led him onto the dancefloor made me laugh.

It wasn't until no one was looking that I let my smile slip.

I studied the horde of dancing teenagers. They pressed so close to each other, skin grazing, bodies grinding, stranger to stranger, friend to friend. Faces bright with pleasure, unshadowed by the burden of care. The beat became the pulse that pumped blood through their veins, the melody the electrical signals of their hearts.

I wished I could feel what they felt. Wished I knew what it was like to be that free.

But I didn't.

The music—*this* music—washed over me, around me, and left not a trace of itself behind. The joy I saw shining out of everyone else's eyes did not reach me where I sat at the edge of the room, away from them. On the outside, looking in.

I never felt so alone as I did in a room full of people.

I never felt so…apart.

Bringing the can to my lips, I gulped down the last few sugary drops and crushed it in my hand. I tossed it onto the table beside me, where it disappeared among a mountain of red plastic cups.

Almost against my will, my eyes were drawn to Remy. He was with Jake near the centre of the dancefloor, barely visible amidst the tangle of bodies between us, yet somehow impossible to miss. Remy danced as if today was the happiest of his life, head thrown back euphorically and hips swinging in a way that ought to be illegal.

I shifted in my seat, feeling hot all over. I was a fly trapped in a spider's web, stuck, unable to move but desperate to. Knowing that something terrible was coming for me, that nothing good was going to come from the situation.

I was a moth drawn to a flame, yearning for one last flash of brilliance before the fire burned me to ash.

With a jolt, I realised he was moving towards me. The strobing lights rendered his hair in shades of deep indigo and pale gold, the glint of his piercings like pyrite flecks in drab grey pavement, catching the midday sun. His cheeks were flushed, eyes glowing, smile split across the lower half of his face. He was radiant. Breathtaking.

He's beautiful.

I hated myself for even thinking it.

Remy came to a stop so close to me his knees almost knocked into mine. "What are you doing over here all by yourself?" he yelled over the cacophony of noise. "You're missing out on all the fun!"

I shrugged and tucked my hands under my arms. "I'm not a fan of dancing."

"Oh, come *on*." He hopped back, arms spread wide. He was practically vibrating with delight. "*Everyone* loves dancing!"

"I'm not very good at it," I tried again. Thick bands clamped around my chest and squeezed, the force of it nearly shattering my ribcage. My hand flew to my heart at the sudden pain.

Remy didn't seem to notice. "No one cares about that. Come and join us for a bit."

I shook my head, barely managing to draw in a breath through lips turned numb and cold.

"Come on, Carter. Don't be a downer!"

Just leave me alone, Remy. Leave me alone leave me alone leave me alone leave me a—

"It'll be fine," he said, then reached out and grabbed my arm.

"*I said no!*" The words exploded from my mouth in a torrent of panic and rage. I lurched away so violently, I clipped the edge of the table and sent cups raining down to the floor.

Remy staggered back as if I'd dealt him a physical blow. The colour drained from his face, leaving confusion and hurt in its wake. He stared at me like he didn't know who I was.

58

He *didn't* know who I was.

Without another sound, he spun on his heel and stalked back into the crowd.

I sank down into my seat again, fingers curling into fists so tight my nails bit into my palms. They trembled. They felt like ice.

The memory came out of nowhere.

My ninth birthday.

We were at home, just the four of us, and Mum was in the kitchen preparing a special meal. Dad pointed the remote control at the stereo and a song came on, something upbeat and catchy that instantly snagged my attention. I lifted my head out of my book, liking the way the music shivered through my limbs.

Dad held out his hand. "Come on, Carter. Dance with me."

It took no small amount of coaxing, but eventually, I let him pull me to my feet. Me, his painfully shy boy, plagued by self-consciousness and doubt. He drew me out of my shell slowly, carefully, with encouragement in his smile and gentleness in his eyes.

And I danced. It was glorious.

Then it all came crashing down.

I was wriggling my body, some sort of silly kid moves that made my dad laugh and clap, when Mum entered the room. She froze when she saw us, and a frightening scowl pulled tight across her face. "What is going on in here?" she demanded. "Ronan, you shouldn't be encouraging this behaviour. He looks ridiculous!"

I stopped. Everything stopped.

"Christ, Andrea," Dad breathed. "He's nine years old. We're just dancing."

"You know that's not all it is!"

Miles ushered me into his bedroom while they fought. "It's all

59

right, little bro," he said quietly, wiping the tears off my cheeks. "Don't listen to her. You didn't do anything wrong. You can dance whenever and however you want to."

But I shook my head and buried deeper into his arms. I wouldn't try to dance again, not when my mother thought it made me look stupid. For a short time, the dancing had been like magic, but she had taken that magic away.

I'd never found it again.

My eyes followed Remy back into the writhing throng. Another boy came up behind him and placed his hands on Remy's hips. He was the same height as Remy, his skin a dusky brown and his hair as dark as coal. Matteo, I presumed. Piper's cousin.

I stared as Remy spun and hooked an arm around Matteo's neck, drawing him closer until their stomachs were flush. Encouraged, the other boy's arms curled around Remy's waist.

My chest ached. I couldn't breathe, couldn't hear the music past the roaring in my ears.

Remy's head turned, and our eyes locked.

I felt my face crumple.

Shoving back my chair, I scrambled through the crowd towards the backyard, needing air, needing to get away, needing space to pull myself together before I completely flew apart. My eyes stung, watered.

The smoke. It's the smoke.

Piper's tiny backyard was empty. I staggered past the lone cluster of trees and braced myself against the fence, gasping, wishing I could play away the tempest rising inside me like I could a song.

The back door slammed shut. I jerked around and saw Remy storming after me, thunder on his face and lightning in his eyes.

"What's wrong?" he demanded. "Seriously, Carter, what the hell is going on with you tonight?"

I've had a long day.

Parties aren't my thing.

You didn't listen when I said I didn't want to dance.

All valid answers, but what came tumbling out of my mouth was: "He had his hands all over you."

"Matteo?" Remy laughed. It was a bitter sound, tinged with disbelief. "Are you kidding me? So, I'm not allowed to dance with anyone else just because you turned me down?"

I dragged in a gulp of air. "That's not what I meant."

"No? What *did* you mean?" Remy advanced, crowding me up against the fence. He was like a bushfire, eerily beautiful, burning bright, but destroying everything in its path. "Go on. I'd love to hear it. Don't be shy." He poked me in the chest. Hard.

"Stop it." I smacked his hand away. He was so close, I could smell the faint, stale scent of beer on his breath and the heavy metallic fragrance of his hairspray.

I felt like I stood on the edge of a cliff, teetering, about to fall.

Remy growled in disgust. "You know what? Fuck this. I don't know why I bothered. I'm going to go and dance some more with Matteo." He took a step back and started turning away.

My mind went blank.

I lurched forwards and seized him by the front of his shirt, clenching the thin material in shaking hands. I shoved him back against the fence and trapped him there, just like he'd been trapping me.

Remy's eyes widened. "What are you—"

And then I kissed him.

five

I spent my ninth birthday cowering in my brother's arms while our parents fought. Miles stroked my hair and held me close without so much as a hint of complaint as my tears soaked through his shirt.

"*I won't let him turn into a faggot!*" my mother's screech echoed down the hall.

Miles gasped. His embrace became unbearably tight. I didn't understand what Mum was talking about, didn't know what that word meant, but the look on my brother's face—like he'd taken a hit in the solar plexus—told me it was nothing good.

My sobs grew louder.

"*What?*" Dad cried. "How can you even—? How *dare* you!"

I'd never heard Dad so angry before. I'd never heard *anyone* so angry before. Dad was mad. Mum was mad. Miles' eyes glittered with rage.

All because of me.

Because there was something wrong with me.

That memory was nothing but mist as I crushed my mouth to

Remy's. The force of it was bruising, near-savage in its intensity, a wild clamour of lips and teeth and tongue. Static surged across my flesh, trailing ribbons of heat that latched on and pulled me closer. Closer. *Closer.*

Hands in my hair tugged harshly, scrabbling for purchase, but I was too far gone to feel the sting. Too far gone in the sensation of another warm body against my own, in the whisper of ragged breaths over my skin, in the desperate ache pooling in my heart. An ache for something I couldn't name.

I'd never *wanted* like this before. Never wanted anything as badly as I wanted this boy, this beautiful *boy*—

The static discharged in a biting spark of awareness, snapping the world back into place.

I tore myself away and staggered backwards, a horrified moan choking out of me. Remy collapsed against the fence, his eyes glassy, lips rosy and swollen from kisses. *My* kisses.

I won't let him turn into a faggot!

"Oh, God…"

"Carter?" A dazed chord resonated in his voice.

"N-no."

Remy raised a hand, reaching for me. "It's okay—"

"*No.*" I stumbled further back, and his fingers grazed empty air.

"Don't run," he said.

But it was too late. I spun and crashed through the trees, thinking of nothing but escape. I elbowed swaying bodies aside as I plunged through the house, ignoring their cries of protest until at last—*at last*—I broke out into the cool night once more.

Then I ran. Just like he asked me not to.

I ran hard and far and fast, feet pounding the pavement, a single-man stampede. Breath rasped through my throat like sandpaper until white stars burst behind my eyes.

I didn't recall getting home. I didn't recall letting myself inside or racing down the hallway to the bathroom. I didn't even realise I'd shucked my clothes and climbed into the shower until the deluge of frigid water shocked me back to reality.

My knees gave out. Slick tiles cradled me as I curled into a ball, fingertips searching for the long, thin scar down my inner thigh. It had been there almost as long as Miles had been gone, a silent reminder of all I wanted to forget. A secret accusation, forever branded into my skin. I pressed hard against it, felt the pulse of my femoral artery beneath it.

Icy needles drilled into the back of my neck. I squeezed my eyes closed and saw Remy staring back at me, stunned, his clothes rumpled from my hands.

I won't let him turn into a faggot!

A scream bubbled up inside me, but I had no strength left to free it. I couldn't speak, couldn't *breathe*, and I clawed at my throat to try and draw in air. My vision tunnelled until the world was consumed by darkness.

The weight of the sky, of the whole world, was pushing down, and it was crushing me.

Oh God.

What had I done?

I avoided Remy for over a week. At school, during recess and lunch, I found excuses to stay away from him and the rest of my friends. I arrived as late as possible to the classes we shared so I could choose

64

a seat on the opposite side of the room. I ignored his calls, and his text messages went unanswered.

It was a cowardly, immature thing to do, but I couldn't face him after what I'd done.

I couldn't face myself.

No one called me out on it until cricket training on Thursday afternoon. "So," Jake said, voice muffled beneath his helmet, "are you going to tell me why you're ignoring Remy?"

I kept my eye on the ball spinning towards me, stepping forward at the right moment to make a block with my bat. The ball ricocheted off the smooth willow surface with a satisfying *crack* and bounced back along the ground to Matt Phillips, who was taking his turn at bowling.

I straightened, glancing at Jake where he crouched behind the wicket. "I don't know what you're talking about."

"Uh huh."

Matt paced back out to the start of his runup. I made a few adjustments to my stance and flexed my hands. The rubber grip on the bat's handle was worn so thin, I could almost see the brownish cane beneath, but I couldn't bring myself to replace it. The bat had been my brother's.

The ball came hurtling towards me.

Crack.

Jake groaned. "Come on, Carter, I'm your best mate. What gives? You've been ignoring him all week, and he's been miserable."

Remy was miserable? I hadn't noticed. Then again, I *had* been avoiding him, so that wasn't exactly surprising. "I don't see how that's any of your business, my best mate or not."

I struck the next ball hard, a low drive that flew straight back at

65

Matt and forced him to leap aside to avoid getting hit in the groin. "Hey!" he squawked. "What the hell, Cantwell? Are you *trying* to maim me for life?"

"Sorry!"

Matt muttered something under his breath and jogged off down the embankment to fetch the wayward ball.

"Seriously. What's got you all worked up?" Jake rounded the wicket and leaned back against the chain-link wall of the batting cage. "Did…" He lowered his voice, a hint of caution creeping in. "Did something happen on Saturday at Piper's party?"

I whirled on him. "What? *No!*" Cold dread draped itself around my shoulders. "Why would you ask that?"

"He looks at you a lot. Like, *a lot* a lot." Jake removed his helmet and peered at me through his fringe of sandy hair. "I suspect he has a crush on you, and since you started ignoring him after the party, I thought maybe…" He shrugged.

"No, it's nothing like that." The lie sat heavily in my chest. I licked my lips, knowing I had to offer him something more, or he might just keep pushing until I cracked. "We had a misunderstanding, that's all. I'm dealing with it, and I'll speak to Remy when I'm ready." Not that I knew when *that* might be.

"Okay."

"Okay?"

"Yeah." Jake grinned. "I like that kid. I didn't want to have to kick his scrawny little—"

"Hey, Brenner!" Matt's shout preceded him up the rise. "You're up, man. I am *not* giving Mr Aggro another shot at my favourite parts."

I felt a guilty sort of relief as Jake turned away.

I knew I wouldn't be able to stay away from Remy forever, no matter how much I wanted to. But every time I thought about approaching him, *talking* to him, a wraithlike hand took hold of my windpipe and squeezed. I told myself I'd use the weekend to get it together, to figure out what to do, but by the time Sunday afternoon rolled around, I was no closer to answers than I had been eight days before.

Lying on my back in my childhood bed, I stared up at the ceiling. My vacant eyes traced the pattern of the glow-in-the dark galaxy Dad stuck up there when I was little. Its soft gleam beckoned, waiting for me to reach out and touch it.

But it was so far away, and the years had dulled its shine

I was like those stars and moons, like those planets and suns. Faded. Remote. Tired in a way that went bone-deep.

Then I felt sad.

It was the type of sadness that seized my heart and never let go, the type that slipped into my bloodstream like ice shards, ripping through the fragile walls of my veins. It was the type of sadness that stole my breath, a thief in a moonless night without end.

I was a collapsing star, sucking everything into itself as it died. Even the light.

You know I'll always be here for you, right?

I thought I did. I thought Miles would be here forever. But he wasn't. He'd left me to fight this battle on my own.

At the other end of the house, the doorbell rang. I ignored it. Mum was out in the living room—she could get the door. I heard it open, heard the murmur of hushed voices, then footsteps heading my way. "Carter," Mum called. "Your…friend has come to see you."

Was it just me, or did she sound stiffer than normal?

67

Daylight flooded my room. I squinted through the sudden glare and caught a glimpse of my visitor.

I sat bolt upright. What was *he* doing here?

Remy Montrose stuffed his hands into the pockets of his jeans. "Hi," he said.

My eyes went straight to Mum. Her mouth was a thin, bloodless line, and her face was dead white, auburn brows slanting down in a pointed glare she aimed at Remy's back. I knew if I asked her to send him away, she would. She'd *jump* at the chance.

And then as soon as the door closed behind him, she'd be on me like a hawk.

I forced a smile. "Thanks Mum."

She huffed, gave me a look that made my stomach roll, and disappeared back down the hallway. I swung my legs over the opposite side of the bed to the door, turning away from Remy. I wasn't ready to meet those disarming leaden-blue eyes. I knew they tracked me as I stood and drew back the curtains, their weight easing only slightly as the darkness withdrew.

Sweat broke out on my palms. "What are you doing here, Remy?"

"You've been ignoring me."

I didn't respond. How could I, when we both knew it to be true?

Remy sighed. "I guess I understand why, but we need to talk."

"Do we?" Talking was the last thing I wanted to do right now. Sure, it had been my plan to stop avoiding him sometime soon, but it was supposed to be on *my* terms, when *I* was ready. Not here, in my bedroom, with my mother waiting down the hall.

"We do," Remy said earnestly. "I don't want to lose your friendship over this, Carter. Please. Please talk to me."

Those words, brutally honest, convinced me to turn back and face him. For a moment, Remy seemed so vulnerable, so young, standing there in his ripped-up charcoal jeans and tie-dyed rainbow tee-shirt. There were faint shadows beneath his eyes that bespoke sleepless nights, and he gnawed anxiously on his lip ring as he awaited my response.

Something inside me pulled taut. "Not here."

"Then…" He flashed a hopeful smile. "Will you come over to my place for a bit? My family is out. We'll be alone."

Being alone with him probably wasn't the wisest idea, but… "Fine."

"Thank you."

Remy waited while I found some shoes and scrounged around on my desk for my phone and house key. I didn't look his way again as I led him from the room, wrestling down the blind panic coiling tight inside my chest. "Mum, I'm going to Remy's for a bit," I told her as we passed by the lounge room.

Her fingers froze over the keyboard of her laptop. "What for?"

"He's going to help me with my psychology homework, ma'am," Remy said with easy charm. "I'm struggling a bit, to be honest, and Carter knows his stuff."

That was an outright lie. Psychology was Remy's best subject.

"Very well," said Mum, but she didn't look happy about it. "I want you home by six though, Carter. It's a school night."

"Of course. I'll see you later."

Her eyes followed us all the way out the door.

The walk to Remy's house was silent. Uncomfortably so. Tension mounted with every passing moment, gathering close and still like the calm before an encroaching storm. My skin itched with unease,

69

and I couldn't shake the feeling I was making a terrible mistake. A mistake worse than the one I'd already made.

But Remy said he didn't want to lose our friendship. Though it was new, still taking its first few shaky steps forward, if I was honest with myself, I didn't want that either. So I kept my mouth closed and walked, fighting the urge to bolt for home like I had all those years ago.

When we got to the Montroses' place, Remy took me straight to his bedroom. I was glad he didn't offer me anything to eat or drink; my stomach churned as I perched on the edge of his bed. The mattress was soft and comfortable, but firm too, the bedspread subdued in shades of pale blue and grey. That surprised me. In fact, looking around Remy's room, I found it wasn't at all what I expected. I thought his inner sanctum would be wild and vibrant, like Remy himself, but instead, it was shockingly mature.

His desk was dark, sleek wood with tidy stacks of paper at each corner, and the bookshelf beside it boasted rows of books organised by colour and height. There were no clothes strewn across the spotless cream carpet, no makeup or jewellery scattered on every flat surface, and the only poster on his walls was a framed rendition of Queen's *Bohemian Rhapsody*.

I felt a queasy pang of guilt at the realisation I'd been stereotyping him.

Remy threw himself into the swivel chair behind his desk and kicked off his shoes. My eyes drifted to the trees outside the window. Their leaves were mottled green and gold, caught partway between summer and autumn, and their slender branches tapped out an irregular rhythm as the breeze blew them against the glass.

It was the only sound around for miles.

The silence stretched, ringing in my ears like the muffled echo of a tolling bell. My mouth had gone as dry as powdered ash. I didn't know where to begin.

"I'm sorry."

My gaze snapped away from the window. "What for?"

"For the way I spoke to you at the party." Remy's shoulders curled inwards as he grimaced. "I was upset and angry and had had a bit too much to drink, but that's not an excuse. Taunting you like I did was unfair, and I'm sorry."

I gaped. I hadn't expected *him* to apologise. As far as I was concerned, he had nothing to be sorry *for*, and I hadn't considered the possibility he might feel just as guilty as me.

"Say something," he whispered.

I hung my head. It was now or never. "I'm...sorry too," I forced out. "I didn't mean to...accost you."

"Accost me?" Remy barked out a laugh. "You didn't *accost* me, Carter. You kissed me, and...well...it wasn't at all unwelcome."

I found myself suddenly captivated by a loose thread on the knee of my pants.

"Had you ever kissed another boy before?"

I swallowed convulsively and tugged at the thread, watching with detachment as it pulled away from the seam. "No."

Remy hesitated, then asked, "Have you thought much about it? Our kiss?"

Thread still pinched between my fingers, I glanced up at him. The last week replayed through my mind with painstaking clarity: long days, desperate to be rid of the unfamiliar yearning that writhed in the pit of my belly; longer nights, unable to find a reprieve from the frenzied images dancing behind my eyelids. Mornings, waking

71

with my heart racing and my body aching to be held, touched.

"Yes," I said hoarsely.

Remy's smile was like lightning, a brief flash of splendour, there one moment, gone the next. I hated to see it go, hated the solemn curiosity that took its place. "And? How did it compare to kissing girls?"

I stared at him. Heat rose to my cheeks.

He blinked. "Wait. That was your first kiss *ever*?"

"I'm not gay!" The words spewed from my throat, almost strangling me on their way out. "I'm *not*!" I grabbed at the thread on my knee and *pulled*, yanking and yanking until the weave of the fabric unravelled.

"Hey." The bed dipped beneath Remy's weight. "Stop that." His fingers slid over mine, calming my frantic hand. "It's okay."

I tried to withdraw, to escape, but he held on tight, refusing to let go. The warmth of his palm seeped through my skin and my struggles weakened, then ceased. Angry tears pressed at my eyes. "I'm not—"

"I heard you the first time, mon chou," he said softly. His thumb stroked the edge of my wrist, and I felt it shudder all the way up my arm.

"Remy..." I didn't know whether it was a warning or a plea.

He sighed. "People are so quick to put labels on things. Male or female, gay or straight, as if there can't possibly be anything in between. Are you really that eager to paint yourself into a box?"

If only he knew. I was already *in* a box. Sometimes, the box was the only place that felt safe.

"I can't do this with you," I croaked.

"Do what? We're just talking."

I looked pointedly down at his hand, twined around mine.

"Okay." He cracked a grin. "We're talking *and* I'm holding your hand. You can pull away at any time, you know."

But I didn't. And I thought, somehow, he knew I wouldn't.

Remy shifted, half-turning towards me so I could see the play of sympathy and concern across his face. "Can you tell me why, at least?"

"Why what?"

"Why *can't* you do this with me? Whatever *this* is."

I won't let him turn into a faggot! It hissed through my ear, like she was standing in the very room with us.

"She wouldn't understand," I mumbled.

"Your mum?" Remy asked. "She's the reason you're so twisted up about this?"

I was hyperaware of every place my side brushed against his, of the pressure of his palm on the back of my hand, and I allowed myself a fleeting moment to wish things could be different. To wish that *I* could be different. That *she* could.

"Carter?"

"I can't let her down," I told him. "She's all I have left."

Remy stilled. "Left?" he echoed carefully. There was a long pause, caution warring with the question he so obviously wanted to ask. "What happened to your dad?"

I sucked in a breath and held it while a familiar ache panged through my chest. No matter how many times it happened, I was never ready to hear those words. I was never ready to answer.

I peered at Remy past the stinging in my eyes. He looked back the way he always did, like he was unearthing all my secrets...like he could really *see* me. But he didn't. He couldn't. He only knew

73

the parts of me I'd chosen to show him, the parts I'd chosen to tell him.

He didn't know all the rest.

The tremor started in the tips of my fingers. I turned my hand in my lap so our palms met and threaded my fingers through his. Remy gripped me tight. "He died," I heard myself say, staring down at our joined hands. "My dad and my brother were killed by a drunk driver."

six

Mum had forgotten to get the Pringles.

She was distracted after an altercation at the soup van the night before, and when she stopped at the supermarket in the morning to buy food for Miles' pre-graduation drinks, she'd forgotten the damned Pringles.

Miles was magnanimous about it, like he was about almost everything, but on this one occasion, he couldn't quite hide his disappointment.

Dad sighed. "Come on, then. I'll run you down to the supermarket, and you can pick out whatever you want. We can't have you going without your favourite treat on your big day." He removed his reading glasses and rubbed at his weary eyes. "Let me just go and find some shoes."

"Thanks, Dad. You're the best!"

"Uh huh."

My chest tightened. I was curled up in my usual corner of the couch, flipping through a book of baroque music I received for my twelfth birthday. I stared down at the pristine white pages until the notes blurred together, hoping no one noticed my quiet distress.

But my brother seemed to have a sixth sense when it came to me. The next thing I knew, Miles was crouching right in front of me, his hands braced on my knees. "What's wrong?"

"Nothing," I mumbled.

"Carter, anything that makes you look like someone's kicked your puppy is not *nothing*."

Head still bowed, I glared at the sonata in my lap. "We don't have a puppy. Mum's allergic."

Although I couldn't see his face, I *felt* him roll his eyes. "Tell me what's wrong."

"It's stupid."

"*Tell me.*"

I knew he wouldn't let it go; my brother was nothing if not persistent. With a sinking feeling in my belly, I forced myself to meet his eyes. "It's just…it's happening too fast. You've turned eighteen, soon you'll have your licence, and now you're done with school. All you have left is your exams. Next year you'll be at uni."

"Well…yes," Miles said slowly. "That's what usually happens when you finish year twelve. Why are you upset about it?"

"I'm not ready for you to leave me!" I burst out.

Miles blinked, brows lifting in surprise. "Who said anything about leaving?"

"You're almost grown up, Miles," I said, "and grown-ups leave home. I've heard you talking with your girlfriend about mov—"

"Stop."

I gave him my most pathetic look.

"That's enough of that." Miles crawled up onto the couch beside me and drew me in for a fierce hug. "I can't tell the future, little bro, but you know I'll always be here for you, right?"

I buried my face into the crook of his neck, breathing in his familiar scent. His arms tightened, and I calmed. Nodded.

"No matter what happens next year, I'll be here," he said. "I'll *always* be here for you. I promise."

Dad came back into the room then, car keys dangling from one finger. Miles disentangled himself from me and scrubbed an affectionate hand over the top of my head, ruffling my hair.

"Hey!" I protested.

He launched himself over the back of the couch and darted out the door, laughter trailing after him like the tail of a kite.

I watched him go, then flipped over to the next song, thumping my fist against my thigh. What on earth had I been thinking? Of course Miles wasn't going to leave. He wouldn't abandon me, not even if hell froze over. My brother would always be here—no matter what.

Half an hour later, Mum breezed into the room in a robe, hair twisted up in a towel on the top of her head. One dark red strand was plastered against her neck, dripping onto the terrycloth collar. She paused halfway to the kitchen. "Have Miles and your dad got back yet?"

"No."

"I wonder what's keeping them."

I shrugged. "Maybe they had to go to another store?"

"Maybe."

Thirty minutes stretched into an hour.

Mum tried calling Dad, then Miles. Neither of them picked up. One hour turned into two.

We should have been leaving soon. I put away the music book

and changed into my good clothes, running a brush through my hair as I perched on the edge of the coffee table. Mum was on the phone to Uncle Sean, Dad's younger brother, which wasn't a good sign since they didn't get along at the best of times.

Two hours became three.

Mum was pacing up and down the hallway, and my fingernails were bitten down to bloody stubs. Uncle Sean stood stiffly in our kitchen, speaking into the landline in hushed tones.

I didn't hear a word he said. My eyes kept flicking to the front door, waiting for it to open, for them to come home. Any minute now, Miles would burst across the threshold, impish grin on his face, and tease us all for being so worried. He had to.

He *had* to.

Finally, three hours and twenty-seven minutes after Miles and Dad left the house, the doorbell rang. I leapt to my feet with a relieved yell and hurtled towards the door. As I yanked it open, I drew a deep breath, ready to give them a piece of my mind.

At first, I didn't quite understand what I was seeing. Two men in dark blue clothes and neon yellow vests stood beyond the doorway. They both held funny-looking hats under one arm.

"M-mum?"

She was at my side before I could blink, and her face turned the colour of old milk. "Good evening, officers," she said. She sounded strange. "How can I help you?"

The policeman on the left stepped forward, into the thin nimbus cast by the porch light. His eyes were all crinkled up—an expression that, years later, I would understand to be sympathy—and he cleared his throat. "I'm sorry to tell you this, ma'am, but there's been an accident."

"What do you mean?" I demanded.

"Carter, come over here," said Uncle Sean.

I spun around and saw the stricken look on my mother's face. "Mum, what does he mean? What does he *mean*, Mum?"

But, deep down, I knew what the police officer meant. I heard the plea in my voice.

And that was when they said it.

That was when they said the words that tore my life apart.

Mum's legs folded, and she dropped towards the ground in silence. Uncle Sean just barely managed to catch her before she struck her head on the tile.

I didn't recall much of what happened next, except that I screamed. I screamed and screamed and screamed, like someone had punched through my ribcage and ripped the still-beating heart from my chest. I screamed until my voice broke apart and my cries petered out into whimpers.

"It can't be real," I croaked, the lids of my eyes gummed shut.

Uncle Sean's hand shook as it combed through my hair. "It's real. I'm so sorry, kiddo."

But he promised.

Miles had never broken a promise to me before. My brother had promised he wouldn't leave me, but less than four hours later, he had.

Miles and Dad were gone, and they were never coming back.

I barely spoke for the next two months. It was too hard, took too much effort with my wrecked voice and shattered heart. Words were worthless, anyway. They were nothing but hollow, empty lies. Miles had shown me that.

I walked through each day like a ghost. A shadow of the boy who once had a father and a brother. My laughter dissolved into barren silence, food tasted like dust in my mouth, and I no longer felt the comforting touch of Jake's hand on my shoulder. I never even looked at my violin. It was the longest I'd gone without playing since the first time I laid eyes on it.

The numbness was both the cause and the cure for my pain.

Eventually, I came out of my catatonic state. It was like emerging from a long hibernation to find that the whole world had changed, that everything I knew had been stripped away while I slumbered, reclothed in colours that were strange and frightening and utterly unfamiliar.

I pieced together what happened that day from the fragments Mum deigned to offer me. Dad and Miles were on their way to another supermarket when they were T-boned by a car that ran a red light. The other driver was seventeen, unlicensed, with a blood alcohol concentration of nearly three times the legal limit. He and Dad were killed instantly.

Miles didn't make it to the hospital alive.

He'd still been in his school uniform, and the new pants and shirt Mum bought him for the graduation dinner hung from his wardrobe door. They were still there, even now, but Miles would never wear them.

So much death, so much hurt, all because of a stupid drink. A stupid drink that turned friends into strangers, men into monsters, and took fathers and brothers away from lonely twelve-year-old boys.

I'd sworn it would never pass my lips.

"God, Carter," Remy rasped. "I don't know what to say." His fingernails dug into the back of my hand so hard, they nearly drew blood.

But I was used to pain. The loss of Dad and Miles wasn't the sharp sting I still felt when I thought of Tim Halloran, but it was a diffusive ache beneath my breastbone that never really went away. I'd been told to give it time, that the pain would fade, but that was yet another lie. The pain didn't fade.

All I could do was shore up the hole inside me and learn to live with being only half the person I used to be.

"You don't have to say anything," I said to Remy. I stared down at our joined hands, at the half-moons he'd gouged into my skin. It had been a long time since someone held my hand, in comfort or anything else. It felt...good. Too good.

I pulled away, and this time, he let me go.

Remy flopped onto his back and stared up at the ceiling. A slight frown marred his elegant features. "I spend half my time wanting to murder Monique in her sleep, but I can't imagine life without her or Sabine. Or Dad."

I thought that was probably the way things were between most siblings. I wouldn't know, because it hadn't been like that with Miles and me. We never fought, never bickered. I was his sidekick, his shadow, his loyal devotee.

And Miles...Miles had been my everything.

Remy propped himself up on one elbow. "So. Your mum."

My face twisted.

"She wouldn't approve of her son kissing another boy?"

"No."

"What makes you think that?"

I won't let him turn into a faggot!

I cringed. Was he really that naïve?

"She was raised in a conservative, religious family, Remy.

They…" I forced myself to glance down at him. "They kicked her out when she got pregnant with Miles. She was only eighteen, and she and my dad weren't married."

"That's rough." Remy was a little wide-eyed, but there was no judgment in his expression.

"My dad stepped up, though," I forged on. "His family wasn't happy about it either, but he moved out and got them a place of their own. He worked nights to support them while he was studying to be a doctor. It just about killed him." My voice cracked on the word.

It wasn't working that killed him in the end.

I cleared my throat. "Even after that, my mum… She just has a very firmly set idea of the way things should be. That's not wrong."

"It's not wrong," Remy agreed. "But it is problematic if it makes you feel like shit about yourself and who you are."

"I…I'm fine."

"Are you?" Remy's smile was tinged with sorrow. He levered himself upright and reached out to press his palm against my cheek. We both heard my breath catch, but he didn't retract his hand. "Wasn't it good? Our kiss?"

My stomach lurched sideways. I tried to rear back, but Remy's fingers curled around my chin, holding me in place.

"That's beside the point. It doesn't matter whether it was good or not. I *can't*."

"Forget *can* and *can't* for a moment. Didn't you *like* it?"

I couldn't do this. I couldn't *be* this. But even with the denial I so desperately wanted to give poised on the tip of my tongue, I couldn't force it out.

Those long, slender fingers caressed my jaw, sending shivers right down to my toes, and against all reason, my eyes drifted closed.

"You turn me inside out," I accused. "I can't stand it."

Springs groaned as Remy shifted closer. His other hand touched the back of my neck, tangled in my hair, and the earth quaked. "I can work with that."

"Remy…"

He hushed me. I was trembling in his grasp, but I didn't have the strength to push him away a second time.

When I opened my eyes, Remy was much nearer than he had been before. His eyes were more blue than grey, the pupils blown wide, and when they dropped to my mouth, my pulse skipped.

"Please," he said. "Let me show you what it could be like." He dragged his gaze back up to mine until I saw my own conflicted expression reflected right back at me. "Please, Carter. Will you give me this one chance?"

I expected Mum to swoop down on me with her questions the moment I got home. I wasn't expecting to receive the cold shoulder.

At ten minutes before six, I let myself in through the front door. Mum was preparing dinner in the kitchen, and she glanced at me as I locked up. Her eyes raked my face, searching for a sign I'd done anything other than help Remy with his psychology homework.

Then she went back to her chopping.

Queasy relief flooded my veins at her apparent lack of concern. I slunk past her to put my things away in my bedroom, then proceeded to the bathroom to shower.

I stood in the glass-walled stall with my head bowed and let the hot water drum against my shoulders. Rivulets ran down my chest and stomach to gather in the hollows above my hipbones, pooling there until the water overflowed and coursed down my legs.

The scar on my thigh was unnoticeable to those who didn't already know it was there—and no one knew about it except me. I lined my forefinger up against it, felt the slightly raised and roughened skin, and remembered when and how it was made.

It had been a relief to find something that could cut through the numbness which pervaded every inch of my useless existence in the months after Miles died.

It was a reminder of a simple truth Mum and I both knew but refused to acknowledge: it should have been us. It should have been us that died, because Mum wasn't made to live without Dad...and I wasn't made to live without Miles.

I rubbed my eyes and shut off the water. It continued to drip from my skin, from my hair. My body felt as light as a feather and as heavy as stone all at once.

Dinner was ready by the time I was done in the bathroom. I joined Mum at our small, round dining table, where we took our seats opposite each other. The meal was consumed in silence. I barely tasted anything, but I made sure to compliment her on the food anyway. Mum didn't acknowledge my comment with so much as a grunt.

Whatever was left of my appetite vanished.

It wasn't until her plate was clean that Mum laid down her fork and fixed me with a look so sharp, I could slice myself bloody on its edges. "Why didn't you tell me you're friends with somebody... like that?"

My eyes dropped to the table. *See what I mean, Remy? She'll never understand.*

"Answer me, Carter."

"I didn't think it was a big deal," I mumbled. "He's new this year, so I've been showing him around. You know, school captain stuff."

"I see."

I dared to peek up and could tell by her flinty expression that she absolutely did *not* see. "My friends kind of…adopted him. He's part of our group now."

Mum's lips pursed. An emotion I didn't recognise glinted in her emerald eyes. "What did he want today?"

"You heard him. He needed help with his psychology homework."

"Why couldn't he just call you?"

"He tried." I shifted uneasily, hands clenching around my utensils. "My phone was turned off."

This time, I recognised her displeasure. It was as familiar as it was unwelcome. "That reminds me. What on earth were you doing in bed with your blinds closed on a Sunday afternoon? Don't you have your own homework to do?"

"I was tired."

Mum studied me, and I forced myself to allow the scrutiny, to let her see my exhaustion for what it was and take me at my word. I'd never given her any reason to doubt me.

Until now.

"Be careful around that boy, Carter," she warned. "I didn't like the way he was looking at you. I don't want you spending time alone with him. Do you understand?"

Every lie so far had driven home another nail in my coffin, but there was no going back after this one. I really was going to do this.

"I understand," I said and was shocked that my voice didn't shake.

My insides clenched. I wasn't sure what was worse: that I'd lied to my mother's face, or that I'd let her say those things against Remy and didn't lift a finger to defend him.

"May I please be excused?"

Mum's shoulders relaxed. "Very well. Off you go."

When I was back in the safety of my own room, I sank down onto the bed and stared at the fading marks on the back of my hand. I didn't tell Remy he'd squeezed me so hard because I knew it would upset him, but I didn't mind. The marks proved that Remy cared. A lot.

I rolled over and buried my face in the pillow, muffling a groan.

I never meant to kiss him. I still didn't understand what came over me at the party, but I would have got over it eventually, could have chalked it up to a one-off adolescent experiment.

Except I'd liked it. I *liked* kissing Remy Montrose.

Today had been the last chance to turn my back and walk away. That was what I'd planned to do. But then Remy asked to show me what it could be like between us, and the offer was as inescapable as gravity's pull.

So I said yes.

seven

A cloud of steam wafted up into my face as I lifted the lid of the pot. The aroma of hot chicken soup filled my nostrils, oozing down my throat and coaxing a growl from my empty stomach.

Anna chuckled and glanced at her watch. "This is the last stop for the night. Think you can hold out for another half an hour?"

"I'm sure I'll live."

"Good. I don't want you keeling over before your friend comes to pick you up."

Biting back a grimace at the reminder, I plucked a Styrofoam cup from the table and ladled in the soup until it was nearly full to the brim. The line was long this evening, a gaggle of bodies slumped against the graffitied shopfront, glaring at the horns of passing cars as they echoed off the high-rise commission flats on the other side of the road.

I handed the cup to a gaunt man wearing a moth-eaten charcoal beanie, who accepted it with a husky murmur of thanks.

As I prepared another cup, I peered sidelong at Anna. She

was a bright-eyed, brown-haired woman in her early sixties with deep grooves bracketing her mouth from a lifetime of smiles and laughter. Mum first met her years ago, shortly after Miles was born, and it was due to Anna's influence that we'd all become involved in volunteering.

Anna caught me looking and paused, her own ladle poised in mid-air. Her eyebrows lifted. "Something on your mind, Carter?"

The lie leapt unbidden to my lips. "No. Just thinking about everything I need to do before school goes back."

Anna pointed the—thankfully empty—ladle at my chest. "You need to slow down, young man, or you'll burn yourself out. School doesn't start back for another week. If you weren't staying at your friend's house tonight, I'd complain that you don't make enough time to relax."

I barely made *any* time to relax. Time was not something I had in abundance these days. Even now, during the Easter holidays, I was busy. I'd spent much of the first week working at the shelter or studying, and I picked up several extra nights at the soup van to avoid spending evenings at home. To avoid my mother.

The churning in my belly morphed from hunger to nausea.

Remy had convinced me to come over to his house tonight, and I told Mum I was spending the evening at Jake's. Lying to her— *deceiving* her—didn't sit well with me, but I had no other choice. Staying away from Remy was no longer an option, and I couldn't explain this…this *thing* to her when I couldn't even explain it to myself. She wouldn't understand.

And now I couldn't meet her eyes without the anchor of guilt threatening to drown me.

I sighed as my ladle scraped the bottom of the pot. The soup dregs were light on chicken but heavy on lentils, and they made a nasty squelching sound when poured into the last cup. I held it out and was unsurprised by the youthful hands that grasped it.

The boy always hovered at the end of the line. Unkempt strawberry-blond hair framed a pale, freckled face, obscuring his wary light-green eyes. He couldn't be much older than I was, but he'd been a regular at the soup van for almost two years now. I often wondered what had forced him onto the streets, but any attempt to engage him in conversation invariably ended in failure. He never spoke.

I didn't even know his name.

The boy took his soup with a nod and a small, tired smile, then turned and melted into the shadows of a nearby alley. I watched him go, swallowing past a crushing sense of uselessness.

Remy arrived just as we were locking up the van. The mere sight of him sauntering towards us cut clean through the anchor weighing me down and obliterated my lingering guilt.

In the week since first term ended, he'd dyed his hair alternating stripes of pink and green, and the dazzling colours were bright against the black of his shirt. His entire presence was hypnotic. Mesmerising.

He lured me in like a siren weaving a song.

Breathe, Carter.

He stopped a few feet away, grin tugging at one corner of his mouth. "Bonsoir."

"Hi," I squeaked.

Remy's grin widened. "This lovely lady must be Anna."

I shut my eyes and prayed for a spontaneous bolt of lightning to strike me where I stood. Why did I agree to let Remy pick me up from the soup van? What had I been *thinking*? Anna was friends with my mother!

But Anna, when she stepped up beside me, was smiling. "And you must be Remy. It's a pleasure to meet you, dear."

"The pleasure is all mine, ma'am."

"Oh, pish posh," Anna huffed, flapping a hand in his direction. "Carter, take this charmer and get him out of here. He's too dangerous to be out in public."

The tension in my shoulders eased. It was a relief to know that Remy's presence affected someone other than me. I cleared my throat. "You sure?"

"Of course. We're all packed up now. You boys have a good night."

"Thanks, Anna. I'll see you next week."

I collected my bag from the van and followed Remy back to his car, which he'd parked around the corner. It felt strange sliding into the midnight-blue sedan with someone my own age behind the wheel. Of my close friends, Remy was the first to have turned eighteen and qualified for a probationary licence, and as I buckled my seatbelt, I found myself quashing a mild sense of alarm.

"I hope you're hungry," Remy said as he indicated and pulled out onto the street. "Maman cooked boeuf bourguignon. A lot of it."

"She didn't have to do that."

"Bad luck. It's done. So, are you hungry?"

I shifted in my seat and admitted, "I'm starving."

"Thank God! I don't want to be eating leftovers for the rest of the week."

When we arrived at Remy's place, it was after nine o'clock, and the house was quiet. He told me his parents were in bed since they both had to work in the morning, and Monique was sleeping over at a friend's house. Sabine, his youngest sister, sat cross-legged in the darkened living room, scrolling through movies on the TV.

She glanced up with a hopeful smile. "Can we watch one of the *Thor* movies?"

Remy flipped on the lights. "Sure. Chris Hemsworth is *smoking* hot. You know how much I love a bit of eye candy."

Sabine giggled, but a sharp pang went through my chest. Although I knew Remy was out to his family, the ease with which his sister accepted his comment was bewildering. I didn't get it. How could I, when all I had to compare it to were my mother's caustic words?

Be careful around that boy, Carter.

I don't want you spending time alone with him.

I won't let him turn into a faggot!

"Carter?"

Shrugging off my nerves as best I could, I joined Remy in the kitchen. I leaned against the counter as he heated up our dinner, and when the food was ready, we grabbed the plates and a tub of mint choc chip ice cream and joined Sabine in front of the TV.

Only half my attention was on the screen while the movie played. The other half kept drifting to Remy, slumped on the couch beside me. One long leg stretched out in front of him, foot resting on the coffee table near his abandoned plate, and the other was tucked against his chest. He rested his chin on his knee, giving me an unobstructed view of the flickering light playing across his face. Beneath the glow, his features looked sharper than usual, more fey.

"So, what did you think?"

I jumped at the sound of his voice. "Huh?"

Remy nodded at the TV; credits were rolling across the screen. "The movie, Carter. What did you think?"

"Oh. Yeah. It was good." I hadn't even noticed it finished.

"Il n'a pas regardé le film," said Sabine. "Il était trop occupé à te regarder."

Remy cocked an eyebrow. "Vraiment?"

"Est-il ton copain?"

"Non, il est seulement un ami."

Sabine stared at him for a minute, her expression dubious. "Je ne te crois pas."

Remy laughed. "Believe what you want, ma puce. It's the truth." He stood and stretched luxuriously, spine bowing like a cat's. "Carter and I are going to my room now. Bonne nuit."

I was aware that my face was burning as he grabbed my elbow and all but dragged me down the short hall into his bedroom. He kicked the door shut behind us, and my stomach gave a savage twist. "Um…you do know I took French up until last year, right? I may be a bit rusty, but…"

Remy groaned and flopped onto his bed. "Merde, you understood all that?"

"She asked if I'm your boyfriend," I accused.

"Calm down. In case you didn't notice, I told her you're just a friend."

I bit my lip. "She didn't believe you."

"Well, it's not my fault you spent the whole movie watching *me*!"

Blood rushed to my cheeks so fast my toes tingled. I opened my mouth to say something—*anything*—in my defence, but the stream of my vocabulary had run completely dry.

I covered my face with my hands. *Kill me now.*

The bed creaked as Remy bounced back onto his feet. He pulled my hands down, fingers curling tight around my wrists. "You're adorable when you blush." His head tilted, considering me. "So, all those times I've called you mon chou..."

I swallowed hard, pitched my voice low. "I knew you weren't calling me your 'cabbage' because I remind you of a vegetable."

"Well." Remy's lips curved skyward. He tugged lightly on my wrists, and just as I swayed closer, obeying the silent command, his gaze ensnared mine.

My breath caught.

I'd wondered, in our week apart, whether I'd imagined the draw I felt towards him. I'd wondered whether it had been a mistake, some kind of fluke. But here, now, I couldn't deny the pull. We were the earth and the sun, drawn together by gravity.

I didn't flinch when Remy closed the distance between us.

His mouth pressed into mine, and the world trembled. He tasted like peppermint and chocolate and the warm tang of metal as he moved his lips gently against my own.

This kiss was not like our first. This time there was no rage, no hurtful words tainting the air we shared. The fire in my belly was banked by something sweeter, softer, but just as strong. Stronger, even. Remy's nose nudged mine, and I sighed into his mouth. My eyelashes fluttered over his brow, and his fingertips dragged sparks across my jaw.

Then his hands slid down to my chest, right over my racing heart, and he was pushing me away. There was an indentation on my mouth from his lip ring, and I traced it absently with my tongue, a sharp thrill running through me when his eyes went dark and hot.

"There," he murmured. "That wasn't so bad, was it?"

93

I wasn't prepared for the surge of emotion that slammed into my ribs. Breath shuddered out of me in a torrent, scraping my throat raw.

The longing on Remy's face melted into something far more tender. "Come on," he said. His arm slid around my waist, and he herded me over to the bed. "Lie down with me."

I collapsed against a striped pillow without protest, rolling onto my back to stare up at the ceiling.

Remy crawled up beside me and put a hand on my chest. I tensed. "Is this okay?" he whispered.

The only thing separating the flat of his palm from my skin was the material of my shirt. I could feel his warmth through the thin cotton, sense the splay of each finger across my sternum. Did he feel how hard my heart was pounding?

I was silent too long. Remy withdrew his hand, and I hated the chill that stole through my body at its loss. Reaching blindly, I caught hold of his forearm.

"Carter?"

I turned my head to look at him. His gaze roamed over my face as he worried his lip ring between his teeth. "It's okay," I said.

"You sure?"

In response, I took his hand and pressed his fingers back to my chest. Shivers skittered down my spine and Remy wriggled closer, until our faces were only an inch apart.

Hesitantly, I touched one of the green spikes on his head. "Why do you dye your hair like this?"

"I like it."

I liked it too. More than I should.

"It's not a statement or anything," Remy said. "Some people think it is. Kids at my old school loved to give me hell for my fashion choices, and if I called them out on it, they claimed I made myself a target."

Hadn't I thought the same thing, the day we met? That Remy's appearance painted a target on his back, that he was simply *asking* for trouble? Shame burned like acid in my chest.

A shadow crossed Remy's face, but it passed swiftly, a summer squall blowing over. The smile that followed was wistful. "I'm lucky, though. My parents have never been anything but supportive. I was twelve when I came out to them."

I blinked. *Twelve?*

"Dad signed the two of us up to self-defence classes the very next day. He said that people could be hateful, so we had to be ready to fight for my right to be me." Remy chuckled fondly at the memory. "When I wanted to dye my hair, I worried about what people might think, but Mum told me that life's too short to let others dictate the way I live. She marched me straight to the hairdresser and demanded someone make me look as bold and bright on the outside as I was on the inside."

I thought of myself at twelve. I was the quiet kid who read books and played the violin and hid behind his brother. The kid who was so shy he could barely speak without stuttering, who let others pick on him, push him around. The kid who never lifted a finger to defend himself, because he didn't know how.

I didn't learn until Miles and Dad were gone and Uncle Sean fled overseas, and the only support I had left was a mother who'd sooner scream in my face than hold me in her arms.

My eyes prickled.

"Hey." Remy touched my cheek. His fingers came away wet. "What's wrong?"

I looked at him. He was so beautiful, so unlike anyone I'd ever met before. At first glance, he seemed more delicate and fragile than other boys, but I didn't have to look far to find the steel beneath. I wished I could crawl inside his skin and stay there forever, safe and warm.

But I'd have to settle for something not so far out of my reach.

I licked my lips and dropped my eyes to his mouth. "Can you... can you kiss me again?"

Remy's fingers, still hovering over my cheek, slipped back into my hair. His eyes were bright. "I thought you'd never ask," he said and leaned in.

The next few weeks passed in a blur. My days were occupied by classes and music rehearsals and weekend shifts at the shelter, my nights by homework and chores and volunteering at the soup van. School cricket was replaced by football with the onset of second term, so Saturday mornings were commandeered by matches that left me wet and muddy and aching all over.

Somehow, I still found time to be with Remy. We walked to and from school together when we could, just the two of us, alone. I loved how he could talk and talk and talk, regaling me with outrageous stories that pulled honest laughs from my chest. I lived for the stolen moments when his fingers brushed against my hand or my hip, or his lips grazed over my skin.

Being around Remy made everything feel brighter, more hopeful. Around him, the mounting pressures of the outside world faded into obscurity. He was like a shining light in the darkness that pervaded the rest of my life. The *only* shining light.

If I believed in magic, I might think that Remy had put me under some kind of spell.

One evening towards the end of April, Katie came over so we could finalise planning for the year twelve formal. The event was only two months away, and while the venue had been booked, we still needed to decide on the menu, the music, and the decorations.

"Spencer has been freaking out about what to wear," Katie said as she flipped idly through a catalogue. "I always thought that was *my* job."

"Well, he's supposed to coordinate his outfit with yours or something, right? That must stressful since you'd eat him alive if he messed it up."

She shot me a narrow-eyed look. "Maybe I should take him shopping."

"Poor Spence."

"Hey!" A pencil came hurtling for my forehead. I jerked back at the last minute, and it bounced harmlessly off my chin. "What are you saying, Carter?"

Grumbling, I bent to pick the pencil up from the floor. "Nothing."

"That's what I thought." Katie leaned back in her chair. A frown crept across her face as she studied the magazine. Tucking a loose strand of sun-bright hair behind her ear, she sighed and tossed it onto the pile with the rest. "I don't like that one."

I *thunked* my head on the table. There was only so much browsing through decorations I could take, and I'd surpassed my limit at least five brochures ago. "You do realise that was the last one we have?"

"Well…"

I pressed my face harder into the wood, stifling a groan. "What?"

Katie hesitated. "How about the catalogues your brother collected for his formal? Do you still have those lying around somewhere?"

Slowly, I raised my head to stare at her. "Are you serious?"

My co-captain grimaced, then shrugged, but she didn't retract her question. At least she had the decency to look contrite.

"I'll have a look," I said flatly, shoving my chair away from the table hard enough that the legs squealed against the tiled floor. I didn't glance back at her as I left the room.

I paused for a moment in the hallway right outside Miles' permanently-closed door. It wasn't often that I set foot inside, and I resented being pressured into it by Katie. But my irritation warred with exhaustion, the two clamouring for the upper hand; in the end, exhaustion won out. Hanging my head, I turned the doorknob and stepped into my brother's bedroom.

The thing was, while I told Katie I'd look for the catalogues Miles used for his school formal, I already knew where they were. I knew where *all* his things were.

Nothing that belonged to Miles had been thrown away.

I passed his desk and shelves without looking at them and knelt down by his bed. Beneath it, there was a box full of ideas he had and plans he'd made when he was the school captain five years ago. I dragged it out and wiped away a thick layer of dust before opening the cardboard flap.

The sight of the first file almost made my heart stop:

GRADUATION

I sat back on my heels, holding a hand to my suddenly throbbing eyes. Looming at the edge of my awareness were a plastic-wrapped shirt and pants hanging from the closet door as if Miles left them there yesterday. As if he was still coming home.

"Did you hear that Paige asked Jake to be her date for the formal?"

I whirled with a startled cry, elbow catching the corner of the box and tipping it onto its side. "What the hell, Katie?"

She stood beside the desk, just inside the doorway. One of Miles' photo frames was in her hand. Heat sparked against tinder inside me, erupting into rage. I leapt to my feet and snatched the frame off her. "*Don't touch his stuff!*"

Katie's eyes widened, and she took a half-step back. "Sorry."

The fire extinguished. That quickly, the anger just drained away. All that was left in the ashes was weariness, a hollowness I knew all too well. "I just…"

"No," said Katie. "I get it. I'm sorry."

She didn't get it, but I accepted the apology for what it was. I jerked my head in the direction of the fallen box. "Take what you want from there."

"Thanks."

While Katie searched, I set the wooden frame back on the desk. It held a picture of Miles and his girlfriend on the night of their formal. They were in the centre of a large room, surrounded by others, but they may as well have been in a world of their own. She had her eyes closed, face tilted up towards my brother, who gazed down at her with the smile of one who'd lost his heart long ago.

"Found it!" Katie held up a tattered manila folder that was easily twice as thick as ours.

Sighing inwardly—where on earth had Miles found so many

catalogues?—I nudged the box back under the bed with my toe and followed her into the living room.

Katie dropped the file onto the table, where it landed with a dull thud. "So. Paige and Jake. What do you think?"

"I'm pretty sure she asked him because her parents don't like him."

Katie snorted. "Sounds about right. I bet Jake's thrilled. He does love to make a scene."

"Hmm."

"Who are you going to ask?"

It took a moment for the question to register, but when it did, I felt all my muscles freeze up. "I was just planning to go by myself."

"You always do that," she complained.

"So what?" I said, unable to keep the defensiveness from my voice. "Having a date isn't compulsory, is it?"

Katie blinked. Then she leaned forwards and gently touched my hand. "No, but it's our year twelve formal, Carter. It's like…a milestone. Don't you want to share it with someone?"

There was a herd of elephants running rampant in my ribcage. "I don't—"

"Why don't you ask Piper?" Katie suggested. "You guys get along, and I heard on the grapevine she just broke up with her boyfriend."

"But we're not—"

She waved away my protest. "Then just go as friends, like Jake and Paige. It's not as if it's a marriage proposal, you know. Think about it, at least."

My eyes dropped to the table. I didn't *need* to share the occasion with someone else, not when all my friends would be there anyway.

I didn't even *want* to, because on the night of the year twelve formal, there was only one person I could imagine standing beside me. Only one person who belonged in my own photograph, looking at me with a smile.

And I couldn't take him.

eight

I wasn't sure if I believed in God. Religion didn't play much of a role in my life growing up, despite both my parents being raised in religious households. While neither of them had lost their faith, practicing it simply hurt too much after their devout families turned their backs on us all.

Mum and I only started attending church after the accident. Mum slotted back into the community as if she'd never left, used it to fill the gaping void left behind by her husband and son.

It wasn't that easy for me. I struggled with the concept that God might be testing me, or punishing me for an infraction I didn't understand. The alternative was even harder to accept: that Miles and Dad were taken from us by nothing more than chance. Bad luck.

For years I swung between two extremes, belief and disbelief, faith in God and faith in science, unable to find a balance between the two. In the end, I decided it didn't matter, and I made my peace with the fact that I'd never know for sure.

But after Tim Halloran's death, I realised one thing: if a higher power *did* exist, it harboured nothing for me but hatred.

I was reminded of that every Sunday when I sat in the cold, drafty church next to my mother, keenly feeling Tim's absence on my other side.

I stifled a yawn as today's sermon droned on. The pastor's monotonous voice reverberated off the vaulted ceiling, and with the natural light muted to a variegated glow by the stained-glass windows beyond the altar, it was a battle to keep my eyes from drifting closed. The only thing keeping me awake was the discomfort of the hard pew digging into my back.

It was a relief when the service ended and we retired to the modernised recreation area for morning tea. I stuck to the edge of the room while Mum socialised. Most people my age were involved in the youth group, and though I was glad Mum had never pushed me to join them, it left me in a bit of an awkward position after the service.

A sudden lull in the chatter caught my attention. I followed several furtive glances towards the open door, and my heartbeat faltered when a couple stepped into the room. The pastor greeted them like long-lost friends and ushered them over to the refreshment table. They nodded and smiled at whatever he said, but the smiles didn't quite reach their eyes.

Eventually conversations resumed, but my gaze lingered on the couple. If they were offended or flustered by the scrutiny they received, they didn't show it. They huddled close together, the man peering into his coffee as if it held the answers to the universe, while the woman's eyes darted restlessly about the room.

Until they fell upon me and stopped.

The woman nudged her husband's arm. He looked up, tense expression smoothing out when he spied me leaning against the wall. Then they started towards me, and my stomach leapt into my throat. I scanned the crowd for Mum, hoping she'd call me over, but her conspicuous auburn hair had disappeared from view.

The couple halted only a few steps away. "Hello, Carter," the woman said.

I swallowed. "Hi, Mrs Halloran."

"How are you?"

"I'm well, thank you." I refrained from returning the question. I didn't want to put them in a position where they had to lie and say they were fine.

Mr and Mrs Halloran weren't fine. They couldn't be. They seemed to have aged a decade since I last saw them in December, at the funeral of their only son.

"Good. That's good." Mrs Halloran smoothed her hands nervously over the front of her blouse. "We'd like to speak with you if you have a moment?"

My brain short-circuited.

In the years we'd attended the same church, I'd rarely spoken to either of them except perhaps in passing. But they knew Tim and I had been friends. Not close friends, like I was with Jake, but Tim wasn't in the youth group either, so we'd hang out on Sunday mornings. Have fun together.

I didn't want to talk to his parents, but they looked worn, desperate. Devastated. The least I could do was hear them out, let them get off their chests whatever they needed to say. I owed that much to Tim.

I owed him so much more.

I was hyperaware of all the eyes upon us, watching our exchange with interest. My skin prickled, but I forced myself to give a nonchalant shrug. "Sure."

"Let's go into the church," Mr Halloran suggested.

On wooden legs, I followed them back through the door that led to the main part of the church. I sank onto the front pew, and Mrs Halloran settled down beside me. Mr Halloran remained standing, shifting his weight anxiously from foot to foot.

I laced my fingers together in my lap. "How can I help you?"

Mr Halloran reached into his pocket a withdrew a small, rectangular object. I recognised it immediately; the Winnie-the-Pooh stickers, faded and peeling in several places, were unmistakable. It was Tim's mobile phone.

"He called you...that day."

The world stopped.

"I don't..." My voice was formless, disembodied. "I missed the call."

Mrs Halloran's eyes swum with tears. "But why would he call you? Why *you*, Carter? Why not his school friends? Why not *us*?"

Why? That word struck me with the force of a million tiny daggers piercing my flesh. *Whywhywhywhywhywhywhy?*

Cold flashed through my body from all directions, colliding in the middle of my chest. I tried to breathe in, but it felt like inhaling shrapnel; agony sliced my lungs apart.

As if from a distance, I heard Tim's parents speaking, their tones urgent and low. I couldn't understand them. Everything had gone hazy, dark, and I was shaking, breaking apart.

I'm dying.

"What on earth is going on here?" a harsh, angry voice bit into my blurred edges. Warm fingers grasped my chin and tilted my face upwards. "Carter, look at me."

I opened my eyes. Light refracted around my mother's furious expression, scorching into my retinas.

"Come on. We're leaving." With strength that belied her willowy frame, she hauled me to my feet.

I couldn't feel my toes. I couldn't feel much of anything except the pain.

"Andrea—"

"No," Mum snapped. "You stay away from him. Your boy did enough damage."

It took all my remaining energy to stay upright. Mum's grip on my arm was bruising, but it was also the only thing that kept me tethered to the present, to reality. Whenever I swayed too far to one side, she pulled me back, and she managed to get me outside and bundled into the car before my knees gave out.

I mashed my face up against the cold window. My head spun, the thumping ache so intense I thought my brain would pop like a burst balloon. On the other side of the glass, the world raced by, and I couldn't shake the feeling that I wasn't really part of it. Like I was merely a tourist in my own life, a passing stranger who would soon move on and be forgotten by all who had seen him.

Disjointed images marched before me to the shutter of an old film: stained-grey street—*click*—trees weeping orange leaves—*click*—a driveway lined by cracked bricks—*click*—stooped porch with a familiar door—*click*—narrow hallway, boards underfoot—*click*—then falling…falling onto the softness of my bed.

The galaxy stretched out above me, but even the sun had gone dark.

Mum's frowning face blotted out a patch of stars. "I don't know what they said to you, Carter, but I hope you know his actions had nothing to do with you."

I shuddered, wishing with all my heart that I could tell her everything.

"Will you be all right?"

No. Please help me. But the words were lodged in my throat along with all the other things I couldn't say.

"Do you need anything?"

I needed her to hug me, kiss me, tell me she loved me and that everything would be okay. Even if it was a lie. I wanted her to sit down by my side and drag her fingers through my hair, trace the lengthy shadows beneath my eyes.

But her heavy sigh only proved that was nothing more than a hopeless, impossible dream. "Get some rest, Carter. You have school tomorrow."

Then she was gone.

My ragged sob cleaved the air.

I remembered the last day I spent with Tim Halloran. We sat on a bench out the back of the church, verdant grass beneath our feet and the summer sun warming our faces. It was a welcome reprieve after the pastor's lengthy speech about death.

"What do you think it's like to die?" Tim asked me.

I glanced sideways at him; his eyes were closed, and he was smiling. Light filtered through the trees and dappled his golden skin, casting half his profile in shadow.

I thought death would be ugly, painful, but I didn't tell Tim that. The truth would make his smile vanish, and I hadn't seen it in months.

"I reckon it's peaceful," I said. "Like falling asleep."

Tim called me later that week. I saw his name on the screen of my phone, and I let the call ring out. I knew what he was after. At least, I thought I did, and I didn't want to hear it.

If I'd known what he was planning, why he was *really* calling, I would have done everything differently. But I didn't get a second chance.

The next day, Mum told me he'd killed himself, and I never saw him again.

The tears started as an itching burn behind my eyes. Droplets clung to my lashes, pooling there before tumbling down over quivering skin. First a trickle, then a stream.

Once the cascade started, I thought it would never stop.

I was drowning, sliding down into a pit of ageless despair. I wondered if anyone would care if I never clawed my way out. Sometimes, I didn't much care myself.

Sometimes, I could almost comprehend how Tim found it too much to take.

Time passed.

I continued to breathe, sucking in one tear-swollen lungful of air after another until the storm quietened. Settled. It left behind a stillness more disturbing than the storm itself.

The door slammed open, wrenching the hinges with a sound like a gunshot. "Get up, Carter. You're going to be late for your orchestra rehearsal."

I didn't react.

"Don't ignore me!"

Sluggishly, I rolled over. Mum stood on the threshold with her arms crossed, every inch of her pressed and polished for work. There were silver threads in her hair that I'd never noticed before.

She scowled down at my prone form. "For Pete's sake, you're a mess! Get up and go wash your face. We're leaving in ten minutes."

The thought of moving, of having to fasten on a smile like a piece of clothing, made me feel sick. "Mum," I croaked. "I don't feel so good. Can I stay home today?"

"That isn't how the real world works, Carter. You're not a child anymore. Do you think I get to take a day off every time I'm feeling down? If I did that, we would be out on the streets." Her lips pursed. "No. Unless you're on death's door, you're going to school. Get up."

"I c-can't. Please don't make me—"

"*Get out of bed*!" Mum shouted, her whole face flushed crimson. "There is absolutely *nothing* wrong with you. Miles would *never* have carried on like this!"

The accusation knifed through me. I hated when she did that, when she used my brother against me like a weapon. I hated it more when she was right.

Miles would never have acted like this.

I sat up, still groggy, and lowered my feet to the floor. My joints creaked as I stood, and Mum moved aside so I could hobble down the hall to the bathroom. To wash my face. To do as I was bid, so I didn't let her down again. So I didn't let *Miles* down again.

I went about my morning ablutions as if on an automated sequence. My mind was listless, my thoughts like the wind: hard to catch, impossible to hold onto. But those ten minutes went by lightning fast, and then Mum was herding me out of the house.

It was rare for her to drive me to school. On a normal day, I'd be ecstatic she made the offer, let alone set aside the time.

But today was not a normal day.

When we pulled up outside the front gate, Mum was gripping

109

the steering wheel so hard, the tendons stood out on her hands. She was expecting a fight.

"I'm sorry," I whispered.

Her shoulders slumped. "I know I'm hard on you. But you appreciate more than most how difficult life can be. How unfair." She drew in a tight breath. "There are bad days. There will *always* be bad days, but we have to pull ourselves together and endure them."

She was right. I knew she was right. So I smothered the feeble voice in my head that wondered if others had bad days like mine.

I met Mum's eyes. Other people, other mothers and sons, would never understand how it was between us. We were holding on by the most tenuous of threads. Holding on to each other because that was all that was left. Everyone else was gone.

I opened the door and got out.

"Thank you," Mum said.

I didn't wait around to watch her leave. I glued a mask to my face and strode through the gate as if I wasn't falling to pieces inside.

Jamie and Piper were already in the rehearsal room when I arrived, directing a handful of younger students as they set up for the orchestra. I placed my violin beside a stack of music stands and weaved my way through the growing island of chairs.

Piper noticed me first. She turned in my direction, razor-thin eyebrows angling down. "Carter, you look awful. Is everything okay?"

For a moment, I was trapped by the open concern in her eyes. My pulse accelerated, slamming my heart against my ribcage like an *acciaccatura* in quick time.

I was so tired. Tired from not sleeping through the night, from the drama of the previous day. Tired of guarding my secrets, of trying to untangle the Gordian knot that was my friendship with Remy. Tired of feeling like I was suffocating under the weight of everyone's expectations as they closed in around me.

I wanted, just for once, to feel *normal*.

I didn't realise Piper had moved closer until her fingers tugged at my sleeve. "Carter—"

"Would you like to go to the formal with me?" I blurted.

Across the room, several people sniggered. Piper's eyes went comically wide.

Heat rushed to my face, and I hurriedly added, "Just as friends, of course."

She stared at me—kept staring—then a boisterous shriek pierced my eardrums, and I found myself with an armful of Piper.

"I take it that's a yes?" I wheezed.

"*Yes!*" Piper released me. "That's a *definite* yes. You've literally saved my life."

I rubbed the back of my neck. "Um…glad I could help?"

"How cute."

The smile playing at my lips dissolved. That snide voice could only belong to one person.

Piper rolled her eyes. "Shut up, Jamie. At least now I *have* someone to go with."

"Touché," Jamie drawled. He pressed a hand to his heart. "Please. Don't spare a thought for my feelings."

Piper huffed. "And what feelings would—" Something across the room wrenched at her attention. "Kevin Tran, are you *filming* this? Give me that phone right—"

I didn't hear the rest of her words, because the moment she launched herself at the year eight boy, Jamie's cool eyes drilled into me.

"What?" I demanded.

His expression was pensive. Calculating. "I didn't think Piper was your type."

My heartbeat slowed to a *calando*, falling away with every rhythmic thump. "What's that got to do with anything?"

"Oh nothing, Carter." Lips curling, Jamie turned away. "Nothing at all…"

"So, I just heard that you asked Piper to the formal."

I wilted against my locker. It was only the start of recess, barely two hours since rehearsal, but thanks to Kevin Tran and his covert filming, it seemed the whole school already knew. I shouldn't have been surprised the news had made its way to Remy.

"It's true, then," he said. It wasn't a question.

My jaw worked as I scrambled for an appropriate response. Remy and I hadn't talked about the formal. I'd avoided the subject altogether when he was around, fearing I'd find myself in a situation exactly like this.

Remy elbowed the locker door aside. Metal groaned as he leaned against it, exhaling loudly. "I get it, Carter. I do. I didn't expect you to ask *me*, you know, but I thought I'd at least earned a heads-up."

"I didn't mean to…" I bit my lip before I finished the sentence. There was no good way to end it, no way that would absolve my guilt as well as Remy's hurt.

"You got scared."

I gave him a pained look. Was I truly that transparent to him? Could he really read through the lines I drew around me like a cloak?

Remy's expression softened. "It's okay. It happens to the best of us. Just…talk to me next time, okay?"

"Okay," I promised.

He poked me in the side. "Come on, then. Let's go and join the others."

We found them in our usual spot under the gum tree near the oval. Jake clapped me on the back as I settled down beside him, grinning from ear to ear. "Look who it is! The man himself!"

"Have you guys seen the video?" Paige chortled. "He was so *delightfully* awkward."

I gritted my teeth through my friends' good-natured teasing, but I felt no real mirth. No pride at what I'd done. How could I, when all I could think about was that I'd let Remy down?

I didn't think things could get any worse than that.

"Hey," said Spencer out of the blue. "What's Jamie Ray doing out here?"

My stomach plummeted through the bottom of my scuffed school shoes.

"Hi there, Jamie!" Katie called.

"Katie," Jamie acknowledged her greeting, but dismissed the rest of us as if we were bugs beneath his heel. That suited me just fine.

Until he stopped beside Remy and said, "Would you like to be my date to the formal?"

I froze.

"Your date?" Remy echoed.

"Yes."

For a fraction of a second, Jamie's eyes darted to me, raking across my face before he turned a startlingly sweet smile on Remy. "We're the only queer guys in the year level—the only *openly* queer guys," he amended. "So I figure…why not?"

I was going to throw up. I needed to get out of here *right now*.

I muttered something about going to the bathroom and heaved myself off the ground. I walked away before I could hear Remy's response, knowing he would say yes. Knowing I had no right to wish he would say no.

I couldn't give Remy what Jamie could. I couldn't give him what he deserved.

Ants crawled beneath my skin as I cast my eyes across the schoolyard. Younger kids raced around, dashing through breezeways and yelling as they chased after one another, cheerful laughter brightening the air.

I longed with everything I had to be one of them again. If I ever had been.

Something slammed into my back, right between my shoulder blades. Too stunned at first to react, I was propelled into a shaded alcove beneath the nearby stairs, where I staggered around to confront my attacker—and gaped at the sight of Jamie Ray.

His usually tidy hair was mussed and he breathed hard, as if he'd run a mile. As if he'd *run after me*. A thunderous expression clouded his face, and I did nothing to stop him when he fisted my jumper and pushed me into the wall. "What's your deal, huh? Are you pissed that I asked your guy to the formal, or that you couldn't work up the courage to ask him yourself?"

"W-what?" I choked out. "We're just fr—"

"Don't." The word was low, furious. "Don't feed me that bullshit.

Unlike everyone else at this school, I'm neither blind nor stupid. He follows you around like a lovesick puppy, and you can't keep your eyes off him. You're more than just *friends*."

Panic streaked through my system. "I don't know what you're talking about."

Jamie scoffed. "No? Then look me in the eye and tell me you're not into him."

It was like a slap in the face.

This couldn't happen. This couldn't *be* happening.

Being with Remy was the best part of my day. He was my first thought when I woke in the morning and the last thought I had every night. He was what kept me going when everything else was too much. He was in my dreams, in my very soul, and this strange, undefined thing between us was precious to me. Precious beyond words.

But it was *mine*. I didn't want to share it—share *him*—with anyone. It would be tarnished in the light of others' eyes, and I couldn't go back. I couldn't go back to being the boy people pointed at and spoke about in hushed whispers when they thought I couldn't hear.

"You can't say it." Jamie sounded surprised. His hand uncurled from my jumper.

I shoved him away. "*Fuck you.*"

"No, fuck *you*, Carter, for being a coward." He jabbed an accusing finger my way. "You don't want to be open about who you are? Fine. That's your business. But you can't be with someone as incredible as Remy Montrose and expect to keep it a secret."

An outraged, sputtering noise burst out of me. I'd never hated anyone before, not even the kid that killed my dad and brother. But right then, I thought I might just hate Jamie Ray.

"Oh relax. The quiet, broken ones are more my thing…but I'm still taking him to the formal. He shouldn't have to go alone and watch you parade Piper around." Jamie's mouth twisted into a sneer. "And since you've got that terrified look on your face, I'll have you know that outing people is at the top of my *do not* list."

He leaned closer. The anger in his eyes was gone, but it was replaced with something colder, harder. A warning. "This will stay between us. I just hope you realise that a light like his can't shine in the dark of your closet."

Without another word, Jamie turned and walked away.

I sank to the ground and buried my face in my hands.

nine

Winter came early.

Northerly winds blew in from the Antarctic, dragging misty cold fronts that smothered the city in fog. The fog clung to everything, even the bare-boned trees, and imparted a damp chill that lingered for hours after it finally dispersed.

The nights grew longer, darker, snatching away minutes of daylight with every rotation of the earth. Soon enough, the only time I saw the sun was through a classroom window, and even then, it was muted, its warmth feeble and dull.

The world was an uncanny reflection of the way I felt inside.

Things with Remy hadn't been the same since my confrontation with Jamie. I couldn't shake the doubt Jamie's words had roused in me, couldn't banish the guilt that gnawed at my bones. It showed in the stilted way I spoke to Remy now, in the way I couldn't quite meet his eyes. In the way I'd gone back to flinching whenever he touched me.

It only got worse as the date of the formal inched closer. I tossed and turned most nights, unable to find a reprieve from my harrowing thoughts. They left me strung-out and irritable, and every time Remy so much as looked in Jamie's direction, I wanted to punch the nearest wall.

"Hey, Carter, can you get the door?" Megs' shout echoed down the corridor.

Right. The shelter's doorbell was ringing.

I shook my head as I rose from my haunches. Papers and folders littered the office floor around me; I'd been in the middle of preparing the new filing system Megs had proposed before my treacherous mind whisked me away. I was zoning out like that a lot lately. If I didn't get a handle on it soon, someone was going to notice.

"Carter, don't you make me—"

"Sorry!" I yelled back. "I'm going now." I hurried out into the foyer, fumbled a bit with the lock before I managed to turn it, and threw the door open.

The greeting died on my lips.

The man across the threshold looked like he'd just stepped off the set of an action film in which he had the starring role. He had several inches on me and was built like an Olympic swimmer: broad shoulders and narrow hips, not an ounce of body fat in sight. Dark hair was cropped close to his skull, offsetting a pair of sharp green eyes, and tattoos poked out from the collar and sleeves of the white tee-shirt moulded over his chest.

My stomach took a dive past my knees.

"Um…" The man shifted. "Do you mind if I come in?"

It was only then that I noticed the cane tucked under one sculpted arm and the large cardboard box in his hands. "Oh, of course!" I jumped aside, almost tripping over my feet in my haste to get out of his way.

The man limped through the door and stopped in the middle of the foyer. He nodded down at the box. "I found her on the side of the road."

I approached cautiously and peered inside. It was a puppy—a young one. Young puppies weren't common at the shelter, especially ones as gorgeous as this. She resembled a German Shepherd, but her midnight black coat was longer and her ears floppier, not quite as erect as a Shepherd's were known to be.

I reached a hand towards her quivering flank. The pup wriggled within the box, nose working, and I couldn't stop the gasp that escaped me when I caught sight of her face. "Megs!" I shouted. "*Megs*! I need you out here!"

My boss must have heard the urgent thread in my voice because she came running. Megs skidded to an inelegant halt when she saw the pup, and that *look* she got sometimes bloomed across her face: the look of pity and anger that always overcame her when a new dog was brought in.

I gently ruffled the puppy's ear. It wasn't hard to figure out why she'd been abandoned—she was missing her right eye. The empty, misshapen socket pulled at the whole side of her face, giving her a disfigured appearance that would frighten most people away.

And people abandoned their animals for less.

"You poor thing," Megs crooned.

"I found her on the side of the road," the man repeated.

Megs blinked up at him, as if only just realising he was there. "Thank you for bringing her in…?"

"Ben," he offered.

"Thank you for bringing her in, Ben," said Megs. Her eyes skimmed from his face to his shoulders, following the curve of one tattooed arm down to where he clutched the box against his stomach. She stared at him, at the ridges of muscle plainly visible beneath his thin shirt.

Just like I had.

Only, with her, Ben stared right back.

A stone lodged in my throat. I tried to clear it. Loudly.

Megs flushed. "Could you please bring her through to the examination room?"

"Sure."

I trailed them both to the exam station set up next door to the washroom. The shelter didn't have a full-time vet, but Megs was a qualified veterinary nurse and had training in animal husbandry. She knew what she was doing as she lifted the puppy out of the box and onto the table, murmuring to her in a low, soothing tone.

The dog whined as Megs checked her over. Her single puppy-blue eye fixed on Ben and me, like she was begging us to help her. Save her. I wondered how much she understood about what was happening. Did she know her owner hadn't wanted her and left her on the side of the street like a piece of garbage? Did she know that she no longer had a home?

"She seems okay," Megs announced. "She's a bit young to be away from her mother, and she's dehydrated, but she's not actually hurt. The missing eye is likely a birth defect."

I stretched out my hand again, and the puppy leaned into my touch, butting her ear up against my fingers. My heart did a strange little stutter in my chest.

"What will happen to her now?" Ben asked.

"She'll stay here with us until she's a bit older, and then we'll find her a new home." Megs touched his forearm. "I don't suppose you're interested?"

Ben winced, and neither of us missed the way his eyes drifted to his cane. He was leaning on it heavily now that his hands were free. "I'm not in a position to care for a dog right now," he said, but his voice was laced with regret.

Megs squeezed his arm. "That's okay, Ben."

Something dark coiled beneath my ribs. Why did she keep saying his name like that? And why did she keep *touching* him?

"If you don't mind coming with me, I have some paperwork I need you to fill out."

Ben nodded. He gave the pup one last, searching look before turning to me. "Thank you for your help," he said and flashed me a megawatt smile.

I almost swallowed my tongue. Before I could form an intelligent response, Ben followed Megs out of the room, head tilted to catch her words.

"You idiot, Carter," I muttered. Chomping down on a hysterical laugh, I resumed scratching the puppy's ear. She squirmed in pleasure and half-collapsed onto the table.

Dogs were simple—unlike people.

When Megs returned, her face was red, and her eyes were suspiciously bright. She hummed under her breath as she plucked the box off the table.

"You were flirting with him," I chided.

"Well, can you blame me?" She tossed the box in the corner and spun back around, eyebrows raised. "Don't think I didn't notice *you* checking him out."

"I did not!"

Megs' eyebrows climbed higher. "He was *unfairly* gorgeous, Carter. You'd have to be dead not to see it."

I didn't. I *hadn't*. Just because I was captivated by Remy didn't mean I looked at *other* men. That horrifying thought took root deep inside me, and I threw Megs a baleful glare.

Her mirth waned. "You look so much like your brother when you do that."

Those words dropped between us like a bomb. Every muscle in my body stiffened.

Because up until the day he died, Megs had been my brother's girlfriend. The love of his life. They were supposed to be together forever.

And now all that was left were the dreams of what could have been.

The puppy squeaked. I immediately relaxed my grip, groping for a way to change the subject. My gaze fell to the pup's upturned belly, to the silky coat as dark as the shadows at twilight. "Shadow," I blurted.

"What?"

"We should call her Shadow."

Megs sighed. "Carter…"

In that one word—my name—I heard her unspoken warning to not get too attached. Attachment only ever ended in heartache.

Shadow's tail thumped out a beat on the table, and I stared down at her until my vision blurred.

I was pretty sure that this time, for me, it was already far too late.

I slipped my arm around Piper's waist and smiled into the flashing lights.

The evening of the year twelve formal had finally arrived, and my date and I stood in front of Jake's fireplace while the parents tested their questionable skills at photography.

I leaned down and whispered in Piper's ear, "You look amazing."

She beamed up at me. The cameras went wild.

I wasn't lying. Piper did look stunning in a wine-red dress that complemented her tawny complexion. It was fitted firmly to her chest and hips before flaring outwards, tumbling to her ankles with understated elegance. Shiny silver clips pinned her hair at the nape of her neck, and the delicate ivy and white chrysanthemum corsage I gave her was secured on her left wrist.

"Thanks," Piper said out of the corner of her mouth. "You look quite dashing yourself."

I tried not to pick at my sleeve. I was wearing the black suit and white shirt Miles had worn to his year twelve formal, paired with a tie the same colour as Piper's dress. Neither Mum nor I had wanted me to wear the suit, but we couldn't justify the expense of purchasing a new one when the suit hanging in my brother's wardrobe was in perfectly good condition since he'd only worn it once.

When I saw myself in the mirror, I wanted to claw it off my skin.

By the time we stepped away from the fireplace so Katie and Spencer could take their turn, black spots were dancing before my eyes. I might have been accustomed to the brilliant glare of stage lights, but I'd quickly learned that stage lights had nothing on eight camera-wielding mothers. Even my own mother was in the thick of things, snapping pictures on our ancient camera and fussing over the girls' dresses.

I led Piper over to the dining table where the Brenners had set out drinks and poured her a small flute of champagne from the open bottle.

"You're not having any?" she asked.

"You know I don't drink. Besides"—I placed the bottle back down—"Jake's already had enough for the both of us."

Piper giggled. "He just wants to piss off Paige's parents."

"Well, I think it's working."

I spied my best friend across the room, and my stomach sank. He was with Remy and Jamie, laughing at something one of them said. Both wore tuxedoes—Jamie's black and Remy's charcoal grey—with green carnation boutonnières pinned to their left lapels. They looked good together. Distinguished.

I hated it.

The worst part was knowing that *I* could have been the one standing at Remy's side, if only I'd been brave enough to ask him.

But Mum's presence served to remind me why that could never be. Her entire body had locked up the moment they entered the room. At first, I thought it was the shock of seeing Remy again, until I realised she wasn't looking at Remy at all.

She was looking at Jamie.

Jamie, whom I'd known for years. Who I'd never told her was gay.

"All right, everyone!" Mrs Brenner cried. "The limo is here!"

I took a deep breath and tried to pull my scattered pieces back together.

Piper set her glass on the table. "Ready?"

I took her arm, setting her hand in the crook of my elbow, and we followed the procession out to the front yard where a sleek black vehicle idled against the kerb. We obediently gathered for one final round of photos before the eight of us piled inside: Katie and Spencer, Jake and Paige, Remy and Jamie, Piper and me.

The tradition of taking a limousine to the formal had always seemed somewhat excessive to me, but tonight, I was grateful for the distraction. My friends' animated chatter washed over me as I examined the limo's interior, taking note of the leather seats lined by tiny blue lights, the tinted windows, the panelled doors accented with chrome. It was stylish. Trendy.

It was almost enough to block out the sound of Remy's laughter. Almost enough to erase the image of his thigh pressed up against Jamie's.

Almost. But not quite.

The journey to the venue only took half an hour, and all too soon, the limo entered a broad, semi-circular driveway, pulling to a stop at the foot of a staircase covered in red velvet carpet.

Jake squashed his face against the window and barked out a laugh. "I feel like a movie star right now!"

"Well, you sure are classy enough to be one," Paige quipped, eyeing the smudge his nose left on the glass.

The driver jumped out and sidled around to open the door. "Have a good night, kids," he said with a toothy grin that grated on my already frayed nerves.

I climbed through the doorframe and onto the landing, drawing in a lungful of wintry air. Piper followed, and I placed a steadying hand on her elbow when she stumbled on the edge of the gutter. She smiled at me. I smiled back.

She really was beautiful, both inside and out.

So why didn't Piper make me feel even a fraction of what I felt around Remy?

You know why.

I shunted the thought viciously aside.

We ascended the stairs arm-in-arm, Piper wobbling in her heels even with my support. But we reached the top step without incident, and as we passed through the grand entrance, I allowed myself a moment of deep satisfaction.

"Wow," Piper breathed.

Katie's and my hard work had paid off—the place looked incredible.

Strings of fairy lights hung from the arched ceiling, threading between wrought-iron chandeliers that glowed with soft green light. The round tables, draped in chocolate brown cloth, were arranged in concentric circles around a glossy hardwood floor that would be used for dancing later.

At the centre of each table sat a golden vase filled with white lilies, and matching gold cutlery adorned every setting, along with two crystal goblets and a name tag printed on sparkly silver-white card.

We found our places, and I pulled out Piper's chair for her, trying not to scowl as Jamie did the same for Remy. Jamie murmured something to Remy as he seated himself, bending so close that Remy's hair caressed his cheek. The motion seemed so nonchalant, so comfortable.

So intimate.

In my mind's eye, I saw myself pick up the water jug and hurl it at Jamie's head.

My hands twitched.

Piper bumped me with her shoulder. "Everything okay?"

"Fine." I tore my attention from the pitcher and settled it back on Piper. My friend. My *date*. "Perfect," I corrected.

126

But I wasn't fine, and perfection slipped further and further from my grasp as the hours trickled by. My lips carved a smile through my face, stretching the skin like that of a tepid wax doll, solidifying as it cooled. My friends tossed around jokes between mouthfuls of food, and my laughter rose to join the symphony of theirs, always too sharp or too flat. Feigned, where theirs was true.

How could they not see it? How could they not see the darkness pouring off me in waves? Did their own lights shine so bright, they couldn't see past the glare?

Or was I really that good at deceiving them? Would they really not notice if my brittle shell cracked wide open and spilled out all the ugly things inside?

I didn't know why it hurt so badly; I'd been content to hide for so long.

When the lighting dimmed and the music swelled, I fidgeted in my seat. Couples shoved back their chairs and charged for the dancefloor, whooping and hollering to each other, their animated voices only adding to the din.

I would have done anything—*anything*—to get out of dancing, but I couldn't beg off this time. Not when Piper was waiting for me, warm brown eyes twinkling with excitement.

I stood on quivering legs and offered her my arm. "Shall we?"

"You're such a gentleman, Carter," she said with affection. "Let's just stick to the edge, okay? I'm not too keen on testing out my balance in these heels, and I know dancing isn't your thing."

I almost collapsed with relief.

We approached the fringe of the dancefloor, each of us hesitant in our own way. I gripped Piper's hand and spun her around until she was giddy and breathless, laughing and leaning against me like she'd fall if I let her go. It was a task that deserved my full attention, but my traitorous eyes kept drifting to the very centre of the crowd.

Where Remy and Jamie were dancing up a storm together.

It was like watching Remy with Matteo at Piper's party, only worse. Ten thousand times worse. Now that I knew how it felt to have Remy in my arms, to see him in someone else's, to see him in *Jamie's*…

"Do you think they actually *like* each other?" Piper wondered aloud.

I startled, unaware that she'd been watching them too. They were chest-to-chest now, and my insides cramped at the possible answer to her question. Remy shimmied backwards, face lit up in delight as he crooked a finger, beckoning Jamie to follow. "I—"

A wide hand shoved Remy between the shoulder blades, propelling him into Jamie so hard, they both crashed to the floor.

"Oh *shit!*" Piper gasped.

I barely registered her shock. A singular thought was reverberating through my skull, cramming out everything else:

Remy Remy Remy Remy Remy

"Wait here," I growled and plunged into the crowd.

I didn't care who I elbowed aside as I forced my way towards him. Remy had disappeared from view the moment he fell, but the figure looming over the place where he last stood, fists balled at his sides, lips moving—

"Bite my tight gay arse, Kennedy!"

Remy's voice. I craned my neck and saw the top of his blond head.

"Or maybe not," said Jamie. He reappeared at Remy's side and calmly dusted himself off, turning a cool gaze on their assailant. "You'd like that, wouldn't you, Jonah?"

128

"Think he's after a threesome?"

"I know what it is he's after." Jamie ambled past Remy to Kennedy, and before the bully could react, Jamie grabbed his tie and yanked him close.

Whatever Jamie said next was swallowed by the crowd, but it made Kennedy's face go white. "*Fuck you, faggot!*" he roared, and he clocked Jamie right in the jaw.

Jamie staggered, and Remy lurched after him, catching him around the waist. Remy's expression was trapped between worried and murderous, but he turned his back on Kennedy's retreating form to press a hand to Jamie's chin. "You okay, mon chou?"

I choked. "*No.*"

They both whirled, and a pair of blue-grey eyes met my own.

The pain was sharp inside me, like shattered glass.

Remy's hands fell away from Jamie, but it was too late. The damage was already done. He'd called Jamie by *that name*. That name I hated at first but had grown to love because it was special. Because it was *mine*.

Or so I thought.

I spun and shoved back into the crowd, putting as many bodies between us as I could. I raced for the bathroom, desperate to reach its limited privacy before my chest completely caved in.

The bathroom was empty, but I locked myself in a stall anyway, crumpled onto the lid of the toilet, and clutched at my hair. I yanked hard on the finger-length strands and pain sliced through my scalp, but I welcomed it. *Revelled* in it.

This pain was preferable to the hurt inside.

Footsteps approached. Someone pounded on the door. "Carter?"

I closed my eyes.

129

"Carter Cantwell, open this door!"

I considered refusing, but I was a fool who couldn't deny him anything. I pushed wearily to my feet and flicked the lock open.

Remy stood on the other side like an avenging angel, golden hair rumpled, red splashed across his cheeks. "For such a smart guy," he snapped, "you can be really fucking stupid sometimes."

Then he seized my shirt and slammed his mouth over mine.

I stumbled from the force of it, and Remy pushed me back until I was crushed against the wall. Every inch of my skin thrummed, every nerve ending buzzed as he kissed me, consumed me, *devoured* me.

My knees gave out and I sank onto the toilet seat, Remy landing in my lap. A strangled moan rumbled from my throat, but Remy never broke the contact between our lips. His hands found my wrists and he pinned them against the cistern, holding me captive, completely at his mercy as he set every inch of me on fire.

I shuddered. Heat, pulsing and hungry, raced from his mouth to my chest to my stomach and down and down and down. No words were adequate to describe the intense sensations, the heady mixture of pleasure and pain, longing and fear.

It was too much and not enough, and *I was going to implode*.

"Stop," I gasped. "Remy, *stop!*"

He stopped immediately. His lips released mine and he freed my wrists, one shaking hand moving to cover his mouth. "Shit."

I tried to breathe, tried not to squirm, because—

"Shit," Remy said again. He looked as dazed as I felt, irises swallowed by dilated pupils, mouth slack and swollen and soft.

I wanted to pull him closer. I wanted to push him away.

Remy made the decision for me. He climbed off my lap and

sagged against the door which had, fortunately, drifted closed. "Sorry," he groaned. "You just looked all sad and jealous and *so hot* in that suit, and I...I...God, what a mess."

He scrubbed his hands through his hair, over his face, and lowered them back to his sides. "Before you ask, it was an accident. I didn't mean to call Jamie that name. It's *yours*, but Kennedy punched him, hurt him, and it just...slipped out."

Hope intertwined with the fear singing through my veins.

"I promise I don't feel for him what I feel for you," Remy whispered. "And I really, really like you, Carter."

Tears pricked at my eyes. I didn't deserve this.

You're a coward.

"I haven't been fair to you," I mumbled. "Jamie said—"

"Jamie can mind his own damn business. In case you've forgotten, this"—Remy waved between us—"was my idea. I knew what I was getting into when I asked you to give me a chance. I haven't changed my mind, and even if I do, I'll *tell* you. I'm not going to make you guess how I feel."

He leaned forwards and cupped my cheeks in his hands. "I know how confusing this can be, but I'm here for you, Carter. In whatever capacity you'll have me."

I swallowed back the sob that longed to tear free.

Remy kissed my forehead, then stepped away. "I should go and check on Jamie. Will you be okay here?"

I nodded. I needed to thank him, but my throat was too thick to speak.

"Okay. Take as long as you need. I'll let Piper know where you are." Remy listened for a moment to make sure we were alone, then slipped out of the stall. Out of my sight.

The knowledge settled over me like a pall: Remy Montrose was everything. He was *everything* that I wanted.

And he was everything I could never have.

ten

"Bloody hell, kiddo," my uncle croaked and surged forwards to throw his arms around me.

I grunted at the impact, but as he hugged me against his chest, I found myself fighting a smile. I lost. "You're starting to sound like a Pom."

"Shut your mouth!"

"Well, it's true."

Sean pushed me back, holding me at arms' length with his hands braced on my shoulders. A misty film crept over his eyes. "God, Carter, look at you. You look so much like your dad."

My smile dropped. What was with all these remarks about my appearance lately? First from Megs, now from my uncle—they made my battered heart ache.

Sean was my father's only sibling, younger than him by a full ten years. Despite the age difference, they'd been as close as two brothers could be. They were so close, in fact, that Sean had come to live with us when he was sixteen because of some trouble back home.

Dad had doted on him, just like Miles doted on me.

A few months after they died, Sean accepted a job in London and moved to the other side of the world. We kept in touch by email, mostly, since the time difference and his work made him a hard man to pin down any other way.

It was over a year since we last saw each other in person. My uncle hadn't changed all that much, though I couldn't say the same about myself.

"I'm almost as tall as you are," I pointed out. Sean had always been the tallest of the Cantwell boys—something he'd taken immense pride in—but now we stood nearly eye-to-eye.

My uncle scowled. "Now hang on just a—"

A snort of laughter escaped me. "It's really good to see you, Uncle Sean."

"It's good to see you too, nephew of mine," he said ruefully. He drew me in for another hug before releasing me with a slap on the back. "You're looking sharp."

I glanced down at my concert attire: black trousers, black shoes, and a collared black shirt, its wrist-length sleeves rolled up to my elbows. The only break in all that monotonous black was the crisp white bow tie knotted at my throat.

It was the smartest outfit I owned.

"Is your mum home?" Sean peered into the dark room behind me, like he expected her to materialise from the shadows.

"No, she's still at work."

His eyebrow rose. "Really? Does she usually work so late?"

"Sometimes. What's with all the questions?"

Sean held up his hands in surrender. "Just curious!"

I knew it was more than that. My mother and my uncle didn't

134

get along—they never had. Mum tolerated Sean's presence in our lives because he was Dad's kid brother, and she'd tolerated him living in our house when I was small.

But now that Dad was gone, she wanted as little to do with Sean as possible. Sean managed to greet Mum cordially enough on the odd occasion they saw each other, yet every time they were in the same room for longer than five minutes, an argument was bound to break out.

I didn't understand it. I wasn't sure I wanted to.

My uncle shoved his hands into his pockets. "Would you like to head off, then?"

"Sure. Let's go."

When Sean informed me that he'd be in Melbourne at the start of third term and wanted to come to my school's annual music concert, I was both touched and swamped with nerves. It had been years since a family member watched me perform; the last time, our brothers had still been alive.

Sean held the boot of his rental car open while I wrestled my ratty instrument case inside. He eyed the thing speculatively, skimming over the patches of duct tape and the clasps that were just a little too loose. I'd had this case for even longer than I'd had my violin, and it showed—it was falling apart at the seams.

But we couldn't afford to replace it right now. The good ones didn't come cheap.

Once we were in the car, I directed my uncle through the streets to the school and its on-campus auditorium. He left the radio off as I brought him up to speed on all the things going on in my life. I told him about my classwork and the footy team, Piper and the formal. I told him about the winter holidays and the soup van and

Shadow, who'd been with us at the shelter for a month now.

Sean smiled and nodded along, but I didn't miss the surreptitious glances he threw me every now and then. It was like he knew I wasn't telling him everything.

Like he knew that there was something I was hiding.

My stomach had tied itself in knots by the time we parted ways out the front of the theatre. Leaving my uncle to find his seat, I entered through the centre's rear door and made for the cavernous backstage room allocated to the string orchestra.

Paige and Jamie had already installed themselves in the far corner. They glanced up as I approached, and a wide grin broke out across Paige's face. "My, my, my, do you clean up nice!"

"You've seen me dressed like this a hundred times, Paige."

She shrugged. "*I* have, but our friends in the audience certainly haven't. They're not going to know what hit them!"

My chest constricted at the reminder. As the school captain, Katie was attending the concert, and it came as no surprise that Spencer was joining her. What *had* caught me off guard was when Jake and Remy announced they were also tagging along to show their support.

"Chill," said Paige. "It's going to be fine."

Jamie made a faint scoffing noise, which I ignored.

Things had been tense between Jamie and me since the formal. While I admired him greatly as a fellow musician and had always managed to turn a blind eye to the less desirable aspects of his personality, I found I could no longer pretend. He knew too much. He *saw* too much. I was all too aware that, with a single world, he could knock down the pillars holding the roof above my head.

No matter what he claimed, Jamie could ruin *everything*.

So, in the hope he would forget all about me, I ignored him. Piper and Paige must have noticed that the male half of our quartet was mired in a cold war, but since Jamie and I didn't let it interfere with our music, they were wise enough not to say anything.

I flipped open my shabby violin case and reached for my bow and rosin. With smooth, methodical strokes, I ran the amber-hued block over the horsehair strings and tried to shove all extraneous thoughts from my mind. Worry about the situation with Jamie, about the fact that Remy and Jake *and* Sean were in the audience, had no place here.

Here, where music flowed like the air in and out of my lungs.

Here, the only place I never felt lost.

I took up my violin and focused on the feel of soft hide against my chin, of ebony and maple beneath my hands. Allowed the excited hum to resonate through my chest cavity as we prepared to go onstage.

For someone who had to fight to free his words when he stood before a crowd, I was always remarkably composed when I performed. Over the course of the evening, I played several pieces with the orchestra and my string quartet, and my few solo sections were executed with an inner poise that was absent from every other facet of my life.

Melody after melody sizzled through my veins, and my fingers flew across the strings like a dream. My whole body thrummed with exhilaration, and as the final song reached its *crescendo*, I felt more alive, more real, than I had in months.

I felt like I could take on the world.

And then it was over.

Too soon, I was backstage again, the sudden silence crashing

137

over me like a wave. The fleeting joy fading *a niente*. I cleaned my bow and packed my violin away, every move sluggish and slow now that the music was gone.

Pathetic.

Annoyed at myself, I slammed the case shut and headed for the front of the auditorium. People milled about everywhere, chatting in small groups as they awaited the performers' return. I spotted Sean standing alone by the garden bed in the middle of the courtyard, and I waded through the masses until I reached his side.

"Holy shit, kiddo!" he exclaimed. "That was fantastic! I had no idea you were so good."

I ducked my head. "Thanks. I guess it's been a while since you've seen me play."

"Don't be so modest." My uncle put a hand on my shoulder, his thumb brushing my neck. "I'm proud of you."

Warmth spread through me, but my throat felt uncomfortably tight.

"Carter!" The familiar shout dragged my attention to the left, and I saw Jake weaving his way towards us. "Mate, that was—" he screeched to a halt, eyes going wide and round. "Mr C! I didn't know you were here!"

Sean let out a dramatic groan. "I'm sure I warned you against calling me that, Jake Brenner. It makes me feel old."

"Don't be stupid. Technically, you're young enough to be my brother!"

Ever since we were little kids, my best friend had worshipped the ground my uncle walked on. Sean was young, 'cool,' and had a playful, easy-going manner. He and Jake actually had a lot in common, and they'd always loved to ruffle each other's feathers.

138

But I missed my uncle's grumbled retort because, at that moment, someone else slipped through the gap that Jake had made in the crowd.

Remy.

My heart swooped through the bottom of my ribs at the sight of him. Tonight, he wore black skinny jeans and a grey button-down shirt that clung to every curve from shoulder to hip. His platinum hair was gelled up in artfully arranged spikes, and the smoky eyeshadow decorating his lids made his blue-grey eyes look enormous.

Those eyes raked over me like hot coals. All my muscles strained, battling the urge to drag him into my arms the way I did one night during the winter holidays when I stayed over at his place. Heat radiated from my cheeks at the memory.

As if he'd read my mind, Remy's lips quirked. "Hey."

"Hey," I said hoarsely.

The moment stretched, *shone*, until someone cleared their throat. I flinched at the sound, tearing my gaze away. Fixing it back on Jake and Sean.

A chill chased the warmth from my body.

I hadn't considered what Sean might think of Remy. Hadn't given a moment's thought to how my uncle might react. Remy was looking very…well, *flamboyant*…yet I hadn't noticed that as much as I noticed how he made me feel.

Like I was about to combust.

But Remy's appearance no longer shocked me—at least, not in the same way as it used to—and that could prove to be dangerous because if my uncle's opinion about gay people was anything like my mother's…

I swallowed. "Sean, this is our friend Remy. Remy, this is my uncle Sean."

"Wow," Remy whistled, peering up through his lashes. "Carter, if this is what you're going to look like in another decade, you're going to be *stunning*."

Jake coughed.

Horror seeped through my veins.

But Sean...Sean *laughed*. "I like you, Remy," he said and held out his hand. "You really know how to make a man feel special."

Remy took Sean's hand between two of his own. "Sean, it is my life's mission to make gorgeous men feel special."

Jake groaned. "Remy. Mate. You're flirting with Carter's *uncle*. That is so not cool."

My jaw had dropped so far it creaked. I didn't know whether to be relieved that Sean hardly blinked at Remy's presence or dismayed that he seemed to be *enjoying* the attention of an openly gay kid almost fifteen years his junior. Maybe both.

Definitely both.

Remy relinquished Sean's hand and poked his tongue out at Jake. "You're just jealous that I'm a better flirt than you."

"Lies!" Jake mock-gasped. "I am an *excellent* flirt!"

"I don't think that poor girl at the snack bar would agree."

"Hey! That was supposed to stay between—"

"As entertaining as all this is," Sean cut in, looking back at me, "Carter, I made reservations for us at that Thai place we went last time, but if you want to hang out with your friends..."

I shook my head quickly, and I didn't need to see the relief dart across his face to know I'd made the right decision. "I see these two every day, Uncle Sean. I haven't seen you in over a year."

"We're getting shafted," Jake said mournfully.

"Sorry. Thanks for coming, guys. It..." I bit my lip. "It means a lot."

Remy's smile made me weak in the knees. "You were awesome, Carter. And on the plus side, I got to meet your hot uncle."

"Oh, God. Please stop," Jake muttered.

The two of them bade us farewell before heading off into the crowd, and as they passed by me, Remy's fingertips swept over my waist. "Don't worry, mon chou," he whispered. "You're still my favourite."

My face burned all the way back to where Sean had parked the car.

Neither of us said much else until we reached the restaurant. When we stepped inside, the smells wafting from the kitchen had my stomach rumbling. An older Thai woman with an enchanting smile led us over to a table in the corner, and I fought a yawn as I settled into my seat. The room's dim lighting and cosy warmth were already making me drowsy.

"When was the last time you came here?" Sean asked, leafing through his menu.

"Not since the last time you brought me."

He frowned. "I thought you said it was your favourite."

"It is." I studied the opposite wall. Its surface was rough and painted a deep red, with squarish cotton lampshades framed by bamboo panels spaced evenly along its length.

When I glanced back at my uncle, I saw his bewildered expression hadn't cleared. "Mum and I don't go out for dinner," I explained with some reluctance. "Most nights, we don't even have dinner at the same time. If she's working late, I'll cook, and she'll eat when she gets home. If I have something on after school, she'll cook, and I'll eat when I get home."

"And you're okay with that?"

"Why wouldn't I be?"

Sean shut his menu and rubbed a hand against his chin. "I just worry about you, Carter. From the sounds of things, you have a lot on your plate. You're only seventeen, and you're still at school, and I—"

"I can take care of myself." It came out sharply. Bristling.

Sean paused. "Of course you can. But you shouldn't have to. Not yet."

My eyes dropped to the laminated pages in front of me, and the small black text blurred. "Dad did a whole lot more than I do when he was only a little bit older than me."

"He didn't want that for you," my uncle said quietly.

The response stuck in my throat. Did what my father wanted for me even matter anymore? He was gone, and his absence left a hole in more than just our hearts; I knew how hard Mum had to work just to make ends meet.

Thankfully, the waitress returned before I had to explain that too. She placed a pot of green tea and two small white cups on the table, then pulled out a notepad and pen. Once she scurried off to lodge our orders, Sean lifted the pot and filled both cups to the brim.

I dragged mine towards me, pressing my hands to the ceramic and letting the heat soak into my palms. The awkward, lingering silence chafed at my insides, but I didn't know how to break it. I didn't know what else I could say.

I'd always suspected my uncle felt guilty for leaving. For living so far away when I—or even Mum—might need him. But I imagined it had simply hurt too much to stay, and though I'd desperately missed him these last few years, I never blamed him for running. I would have leapt at the chance to escape had it been offered to me.

I raised the cup to my mouth and took a shallow sip.

"I'm moving back to Melbourne."

Tea sprayed across the red tablecloth. My lungs seized, and I coughed and choked as I tried to draw in a full breath.

Sean gave me a sheepish smile. "Sorry. I kind of sprung that on you, didn't I? But yes, I've put in an application to transfer back to my company's Melbourne branch."

My hands were shaking, so I placed my cup down before I sloshed scalding hot tea over my fingers. I stared at my uncle, eyes watering. "You're serious?"

"As a heart attack."

"*Sean.*"

"Carter," he said, "it wasn't an overnight decision, nor one I made lightly. I love England, and I've needed these few years away, but it's not home. I miss my family. I miss *you.*"

I could barely comprehend what I was hearing. "When?"

"Mid-October. I think I fly in on your last day of school."

"What about Mum?"

"What about her?"

"Does she know?"

Sean rolled his eyes. "Of course she does. God knows I've never been able to keep a secret from that woman."

I have. The thought threw a damper over my welling excitement. As much as a part of me was thrilled by the prospect of my uncle coming home, another part was afraid. Afraid I wouldn't be able to fool him the way I'd been fooling Mum. Not if he was always around.

Our food arrived a short time later. Grateful for the distraction, I helped myself to a plate of spring rolls and chicken satay skewers while my uncle dished out the rice.

"So," said Sean as he stirred the bowl of green curry, "what else is news? Is there a special girl in the picture?"

I fumbled with a skewer, and it almost slipped out of my fingers. "Um…no."

"What about the girl you took to the formal?"

"Piper?" Sweat broke out on the back of my neck. "We're just friends."

"All right, no girlfriend. A boyfriend, then?"

I froze. "*Excuse* me?"

"Hey, I'm just covering all bases here." Sean eyed me warily. "It's okay if you do, you know. Have a boyfriend, that is."

The ground dropped away beneath my feet. I felt like a bird whose wings had failed mid-flight, sending it plummeting back down to earth. My uncle didn't suspect what was going on between me and Remy, did he? He couldn't have figured it out in the space of those few short minutes he saw us together. That would mean…

Panic turned my voice into an angry hiss. "Just because I have a friend who's gay doesn't mean that *I* am."

"I never said it did," Sean replied.

"I am *not*—"

My uncle reached across the table and covered my trembling hand. "Okay. There's no girlfriend or boyfriend or significant other in your life. That's fine. No big deal."

That was easy for him to say. He didn't *know*.

And he couldn't possibly understand.

Gritting my teeth, I wrenched my hand out from under his, ignoring the flash of hurt on his face. It was time to shift the focus off me. "How about you, then? Are *you* seeing someone?"

"Actually, yes."

I blinked. "You are?"

Sean wiped his mouth on his napkin, his eyes bright. "I've found The One, nephew of mine."

"The One?" Shocked, I sat up straighter in my chair. Sure, I'd asked the question—and I did hate to think of my uncle all alone on the other side of the world—but this wasn't the answer I'd expected. "It's…it's serious?"

"Very."

I squinted at him. "Then what does she think of you moving back to Melbourne?"

Sean's smile was crooked. "Charlie's coming with me, Carter."

"Oh." He was right—it sounded *very* serious. "Tell me about this Charlie, Sean. I can't believe this is the first I'm hearing about her!"

My uncle's eyelids drifted closed, grin widening as if he could see her right in front of him. "Black hair, blue eyes, the face of an angel, but with a wicked streak like the Devil…"

I listened to Sean ramble for a while, watched the secret glow wink in and out of his gaze. Judging by the way he talked about Charlie, it wouldn't be long before I gained myself an aunt.

I'd never had an aunt before.

"When do you head back to London?" I asked Sean later as he was driving me home.

"Sunday night," he said. "I'll be house-hunting for the next few days, so I probably won't see you again before I leave. I'm sorry I can't stay longer, but soon enough, we'll be able to see each other as often as we like."

When we pulled up outside my house, Sean shut off the engine and walked me towards the front door. Halfway up the path, he halted me and put his hands on my shoulders. "I meant what I said after the concert. I'm real proud of you, kiddo."

A light came on inside the house, and my mother's face appeared in the window. Sean's lips tugged down at the corners, but he still pulled me in for a final hug.

"Uncle Sean?" I mumbled into his neck. "Why don't you and Mum get along?"

Sean exhaled, gripping me tighter. "It's complicated. And also not a conversation we can have right here and now. There are… things you don't know about our past. After your exams, we'll sit down, and I'll tell you everything, okay?"

My stomach lurched, but I nodded. What else could I do?

"Okay then." Sean released me and stepped away. "I love you, Carter."

It hurt, hearing those words fall so easily from my uncle's mouth when they never seemed to fall from my mother's. I gave him a tremulous smile. "See you in October, Uncle Sean."

He squeezed my shoulder one last time, then turned back down the path.

I stood there and watched his car disappear into the night.

eleven

I used to think my brother was a superhero.

He had a sixth sense when it came to me, a tendency of knowing when I was lost, or frightened, or in trouble. Of swooping in to save the day right when I needed him most.

His uncanny ability was never so apparent as it was one late-summer afternoon in my first term of high school. I was running down the stairs, my too-large school bag jostling around on my back when I stumbled and went flying through the air, landing with a jarring thud on the concrete and scraping a layer of skin off my jaw.

I lay there, face down, winded and too stunned to move. All thoughts of orchestra practice had been knocked right out of my brain.

"Well, well, well, what have we here?" said a nasally voice. "It's Cantwell Junior! Better watch where you're going, Junior. You wouldn't want to…trip."

A second person laughed. "That was quite a fall, Junior. Here, let us help you up."

Before I could protest, I was hauled upright by my backpack, and my violin skittered out of my hand. The boy that picked me up shoved me into the other, who lifted me by the lapels of my blazer until my feet dangled a good two inches off the ground.

I bit my lip on a whimper.

"Where are you off to in such a hurry?" taunted the first boy. He was behind me somewhere, close enough I could feel his hot breath on my neck. "Surely you can give us a minute of your time?"

I wanted to tell them to get lost, but fear had stolen my voice. It had slipped its talons between my ribs and latched right onto my heart.

The guy holding me gave me a violent shake. "I suggest you answer him, Junior."

Don't cry, don't cry, don't cry, I pleaded with myself, but my eyes had already filled with tears. The face before me blurred, multiplied, splintered apart into half a dozen sneers.

"Aww, don't be scared, Junior. We'll take care—"

"What the *fuck* is going on here?"

My tormentors jumped, and the hands around my collar loosened so suddenly I slithered to the ground like a wet rag. Relief sent the pooled tears tumbling down my cheeks.

Then my big brother was there, and it took all my strength not to throw myself at his legs. "Well? You two cowards think it's fun to pick on a kid half your size?"

"Come on, Cantwell, it was just a joke," was the whined reply. "We weren't actually going to *do* anything."

Miles made a noise of disgust. "Get out of here, and stay the fuck away from my brother. If I hear you've messed with him again…"

But he didn't need to finish the threat because they were already gone.

Miles crouched down beside me, his eyes clouded with concern. "You okay, little bro?"

My whole body was shaking, and I couldn't stop the sniffles, but I managed to nod.

My brother slung an arm around my narrow shoulders and helped me to my feet. "You've had a bad fright," he said. "I think everyone would understand if you gave orchestra a miss this afternoon."

"No!" I objected. My voice was hoarse, scratchy. "I want to go."

Miles gave me a searching look. "You're a brave kid."

"Not really." I brushed the dirt off my blazer, gaze dropping to my shoes. "I...I couldn't even...I didn't even try to fight them. I'm such a—"

"Stop." Miles forced my chin back up, and I winced as his fingers pressed against the new graze there. "You're perfect just the way you are. None of this was your fault. They're the ones in the wrong, and you were *smart* not to try to fight them."

I wasn't convinced. I must have done *something* to earn those boys' ire.

"Do you hear me, Carter?"

"I hear you," I mumbled. When it looked like he might pursue the matter further, I turned away and picked up my violin case from where it had skidded to a stop by the wall. Something inside me eased as soon as my fingers closed around the handle.

My brother walked me over to the music building, despite my half-hearted protests that I was fine. The truth was, I was glad he was by my side. I knew nothing bad would ever happen to me as long as he was there. My brother was a superhero.

My superhero.

"Do you want me to stick around and walk home with you?" he asked before I went inside.

The 'no' should have been immediate. Instinctive. I knew Miles had better things to do than hang around the school for the next hour just so he could escort his baby brother home.

But he sensed my hesitation and gave me a reassuring smile. "I'll stay," he said firmly. "Knock 'em dead, little bro. I'll be waiting out here at five."

And he was. Miles never let me down.

Not while he was living.

There were times when I felt so angry at the way he was ripped from the world too soon, when the mere thought of my brother's death poured fire over the crushing sadness, burning away the grief. When the stoked flames seethed inside me until I was nothing but a patchwork of charred hopes and melted dreams.

This was one of those times.

I stood in the kitchen, tension humming through me as I clutched the edge of the sink. Dusk had fallen beyond the window, streaking the sky with the mottled bluish-purple of a fresh bruise. The streets were dull, bleak, their only colour the barest golden glimmer along the branches of the naked trees.

My jaw clenched.

Of all days to come home to a note requesting—no, *demanding*— that I prepare our dinner, it had to be today. Today, when we had little more food in the house than two large potatoes and a container of half-defrosted beef mince. Today, when anger simmered so close to the surface, a mere spark would have made me explode.

Today, when Miles should be celebrating his twenty-third birthday.

On the bench beside the fruit bowl, my phone vibrated. I relinquished my hold on the sink, blowing out a heavy breath, and turned to tap the darkened screen.

REMY: sendingvirtualhug.gif

My anger cracked right down the middle. The boiling rage vaporised in the space of seconds as I stared down at the animation, imagining what it would be like to have him here, his arms around me for real. But Remy wasn't here right now. It was just me, alone in this house full of ghosts.

Dragging a hand down my face, I glanced across at the tub of beef mince. It sat in a pool of condensation that crept closer to the edge of the bench with every minute that passed. Mum normally used it to make Bolognese sauce, but that would be a worthless endeavour this evening, considering we had no pasta to go with it.

Nor did we have any rice or any bread. The only carbohydrates we *did* have in the house were the pair of wrinkled potatoes in the basket on the pantry floor.

A chill snaked down my spine.

Potatoes and mince. Maybe…could I make…?

I crossed back to the pantry and flung the door open. Squatting down, I rifled through the tins of crushed tomato—several nearing their expiry date—until my searching fingers came upon a can of kidney beans. I stilled. Swallowed hard.

My family had rarely gone out to restaurants for dinner, even when Dad and Miles were alive. Even on birthdays, when we eschewed eating out for sharing a special meal at home.

I'd never cooked chili con carne before, but I'd watched Mum make it every year on Miles' birthday for as long as he had birthdays to celebrate.

I rose slowly and placed the can of beans and some tinned tomatoes on the counter. We hadn't eaten Miles' favourite dish since the day those police officers knocked on our door and tore our lives apart. I wasn't sure how wise it was to cook it tonight, but I couldn't dislodge the idea now that it had taken root. It felt *right*, somehow.

And I didn't appear to have many other options.

Before I could talk myself out of it, I switched on the oven and popped the two potatoes in to bake.

Twenty minutes later, I was sautéing the meat in a pan with some spices. The remaining ingredients, scrounged together from our meagre supplies, were chopped up and ready to add, the beans rinsed and straining over the sink. All the smells caught in my nose, in my throat, simultaneously wonderful and devastating with the weight of the memories.

What would Miles do if he could see me now, cooking his favourite dinner on his birthday? Would he hug me tight and thank me like he used to do to Mum? Or would he ruffle my hair and laugh at my attempt the way he did the time I made muffins with the wrong type of flour, and they came out like cookies instead?

My chest twinged with the knowledge that I'd never get to find out.

Mum arrived home as I was dishing up the food. The potatoes I set in the middle of each plate, slicing them once lengthways and once crossways so they could hold the steaming sauce. I ladled generous amounts of chili over the top while sneaking glances at Mum.

She entered the kitchen with her head bowed, her body drawn in exhausted lines. She tossed her handbag onto the end of the bench and reached for the wine rack. Her hand froze halfway to a bottle of red, nostrils flaring as she recognised the distinct aroma of the meal.

Mum turned, and the kitchen lights cast her face into sharp relief. It was dead white—the sickly, grey-tinged white of a gutted fish.

That was when I knew I'd made a terrible mistake.

I placed down the serving spoon and let my hands fall to my sides. "Mum?"

Time lengthened, stretched. Until it snapped.

"*Why?*" she spat. "God preserve me, Carter, why would you make *this?*"

I opened my mouth, but nothing came out. My eyes dropped to the speckled stone of the benchtop, the sense of rightness wilting inside me.

"*You look at me when I'm talking to you!*" She rounded the bench and grabbed my arm so hard I recoiled in pain. I tried to curl in on myself, dread stabbing through me, but her fingers only squeezed harder. "*Look at me!*"

I looked down. Mum had crowded me into the corner, and though I'd outgrown her years ago, I'd never in my life felt so small. Fury twisted her pretty features, transforming her from my mother into a monster I couldn't hope to predict. Storm clouds billowed in her eyes, and lightning speared from her mouth to strike deep into my chest.

"Why?" she snarled.

I shook my head.

"*Speak.*"

I sucked in a breath that didn't fill my lungs and forced out the only words I could: "I'm sorry."

Silence.

And then Mum screamed. She picked up the plate by her elbow and hurled it at the floor. The ceramic shattered against the tiles, red sauce splashing everywhere, striping the ground like blood. The second plate joined the first, and all I saw was Dad and Miles, their bodies smeared across the road like spilt chili.

"You're *sorry*?" she roared. "That's all you have to say for yourself? What is *wrong* with you? Why would you want to remind me of a time when my life wasn't *ruined*?"

Her words were an avalanche as they hit. A whining sound filled my ears.

Ruined.

Mum's chest was heaving. "I just want to *forget*. Is that so much to ask? It's already hard enough with you—"

The whining stopped. My throat ached.

"I just want to forget," she rasped. Her eyes were glassy and her lips quivering, but she didn't say anything else. She just wrenched the bottle from the wine rack and stalked out of the kitchen, slamming her bedroom door shut behind her.

White noise engulfed my head, so loud it drowned out everything else. The rest of the world fell away, disconnecting me from itself until all I saw was the haunted look on my mother's face, all I heard was her words, throbbing through my ears.

Ruined, she'd said. Her life was *ruined*.

It was so…final.

I stared at the mess on the floor. It looked like someone had died there. It looked like I'd *killed* someone. The broken plates glittered like shards of bloodstained bone.

My blank mind ticked over as I sank to my knees. My chest was tight, hollow, but the rest of me was disturbingly numb. I reached out and grabbed a piece of splintered plate. Its edges were sharp and jagged, and I curled my hand around it, squeezing and squeezing until it bit into my skin and blood seeped out between my fingers, mingling with the sauce.

I barely felt it. I barely felt anything beyond a faint twinge.

Acid burned in the back of my throat. I unwound my bloody fingers and let the shard drop back to the ground. It cracked in two. A red trickle ran down my wrist and disappeared into the sleeve of my shirt. I watched it, transfixed.

Then I swallowed and closed my eyes and tried not to think any further.

Tried not to think about the persistent itch between my shoulder blades, beckoning me towards the hallway cupboard where we kept first aid supplies.

Tried not to think about the packet of Dad's razor blades hidden in the back corner.

Tried not to think about the fact I knew exactly how many were left, about the way it had felt when I carved the scar into my leg and shattered the numbness that caged me.

But the vision flashed through my mind anyway: of me, dragging a sharp edge across my flesh, tracing the line of blood from palm to elbow. I would feel *that*, surely. Would it hurt? Would it hurt to the point it took away my breath, my thoughts, the pain inside?

Ruined.

It couldn't hurt more than that word.

But then the world shifted again, snapping back into place. Sights and sounds and smells bombarded me, and for a moment, I was overwhelmed. The kitchen lights glared bright as the sun,

Mum's running shower was as loud as a torrential downpour. The scent of the chili, which had been so enticing while I cooked it, now made my stomach turn.

And my palm stung like I'd slashed it open with a piece of broken crockery.

Wincing, I heaved myself back to my feet and stumbled over to the sink to rinse the blood from my hand. When it was clean, I dried it and wrapped it in a tea towel, not willing to risk getting close to the first aid cupboard and the sharp edges waiting inside.

I tidied the kitchen slowly. Scraping up the mess on the floor, I dumped it into the bin before mopping the tiles and washing all of the dishes. My body felt as if it had aged years in only minutes; every movement was wooden, stiff, creaking like the rustling boughs of an ancient tree.

I knotted the rubbish bag with trembling fingers and took it straight outside. A frigid wind was blowing, the claws of winter still dug deep. I shivered as I trudged to the end of the driveway, where the household bin was waiting for tomorrow morning's collection.

For the longest time, I just stood there amidst the garbage, letting the chill soak into my skin. Letting it turn me numb again since it couldn't touch the cold settling inside.

When I stepped back into the house, it was as still and silent as the grave. The only light left on was the one in the kitchen, which meant that Mum had already gone to bed.

I cursed the sinking feeling in my stomach. I was a fool to hope she would come back out to talk to me, to apologise for yelling, for breaking the plates. She was more likely to tear me apart a second time than she was to apologise for frightening me the first.

But I had to do better. I had to *be* better.

I *was* better than this.

Taking a deep breath, I crept across the living room and into the alcove that led to Mum's bedroom. Her door was slightly ajar, so I slipped inside and peered through the inky darkness.

Mum was lying face down on her bed, clad in her fuzzy green dressing gown. Dad had bought it for her as an anniversary gift one year, claiming the colour made a lovely contrast with her deep auburn hair. The night leached both hair and gown to greyscale tones, but there was still enough light to make out the shape of the wine bottle lying on the floor.

I picked it up. It was empty.

Don't think about it. She'll be fine.

I set the bottle on the bedside table and, ever so gently, rolled my mother over. Her face was splotchy, and strands of hair were stuck to the silver runnels that tears had made down her cheeks. I brushed her hair back with careful fingers. She didn't even stir. The lines of worry she wore during the day were smoothed out as she slept, and her mouth was slack and soft.

She seemed so innocent, so vulnerable, and I was swamped by a wave of emotion. Protectiveness and guilt, anger and sorrow and fear. I loved her and hated her and wanted so badly for her to wake up and look at me and smile.

I would do anything just to see her smile.

I didn't know if she even remembered how.

Dropping to the floor next to her bed, I tucked myself into a ball. I couldn't face the thought of crawling, alone, into my own bed. Not tonight. A part of me longed to join her beneath the covers like I did when I was small, and nightmares kept me awake.

But I was no longer that boy, and she was no longer that woman.

What is wrong *with you?* she'd asked me.

Sometimes I wondered whether the thing that was wrong with me was the same thing that was wrong with her. This elusive but tangible darkness in both our lives that neither of us dared give voice to. Because speaking of it would make it real.

Speaking of it would give it *power*.

Tears were streaming down my face. "I'm sorry, Mum," I whispered into the silence. Salt slipped between my lips, coating my throat and tongue. "I'm sorry I'm not enough."

I held my breath, but she didn't hear me. She never did.

twelve

The empty pages glared up at me, accusing.

From the moment I'd picked up my pen and opened my psychology test, the words smudging across the paper like watercolours, I'd been ensnared by my own wretched thoughts.

Thoughts about the ache in my head and the ache in my neck from the sleepless night spent crouched beside Mum's bed.

Thoughts about my rapidly approaching graduation and end-of-year exams, which would determine the course of my future. All things Miles never got to experience.

Thoughts about the fact Mum believed her life was *ruined*, about how Miles' life was *beyond* ruined, and the way that, one day soon, I would be older than my big brother ever would be.

I thought about all those things, and when Mr Fielding said, "Pens down!" I stared at my test and realised I hadn't written a single word. I hadn't even started. I'd written *nothing* in a paper that would contribute to my final grades, and there was only one mark that a blank test could score.

Zero.

I'd never failed a test before. I'd never even come close. But as I passed my paper up to the front of the room, I was confronted by the horrifying fact that I was going to fail this one.

Mr Fielding scooped the pile of tests up in one arm, a teasing grin sliding across his face. "I hope you didn't find it too bad."

Some students chuckled. Others groaned. I bit the insides of my cheeks to stop myself from screaming.

"I should have these back to you in about two weeks' time," Mr Fielding went on. "Remember, it's not the end of the world if you don't get a high grade on this test. I set our coursework on the harder end of the spectrum, so your marks will be scaled based on how well you do in the exam. If you have any—"

The lunchtime bell cut through his spiel. Before Mr Fielding could finish his sentence, the class jumped to its feet, and the hiss of chair legs on carpet drowned out the sound of his voice.

Not the end of the world, he'd said. But it kind of felt like it was.

I stood numbly and filed out of the room behind Remy and Jake, carried on the tide of students heading for the locker room. My friends' animated chatter washed over me as they debated the answers to the test.

"What did you put for the second multi-choice, Carter?" my best friend threw over his shoulder. "I picked A, but I was tossing up between A and C. I think..." Jake jabbered on without even pausing to hear my response.

A blessing, since it was all I could do to keep from throwing up.

I followed my friends out to our usual spot in a daze. An abyss had opened up where my heart should be, hollowing me out and drawing the heat from my blood.

We sat, and Remy bumped his arm against mine. "You okay?"

"Fine." I twirled my spoon absently through a tub of yoghurt but didn't bring it up to my mouth. I wasn't hungry, despite not having eaten since lunchtime yesterday.

Remy's eyes crinkled with concern. "You sure? You look…"

I didn't want to know how I looked, but I could imagine what my friends saw as they all turned to face me. My cheeks reddened under the weight of their gazes, and I let the spoon sink down into the yoghurt. I wished I could follow it as I took a deep breath and, for once, gave them the truth: "I think I bombed the psych test."

Jake scoffed. "That's such bullshit, mate. Everyone knows you'll top the class. You always do."

"Besides," Spencer added, "you can always make up for it if you do well on the exam, right?"

That endless abyss splintered apart, and anger poured in through the gaps. For a moment, I wanted to hurt them. To make them hurt the way I hurt, to inflict upon them the same pain their words sent burrowing through me.

Because they didn't get it—none of them did. And I would never be able to make them understand.

I couldn't tell them that, to me, there was nothing more important than doing well at school. That getting good grades, getting into a medical degree, becoming a doctor, mattered more than anything else. More than *everything* else.

I couldn't tell them that there was no other way to make Mum proud of me, to put back the light that used to shine out of her eyes whenever she looked at Dad or Miles. I couldn't say how I needed to show her that her life wasn't ruined like she thought it was.

And I couldn't ever hope to explain that blank test paper, still shrieking its way through my mind, without telling them everything else they could never, ever know.

So I swallowed the rage. Seized it and shoved it down deep. "Right," I said. "Never mind."

Curling my fingers back around my spoon, I didn't bother to mention that a zero was a zero, no matter how you scaled it.

The next two weeks were some of the longest of my life. Winter gave way to spring, but the calendar hanging from our kitchen wall was the only way to mark its passing. The air remained brisk, the skies bleak and grey, and after several days of non-stop rain, I started to wonder whether the winter would ever truly end.

I tried to forget about the test. I tried to shunt it from my mind and move on, like a proper adult, but it was always there, lurking in the dark recesses of my subconscious. Every time I lowered my guard, it crept back up on me, a reminder that showered me with dread.

The day we were due to receive our marks, I sat silently in class. My heart hammered out a desperate beat against my ribcage as Mr Fielding traversed the room, slapping test papers on desks. When mine landed in front of me, it took all my effort to keep a straight face.

Our score was usually printed on the front page in red ink, but mine was conspicuously blank. Not unlike my responses. I eased the paper open, and my belly cramped at the sight of the fluoro yellow note stuck inside. At the message scrawled upon it:

Come and see me at the start of lunch. —Mr F.

I didn't hear Mr Fielding go through the answers to the test—*couldn't* hear past the roaring in my ears.

It was worse than I expected. I should have known Mr Fielding wouldn't just let this go, that he'd want to talk to me about those empty pages. But what was I supposed to tell him? How could I possibly explain? And what was I going to tell everyone else when they inevitably asked me about my score?

My eyes burned.

People *always* asked about my grades. It was as if, because my grades were good, my classmates thought they had a right to know them. That it was okay to brag if theirs happened to be better than mine. *I beat Carter Cantwell!* they'd crow, not knowing how it tore me up inside. Not understanding that being a straight-A student wasn't a cause for pride, not for me. It was a necessity.

And now this.

Time stretched out into eternity before the bell went, signalling the start of lunch. "You guys go ahead," I told Remy and Jake.

"Is everything okay?" asked Remy.

I tried on a smile. "Yeah, I just have to speak with Mr Fielding about something."

"Want us to come with?" Jake offered.

"No, that's all right. I'll see you later."

The two of them traded a glance, and for a moment, I thought they'd protest. But then Jake shrugged, and Remy turned and flashed me a grin. "We'll save you a spot," he promised.

I felt unbearably heavy as they elbowed their way out of the room, leaving me to face the consequences of my failure alone.

Mr Fielding had been cornered by some of my peers, so I hitched my pile of books up in my arms and made for his office myself. I slouched against the wall beside the door, trying not to look like a convict awaiting execution. Several sets of eyes grazed over me as people passed in the hall, but they dismissed me just as quickly. Mr Fielding was the head of year twelve as well as a psychology teacher, so my presence outside his office wasn't exactly unusual.

That didn't mean my skin wasn't crawling by the time he came rushing around the corner, teaching supplies spilling out of his arms. "Carter!" he exclaimed. "Sorry to keep you waiting."

"That's okay."

Mr Fielding bent over, his belongings teetering, and unlocked the office door with a key on the lanyard around his neck. He nudged it open with his foot. "Come on in."

I trailed him inside, and when the door clicked shut behind us, a death knell to my ears, I couldn't help it: I flinched.

Mr Fielding's eyebrows rose. "Relax. You're not in trouble." He dumped his things on one edge of the desk and gestured to the seat opposite his. "Make yourself comfortable."

His words did nothing to soothe my frayed nerves. Stiffly, I placed my own pile of books on the floor and eased myself into the chair. My palms were clammy and cold as I rubbed them together, fingers snagging, catching. Clinging on to each other.

"I take it you know why I asked you to come and see me?"

I nodded, but I couldn't bring myself to look at him.

"What happened?" he asked.

A violent tremor ran through my hands and up my arms. I pressed my wrists between my knees to stop the shaking, hard enough that my carpal bones groaned.

Paper rustled as Mr Fielding produced a copy of the test. "I know you know this stuff, Carter. You're my best student, and you didn't just make a simple mistake."

But it was just a mistake. Maybe not a simple one, and maybe not in the way he meant it, but the reason behind that blank test was just one great, big, terrible mistake. A mistake that started with the decision to cook a forbidden meal and ended with me so weary and distraught that I zoned out for an entire fifty-minute period.

I glanced up at my teacher and found him watching me with an open expression. "What happened?" he said again.

"I...I think I dozed off or something." The lie tasted better than the truth. "I barely slept the night before, so..."

Mr Fielding leaned back in his chair, rubbing his chin. "Why didn't you come and tell me this right after the test?"

I shrugged. How could I say that I was too mortified to even entertain the thought?

"Carter, you know how strict the rules are about school-assessed coursework. We could have done something about this had you approached me on the day, but now that the tests have been marked, it's too late for special consideration."

Special consideration. I hated those words. Mr Fielding must have thought I was such an idiot.

"I know this time of year is stressful, especially for you school captains," he said in a softer tone. "Has this been happening a lot— the not sleeping at night?"

My throat constricted, and my gaze fell back to the desk. The cheap wood surface was rough and pitted, marred by coffee stains that twisted and whirled before my eyes. All the blood seemed to drain from my extremities, leaving my hands tingling, my head too light.

"Because we have help available if you need it," said Mr Fielding.

Please, no.

I tried to take a breath. Found I couldn't.

"Is there anything going on in your life that I can help you with, Carter? At school...or at home?"

"No!" I rasped. Around me, the world had started to spin.

Mr Fielding blinked, then blinked again before his brows pulled close together. "Are you all right?"

No, no, no, this could not be happening. Not now. Not here. Fingers scrabbled at my tie, tugged at the collar of my shirt, trying to loosen the pressure on my windpipe. Fingers that must have been my own, though I couldn't feel them. Didn't care.

I couldn't *breathe*.

"Carter, what's wrong?"

"I...I don't feel too good..." The words came out mangled.

Sounds grew dull and muted. The walls were closing in. I lurched out of my chair, intent on getting out before I was smothered by those encroaching walls. For once, I didn't care how I looked as I crashed out of Mr Fielding's office and stumbled desperately away.

Bile rising in my throat, I made it to the nearest bathroom just in time. The ground raced up to meet me, and I gagged so hard my vision went black.

Someone shouted. A door opened, then closed.

My ears rang, my chest spasmed, and I forced my lungs to expand until slow, gradually, the darkness eased. Dissipated. Curling into a ball beside the toilet, I buried my face against my knees and wrestled back control over my ragged, sobbing breaths.

"Carter?" The stall door screeched as it was pushed open, and Mr Fielding's shadow fell over me. "Come on," he murmured. "Let's get you to the sickbay."

Everything felt heavy and sore. My entire body cried out in anguish, even more than it did after I'd played a full game of football, and my thoughts were muddied and slow. I barely remembered Mr Fielding helping me to my feet or leading me through the maze of corridors to the sickbay.

I wasn't really aware of anything until I was nudged down onto a bed, and I pressed my face back to my knees, so closely I could almost taste the polyester of my school pants. I didn't want anyone to see the humiliating tears sliding down my cheeks.

"There's no need to be embarrassed," said a kindly voice. "Can you look up here for me, dear? Mr Fielding has stepped out for a moment, so it's just the two of us."

It took all my strength to drag my eyes up to meet those of Mrs Taylor, the school nurse. I wanted to run, to get the hell out of there, but all of a sudden, I felt as weak as a lamb. There was no way my legs would hold my weight again.

Mrs Taylor's eyes were warm with compassion. "I'm told you were sick?"

Remnant sourness coated my tongue, but a distant part of me was relieved—relieved she thought that *sickness* was all this was. "Must have been something I ate," I muttered.

A knock sounded at the door, and Mr Fielding slipped back inside with a cup of water. He was unable to hide his concern as he passed it to me.

"Thank you," I said roughly. I took a tentative sip and sighed at its soothing coolness. My throat felt like someone had attacked it with sandpaper.

Mr Fielding propped his hip against the edge of the nurse's desk. "I've called your mum. She's on her way to pick you up."

I froze. It was a comment that was meant to give comfort, I knew, but it was of little comfort to me. Mum wouldn't care that I'd been sick. All she would see was that empty test paper…and that I'd made such a scene they had to bother her at work.

She was going to kill me.

Right now, I thought I would probably let her.

I rested my head back on my knees and didn't offer Mr Fielding or Mrs Taylor another word. They let me be, but I still felt their watchful eyes upon me, still heard the hushed murmur of their voices. I drifted for a time.

I was so, so tired.

So tired…

"Carter."

I startled awake from a light doze. My head was pounding, and my muscles ached even worse than before. I tilted my chin, squinting in the harsh fluorescent light, and then I saw her.

"Mum," I croaked.

She stood beside Mrs Taylor, while Mr Fielding hovered at the door. Her expression wasn't overtly angry or annoyed, but I noted the forced smoothness to her features, the tightness at the corners of her eyes. A storm was brewing. "Let's go," was all she said.

I wiped my face with the sleeve of one quivering arm and heaved myself off the bed. A wave of vertigo struck me as I got to my feet, but it passed with a few deep breaths, and then I was ducking through the door past Mr Fielding. I nodded when he wished me well.

I couldn't get out of there fast enough.

Classes had recommenced, so it was eerily still as I followed Mum back through the schoolyard after a detour to fetch my bag. The uneasy silence pressed on all the tender places inside me, making them twinge, but I didn't dare disrupt the quiet with words.

I doubted there were any words I could say that would reassure my mother.

Neither of us spoke on the way home, but the moment we walked in the front door, Mum stabbed a finger at the kitchen bench. "Sit."

I sat.

She rounded the bench and fixed me with a probing look from across the granite island. "What's wrong?" she demanded. "You've never had to come home sick before. Never."

I didn't know how to respond, so I said nothing.

A wad of paper slid across the smooth stone surface between us, and any illusion I'd clung to that I could hide this—*any* of this—from her shattered. It was my blank psychology test.

"You've never done this before, either," said Mum. "What happened?"

It was the same question Mr Fielding had asked. I didn't have a proper answer for him. I didn't have one for her either. Not one that she'd want to hear.

"I thought I could trust you to keep out of trouble, Carter."

My stomach lurched. "You can, Mum. I—"

"Then what is this all about?" she snapped. "Failing a test, coming home when you're not even sick—it's not like you. Is this some kind of belated rebellion? A cry for attention? Well, you have my attention now, so start talking."

I stared at her. She glared back.

Now would be the time to tell her.

Now would be the time to tell her about the phone call I received last December, the day before Tim died. Now would be the time to

169

tell her that I'd kissed a boy and liked it. Now would be the time to tell her that I couldn't sleep, that I felt pieces of myself falling away every day, that I was lost in a long, dark tunnel and couldn't find the light at the end.

Now would have been the time to tell her all those things—if she were any other mother, and I was any other son.

"I…"

Mum crossed her arms. "Yes?"

But the moment passed, and the opportunity was gone.

She wasn't any other mother, and I wasn't any other son.

"It's nothing," I mumbled. "I…I messed up. It won't happen again."

My words only seemed to anger her more. "I can't take anything else, Carter," she hissed. "There is enough on my plate without worrying about what you're up to or having your school on my back. It is a constant battle just to keep from losing this house, despite how hard I work. Failure is *not* an option."

The house? What on earth was she—?

"Tell me you understand."

I opened my mouth, closed it. Swallowed hard. "It won't happen again," I repeated.

"Good." Mum came back around the bench now, handbag slung over one shoulder, and she regarded me through slitted eyes. "I'm going back to work for a few hours. I trust you have work of your own to get on with if you want to make up for this *disappointment*."

She didn't stick around to watch her parting blow land. It fell like an axe that severed my spinal cord; everything went numb.

Disappointment.

I'd always known that's what I was to her, though she'd never said it aloud. Not until now.

The chasm inside me yawned wide. Sometimes, I wondered whether it wouldn't just be easier to follow Tim's example. To let the darkness consume me and slip into sweet oblivion where there was no guilt, no shame, no pain.

Mechanically, I stood and found my legs guiding me to the cupboard in the hall. I opened the door, reached in, and the packet I sought all but leapt into my hands. I carried it into the bathroom and placed it down beside the sink, filled with an odd sort of relief.

I shed my school shirt and let it tumble onto the ground. I'd lost weight in the last few months. My chest was all sallow and sunken, my ribs jutting out against the nearly translucent skin.

The boy in the mirror stared at me with dull eyes. "What are you doing?" he asked me.

I hated the sight of him. I hated everything about him.

There had been ten razors in the packet when Dad died. Eight weeks later, that number had dwindled down to nine. Just shy of two inches long, each razor was double-edged and wickedly sharp, the blade so fine it vanished into the air.

Don't do it.

Not even a ripple in the numbness when I opened the packet and withdrew another blade. The metal was cool and smooth against my fingers, light as a feather as I rested its edge against my arm. The contrast between the pale, unblemished skin and the silver of the razor was haunting. Captivating.

It was so close I could almost taste it. All my worries would drop away as the ropes binding me to this pained existence unfurled.

Don't.

I wasn't thirteen anymore. I wasn't thirteen, and I wanted to be a doctor. I knew exactly how and where to cut—which way to die, which way to simply maim.

And I didn't want to die today.

I pressed down hard. The pain was blinding. It filled that gaping chasm and smashed through every empty place inside of me. It stole my breath, stole my thoughts, stole the very rhythm of my heart. Obliterated the numbness which was throttling the life from my bones.

For a moment, there was nothing but peace. Blissful, wondrous peace.

Then the weight of the world slammed back onto my shoulders. I should have known the peace would be so fleeting.

Dropping the razor, I clapped my right hand to the wound. Blood seeped between my fingers and fell in scarlet drops, splashing the white-tile floor.

I followed the droplets down and laughed and laughed and laughed until my laughter turned to tears.

thirteen

Shadow whined and licked my hand as I bathed her. I lathered her up in smooth, methodical strokes, one body part at a time, and when her midnight-hued coat was dripping with suds, I rinsed her off in the shelter's purpose-built bath. She sat there placidly and allowed my ministrations, those occasional whimpers her only complaint.

The pup had been with us for close to three months now. She'd grown like a weed with the necessary care and attention, and she was really coming out of her shell. I loved little more than to watch her run about, her gait so crooked and lumbering she often toppled right over.

I barely even noticed her disfigured features anymore.

But Megs had given me some bittersweet news this morning: she'd found Shadow a home.

Good, I told myself. Shadow would make a wonderful pet. She was curious and friendly and so very gentle, and she'd thrive under the care of a loving, doting family.

I heaved a sigh. "You're a good girl, aren't you?"

Shadow shook, spraying water everywhere.

"Hey!" Droplets spattered my waterproof smock, and her tongue lolled out in a wolfish grin. "Bad dog! I take back every nice thing I ever said about you!"

A lie—not that she knew that.

It was going to kill me when Shadow left. The thought of never seeing her again—of never again rubbing her ears until her tail thumped on the ground or seeing that sweet, misshapen face light up when I brought her food—hurt more than I could bear.

But I wanted the best for her, and she deserved better than what the shelter could offer. She deserved better than what *I* could offer. It wasn't her fault I'd broken the rules and become attached or that I secretly longed to take her home myself.

Mum would never allow it.

My left arm gave an unpleasant throb.

I peered down at my sleeve as if I could see through it to the bandage beneath. I'd had to wrap it tight to stop the bleeding, but it had, eventually, stopped.

The shame hadn't come until later.

It took a concerted effort to shove the memory aside and focus on something else. Like the fact I actually felt better today. A little reckless, perhaps. A little less in control. But more myself. The frightful numbness that had seized my body was torn away and faded more with each aching pulse of my hidden wound.

I scratched Shadow behind one floppy ear. "What do you think?" I asked. "Is it time to get you out of here?"

The water roiled as she wagged her tail.

Getting Shadow dried off and groomed and back into her kennel was more of a struggle than washing her. She always went a bit crazy after bath time. She wanted to play, wanted to snatch up anything I brought near her head, and the whole routine took ten times longer than it did for any of the older dogs.

Exhaustion nipped at my heels by the time I wrangled the door shut behind her. It was mid-afternoon, and I'd been washing and brushing all day; the reek of wet dog clung to me like a second skin. I glanced out the window at the dreary, steel-grey sky. I was not looking forward to the ride home—or the mountain of homework that awaited me there.

When the clock chimed the hour, announcing the end of my shift, I rubbed at my eyes and started down the hall to Megs' office. As I grew closer, I noticed the rumble of lowered voices coming from inside the room. Odd, since I wasn't aware that Megs had company.

Then there was a dull thud, like flesh slamming against wood, followed by a startled cry. Heart leaping, I flew the last steps to the open door—and froze.

There was Ben, the man who brought Shadow to the shelter all those months ago. Even in a black skivvy that concealed his sinewy frame and with hair at least an inch longer, I recognised him on sight. He had Megs pressed up against her desk and was cradling her face in his hands.

"Megan," he breathed and kissed her.

Time stopped.

He kissed her, and she twined her arms around his waist to kiss him back, and it was beautiful. And it was so, so wrong.

"*Megan?*" I growled.

They both jumped. Ben pulled away, though not entirely out of

Megs' arms, and colour climbed up his cheeks. The blush looked out of place on a man of his bearing—endearing, even. But it did not endear him to me.

Not when I wanted to launch myself across the room and throw him to the floor.

I jerked my eyes to Megs, hating that they grew damp. "You let him call you Megan?" That was the betrayal that cut the deepest, hurt the most.

"Carter…" Megs said gently. She released Ben's waist and took a step towards me.

I staggered back. All I could see was her kissing a man who wasn't my brother.

Silence beckoned. I squeezed my left arm, shooting the pain down to my fingers, and forced the silence back. "How could you?" My voice broke. "How *could* you?"

"Hey—" Ben started, but Megs shushed him.

"No," she said, "it's okay." Her eyes were sad as I backed away. "Let him go."

I was already halfway out the door. Already bolting from the shelter and out into the cold spring air. I fumbled to unchain my bike as hot tears spilled down my face. Angrily, I swiped them away.

I'd always been afraid this day would come. Now it was here, and I wasn't ready. I hadn't been prepared for how much it would hurt to see her with somebody else. How much it would hurt to hear her full name when for so long, the only one she'd let use it was Miles. A boy she'd deemed the love of her life, who'd loved her back with everything he had.

He left her, just like he left me, but now she was moving on.

Once again, leaving me behind with nothing but my memories for comfort.

✦

"I need to talk to you."

Remy glanced up from where he was trying to cram a four-ring binder into his overflowing locker. "Okay...?"

I fidgeted with the hem of my jumper. "Um...in private."

"Oh. Right." He looked bemused, *sounded* bemused, but he stuffed the folder into a narrow gap and let me drag him out into the breezeway. It had been drizzling all day, so most of the school had taken shelter indoors; the breezeway was deserted.

An icy wind gusted past. Remy shivered and inched closer to me, his ears and nose already pink with cold.

"I miss you," I said.

His eyebrows quirked. "I miss you too. I feel like we haven't spoken in weeks." My guilt must have shown on my face because he reached out and touched my elbow. I felt the light pressure even through layers of clothes. "It's fine, Carter," he said. "I know you've been busy."

The words were soothing and said so earnestly too, but I hated the glimmer of sorrow in his blue-grey eyes. I hated that I'd put it there.

"I want to take you out somewhere tonight."

Remy blinked. "Like...on a date?"

"Yes."

The word hung there for a moment, suspended in the air between us.

I didn't recognise this version of myself—this bold person who

177

abandoned all caution and was direct about what he wanted. He felt wild. Dangerous. I wasn't sure I trusted him.

But today was the last day of third term, and after staying up half the night to finalise plans for graduation, I felt...on edge. I'd been angry and tense all week, and tonight I just wanted to let everything go. To get lost in someone who'd never let me down.

I wanted it so badly I physically *ached* for it.

A smile dawned on Remy's face, like the first ray of sun after a long polar night. "I'd love to go out with you," he said. "I...what..." His lashes lowered, fluttered. "Where are you taking me?"

"It's a surprise."

"*Is* it now?" Remy pouted a little.

I bit back a grin. "Make sure you bring a warm jacket. I'll pick you up at five."

The rest of the day dragged by, and after school, I hurried home to shower and change and shoot off a quick message to Mum, telling her I was going out with Jake. Right on the dot of five, I stood outside the Montroses' place, shifting nervously from foot to foot as I rang the doorbell.

Remy answered only moments later. He looked very sophisticated in grey jeans, a snug black peacoat, and—

A laugh ripped out of me. "What on earth is *that*?"

Affronted, Remy raised his hands to cover the fuzzy rainbow earmuffs clamped around his head. But no matter how he tried, he couldn't hide the sparkles amidst the fluff...or the set of cat ears protruding from the band.

He dropped his arms, muttering, "I'm still not used to this cold weather."

"Haven't you heard of a beanie?"

"I…" Remy paused. "Do you…mind?"

My smile fell. I didn't like that. I didn't like that he'd stopped to ask if I approved of his choice in clothing. It didn't feel right.

A light like his can't shine in the dark of your closet.

I shook the thought away. "No. Keep them," I said hoarsely. He was going to kill me one of these days, but at least he'd look damn cute while doing it. "Just so you know, we're catching a tram. Where we're going is not an easy spot to get to by car, and I don't have my licence anyway."

"Well, I'm intrigued." Remy jerked his chin at the waterproof sheet tucked under my right arm. "What's the tarp for?"

"You'll see."

He huffed. "Fine. Keep your secrets. Let's go."

The rain had cleared in the last hour, but the biting chill still lingered. Fog plumed in the air with each breath, and the ground was damp underfoot, the pavement slick and shiny. Shafts of sunlight filtered through the clouds, but they were lukewarm and tepid at best.

Remy talked non-stop, even as we hopped onto a citybound tram packed like a tin of sardines. I could listen to him talk for days and never get tired of it. I loved the way his voice soared and swooped as he spoke, loved how he used his whole body to emphasise points. I loved that he didn't care I added little to the conversation, that I preferred to stay quiet and listen.

Since it was peak hour on a Friday, twilight had crawled across the sky by the time the tram pulled up outside Flinders Street Station. There were people everywhere despite the cold. A handful of cars crept past, blaring their horns at the milling pedestrians, their tyres flicking moisture up off the bitumen road.

It was a magical feeling, being in the heart of Melbourne at dusk. Lights glowed against a skyline of deepest azure, scattering colours across the glassy surface of the Yarra. Buskers of all ages lined the riverside path, and the tantalising scent of cooking meat wafted from somewhere close by.

Remy gave the tarp a second glance. "Are we having a picnic?"

"Something like that."

We followed our noses to a row of food stalls set up near Birrarung Marr. Remy's stomach was already growling, so I bought us each a kebab and then led him down to the thin strip of green by the river's edge. Shimmering droplets clung to the blades of grass.

"You really do think of everything, don't you?" Remy teased as I spread out the tarp.

I shrugged, smiling. "I try."

The sparse trees provided some shelter from the wind, but Remy still shifted closer to me as we munched on our dinner. He sat close enough that his earmuffs brushed my cheek whenever he twisted his head, but I didn't mind. I didn't mind at all.

As we huddled together, gazing out at the glittering city, it suddenly struck me how…romantic this was. And thoughts of romance led me straight back to Megs and Ben.

The food turned to lead in my stomach.

Remy pinched my hip. "Everything all right?"

"I…" I bowed my head and let my eyes fall closed. "I caught my boss kissing this guy on Saturday."

"Um…okay."

I ran my hand absently over the grass. "She was my brother's girlfriend. They were together almost two years."

Silence, and then: "Oh."

I turned towards him, wanting—*needing*—to make him understand. "Megs meant the world to Miles, and I know she loved him too. He told me he was going to marry her one day. He was going to take her to Paris and propose under the Eiffel Tower and buy her a house with a big yard so she could adopt as many animals as she wanted.

"And seeing her with this other guy…it's not *fair*." My voice cracked. "It's not fair that he might get to do all those things with her when Miles didn't. And it feels like she's betrayed him, which is stupid because my brother is…he's…"

Remy put down the remnants of his kebab and took my hands in his. "It's not stupid," he said. "You're still mourning him. Of course it hurts to see his girl moving on."

I opened my mouth to protest—Megs was a strong-willed and independent young woman who didn't belong to anyone, let alone my dead brother—but nothing came out. Maybe it was true. Maybe, after all this time, I still saw her as *his*.

"If Miles loved her as much as you say, don't you think he'd be happy that she's found someone to care for her? That she's not alone anymore?"

"I guess." But that didn't mean it was easy to accept. I sighed and leaned into Remy's side, trying to soak up his warmth. "I'm sorry for being such a downer."

"No," he said sharply. "Never apologise for telling me how you feel. It means a lot that you trust me with this stuff, Carter." His arm slid around my waist. "This means a lot too—that you brought me here, I mean. It's really nice."

I glanced down at my watch. *Any second now.* "The best bit hasn't even started yet."

181

"What do you—oh!" Downstream from where we sat, a sharp beam of light flashed from one side of the river to the other. "What was that?"

"That," I said, "is your surprise."

Another blue-green thread arced up from the roof of a building in the distance. It was soon followed by a third thread with a deeper, purplish hue.

"What is it?" Half Remy's face was in shadow, but there was no mistaking the wonder etched across his skin.

"It's called Sky Light. There are a bunch of lasers on the top of a tower at Southbank," I pointed, tracing the ebb and flow of the lights as they crisscrossed the sky, "and they shine onto some iconic buildings further north."

"What's it for?"

"The Melbourne Fringe Festival." At his blank look, I elaborated, "It's an arts festival. This year's theme is 'step into the light.' It's… um…" My eyes darted to his lips, then away. "It's supposed to be about giving a voice to minority groups who often go unheard."

Remy gulped. Warmth flooded my chest, and I itched with the need to lean forwards, to touch his throat as it bobbed. "No one's ever done something so thoughtful for me before," he whispered, a wet sheen to his eyes. "Thank you."

I peered back at him, at the dazed smile gracing his mouth, at those ridiculous earmuffs atop his head, sparkling in the lights up above. With a cough, I said, "Let's go for a walk. Get closer to the lights."

Sensing I needed a moment, Remy carried the rubbish from dinner over to the bin while I shook out and folded the tarp. There were more of the laser beams now, almost a dozen jewelled serpents burnished against the velvet of the night sky. They were beautiful—

and fragile, too. Lights cutting through the darkness like knives.

When Remy returned, we made our way along the path towards the display, only stopping briefly back at the food stalls for a plate of tiny Dutch pancakes. They dripped maple syrup and butter, and Remy managed to smear the sticky syrup down his chin on the very first bite.

I snorted. He elbowed me in the side. I didn't dare tell him how catlike he looked as he tried to clean up the mess with his tongue.

The filaments of light streaking overhead were invisible from certain angles, so they flickered in and out of view as we walked. I strolled along with my head tilted back, looking upwards, so I didn't notice at first when Remy drew to a stop.

When I *did* notice, I turned and found his eyes shining like stars. "This is amazing," he said. "*You're* amazing."

I sucked in a startled breath. *Amazing.* Such a different word to *disappointment*.

Pulse racing, I moved closer. Until we stood toe-to-toe. The tarp dropped to the ground as I pulled him into my arms.

I hugged Remy to me tightly—tighter than I'd held anyone in a long, long time. He tucked the top of his head beneath my chin, those fluffy cat ears bracketing my jaw as he nuzzled into the crook of my neck.

This—holding him like this—felt good. Felt right. I could imagine doing it every day for the rest of my life. It was a terrifying thought since most days, I couldn't see past the storm clouds looming on the horizon.

I squeezed my eyes shut. Remy deserved better than what I gave him. He deserved more than I could give, but I couldn't bring myself to let him go.

And it was then, in that moment, that I realised: I was in danger of losing my heart to this boy. If I hadn't already.

God help me.

My hold loosened, just enough that I could pull back and see his face. He blinked at me, slightly owlish, and I bent down.

He halted me with a palm on my chest. "You sure? Out in the open like—"

"Remy?"

"Yeah?"

I stroked a finger down his cheek, along his jawline, over the bow of his lips. "Stop talking," I said and replaced my hand with my mouth.

I kissed Remy Montrose right there out in the open, on the banks of the Yarra under a sky filled with glimmering lights. He tasted sweet, like syrup and butter and powdered sugar, and his hair was gold silk as it slid between my fingers.

The rest of the world fell away, and there was only this. Only him and me and the blooming pressure in my chest. Only this overwhelming, unbearable feeling that was too big for one heart to contain.

"You're amazing," Remy said again, his voice resonating against my lips.

He was the best thing in my life. The only thing that didn't feel spoiled.

And maybe it was just a dream; maybe the morning would herald reality with all its sorrow and guilt and the truth of the cut on my arm. But I was going to hold onto it for however long it lasted.

fourteen

I should have known it wouldn't last long.

The good things in my life never did. For years it had seemed like, every time I crested a hill, the world set another at my feet. Another hill, bigger and more treacherous than the last, blocking my view of what lay on the other side.

Denying me a glimpse of the better life beyond.

So I should have known it was only a matter of time before the peace and joy slipped through my fingers. Before I was woken from that wonderful dream by a trio of painful blows.

The first blow came when Shadow's adoption fell through.

According to Megs, the prospective family had been interested, excited, but when they came to visit, they faced a dilemma no one had foreseen: their kids were terrified of Shadow. Their little boy took one look at her disfigured eye socket and burst into tears, throwing himself at his mother's legs as if Shadow was a monster come to gobble him up for lunch.

I was glad I wasn't there to see it. I was glad I only heard about

185

it second-hand from Megs, who informed me the family chose another dog—a *prettier* dog—instead.

I didn't know what I would have done if I'd witnessed that rejection.

"We'll find her a home," Megs promised. "We always find our dogs a home."

I couldn't meet her eyes. I'd barely said a word to her since catching her with Ben three weeks before. The September holidays had come and gone, and even after taking on additional shifts over the break, I hadn't spoken of that day. Neither had she.

She wouldn't bring it up until I did.

Megs sighed at my lack of response. "I'll let you get to work, then. All the kennels need cleaning today."

"Okay. I'll get on it."

That was how I spent the next several hours. Cleaning the kennels was exhausting, mind-numbing work, the kind I either appreciated or dreaded depending on my mood. Today was definitely the latter. I made my way down the row, dusting and sweeping and scrubbing at floors until they were spotless and it felt like every speck of grime had stuck to me instead.

When I reached Shadow's kennel and saw her sweet face beaming at me from where she lounged in her bed, I sank to my knees. The pup belly-crawled across to me, yipping in delight, and shoved her narrow snout through the bars. I offered my hand, the ghost of a smile touching my lips as her tongue rasped over my fingers.

Shadow whined, and the smile faded.

I gazed down at this beautiful creature and was swamped by a wave of anguish. To think that she could be at a new home right now, curled up on someone's couch or sprawled across their lap, were it not for a flaw she was born with...

I hunched over and buried my face in Shadow's black fur, squeezing my eyes shut to hold back an onslaught of tears. *Not fair*, I thought. *Not fair.*

But Shadow didn't realise the chance she'd lost. Her wagging tail tapped out a rhythm on the cold stone floor. I echoed it in my head, copied the cadence beat for beat until my muscles relaxed, unclenched, and the tight band around my chest loosened. I breathed in, out, in again...and drifted away...

"Carter?"

I jerked, slamming my forehead against the kennel bars.

"Are you all right?"

Gingerly, I sat up. My spine creaked and groaned in protest as if I'd been slumped there a while. The thought chilled me. Had I... fallen asleep? *Oh no...*

"*Carter*," said Megs. She was crouched beside me now, her face creased with worry.

I rubbed the back of my neck. "I'm fine."

She studied me, no doubt observing the dried tears on my cheeks, the dark circles beneath my eyes. Instead of pushing me about it, instead of telling me off for snoozing on the job, my boss settled down on the floor and reached over to scratch Shadow's ear. "This one has really gotten under your skin, hasn't she?"

"Nobody wants her," I whispered.

"We haven't been looking long. Someone will snatch her up, believe me."

But I shook my head. "Nobody wants something that's not perfect."

187

Megs' hand froze. It hovered there for a moment, above the pup's now-upturned belly, and when she spoke, her words were careful, cautious. "Are we still talking about Shadow?"

I curled in on myself, knees to chest and arms draped around my shins. "How did he do it, Megs?" I asked softly.

"How did who do what?"

"Miles." His name fell heavily from my tongue. It was followed by a stillness that sucked the air from the hall like the name was some forbidden thing. Perhaps in a way it was: since his death, neither Megs nor I had uttered it in each other's presence. "How was Miles so perfect at everything?"

A pause, and then Megs withdrew her hand from the kennel. "Miles wasn't perfect, Carter."

"He—"

"Stop." She blew out a breath. "It's the truth. He was your big brother—your hero. You were blind to his faults, and I know he tried to hide them from you anyway. He always felt he had to be strong for you."

Her truth was a knife, twisting between my ribs. I'd worshipped Miles; that was never in doubt. I *still* worshipped him. But to think it meant I'd failed to see him for who he really was?

No. It was unimaginable.

"Don't look at me like that," Megs said. "You look like I've stabbed you through the heart."

She wasn't far off base.

"It's not a *bad* thing, Carter. In fact, I used to envy how much you two loved each other."

My eyes slid across to her. "Really?"

"Really. You know I'm an only child." Wriggling closer, Megs put a hand on my knee and squeezed. "Listen. Miles was special. He was talented and kind and just one of those people who was genuinely *good*. But he was also a perfectionist. He was always so desperate to do well, to be better, and he always felt that his best wasn't good enough. It used to drive me mad."

Something in her expression shattered. "Christ," she breathed. "I miss him. So much."

The rest of her words had bounced straight off me, refusing to take hold, but those ones caught. Stuck. "Then why are you with Ben?"

Megs winced. "I wish you hadn't found out like that. I was trying to find a way to tell you, but I…I didn't. And then he surprised me by showing up that day, and I just…well…"

She tugged on the ends of her hair, her mouth twisting as she considered how best to explain. "Screw it," she swore. "I loved Miles. I would have married him if he'd lived, and we would have been blissfully, blissfully happy. But he didn't. He died, and I was broken, and I will probably never fully get over it.

"But I also know he loved me back. He wouldn't have wanted me to be alone forever. He would have wanted me to be happy, so I promised myself I wouldn't give up on love. And Ben is the *only* guy in five years who's made me feel anything remotely close to what I felt for Miles."

My heart withered in my chest. I wanted to be happy for her, for the hope in her voice, the tentative warmth. But I didn't have it in me. Not now. Not yet.

"Carter?"

"What?" I mumbled. I couldn't even lift my chin from where it had dipped towards my chest. I didn't have the strength.

189

Megs slid her arm across my shoulders. "Ben isn't taking Miles' place," she said. "There will always be a part of me that belongs to your brother, and Ben gets that. He's known about Miles from the start. Okay?"

I didn't respond.

"God, you're stubborn." Fingers curled around my bicep, the nails snatching in my sleeve. "You're just like your brother, you know. Right down to the perfectionist tendencies and the soft spot for unwanted things. But don't make the same mistakes that he did. He felt guilty for ruining your mum's life, not that being born was *his* fault but—"

"*What* did you just say?"

Megs blinked. "Um...I said that it wasn't his fault for—"

"No. About my mum."

"Oh." She dropped her arm. It slithered down my back like a snake before coiling back up in her lap. "Carter, your folks made no secret of the fact Miles was an accident. I know they loved him, but he always felt guilty about it, like he was personally responsible for how his birth affected their lives. Especially your mum's."

I couldn't think. I couldn't speak. All I could do was play that word around and around and around in my head, code on an infinite loop. *Ruined ruined ruined ruined ruined.*

Miles thought *he* had ruined Mum's life? How could that be? Mum loved him. She *still* loved him. More than she'd ever loved me.

Megs sighed. "All I'm trying to say is, you don't have anything to prove, so don't be too hard on yourself. And don't worry about Shadow so much. She'll be absolutely fine." She untangled her legs and carefully climbed to her feet. "Carter?"

I forced my chin up.

"You would have been my little brother one day," she said quietly. "If there's ever anything you need to talk about, you know I'm here for you, right?"

It was rhetorical—maybe. I nodded anyway.

"Good. Now, why don't you head home? You've only got half an hour left on your shift, and you look dead on your feet."

For once, I didn't protest. I needed to leave before she saw how her words had slayed me. But as I heaved myself upright and made for the end of the hall, I felt her eyes tracking me and wondered if she knew more than she let on.

I didn't know if it even mattered anymore. If it ever had.

Outside, it was raining again. I stood beside my bike and let it drench me to the bone.

The second blow came when it all went wrong with my music.

My music—my joy, my refuge, my escape, where I was lost and I was found and I was subsumed by the spirit of the song.

Nothing was more sacred than when I played with my string quartet. We'd worked together for years—for close to a third of our lives—and by now, we were practiced, accomplished. We were a coordinated, well-oiled machine:

Paige and me on the violins, our scores waxing and waning, threading through and around each other in an endless cycle of melody and harmony.

Jamie on the cello, his deep, smooth tones as steady and sure as a heartbeat, a grounding force, our anchor.

And Piper on the viola, drawing together the high and low, bridging the gaps between us.

In everyday life, the four of us couldn't be more different. But the moment we took our seats, the moment we lifted our bows and placed them to our strings, those differences melted away. Vanished. We became one entity, one soul, rising and falling together.

So it was always painfully obvious when something wasn't right.

On the Tuesday of our last week of classes, the quartet stayed back after school to rehearse the pieces we were playing for the graduation assembly. As we went through them over and over and over again, I noticed a rough, jagged edge to the music. Fissures opened up between each part, and notes leaped across the clefts like the tune from a scratched record, jarring the usual smoothness of our sound.

Something was off—something was wrong.

And it wasn't until I stumbled over my part for the fifth time and brought the song to an awful, screeching halt that I realised that something was *me*.

Somehow, I was no longer in tune with the rest of them. I no longer seemed in sync.

"What the hell, Carter?" Jamie demanded, lowering his bow to glare at me. "What's going on with you? You're playing like shit today."

"Jamie!" Piper scolded.

Cheeks burning, I shot out of my seat and stumbled from our half-moon of chairs.

"Where do you think you're going?"

"I need a break," I said. I lay my violin back in its case and curled my aching fingers into fists. It wasn't like I'd never made a mistake before, but never had I stumbled so many times over a set we'd been practicing for weeks.

Jamie's chair squealed on the floor as he shoved it aside. The sound was so harsh, so loud, it almost drowned out the scathing words that followed. "A break? Are you serious? We're performing this stuff in *three days*, and you keep screwing it up!"

Paige rolled her eyes. "Stop being such a drama queen. We'll be fine. We've got this. Besides, Carter has far more important things to be worrying about, like—oh, I don't know—*organising the whole goddamned graduation day*."

But footsteps stalked towards me now, raising the hairs on my nape.

"Jamie, cut it out," warned Piper. "Leave him alone."

I could picture what he looked like, even though my back was still turned. I could *see* it in my mind's eye: Jamie marched at me like a soldier ready for battle, righteous indignation swirling all around him. Despite the late hour, his uniform was crease-free and spotless, his hair slicked back with not a strand out of place. Neat. Proper.

Perfect.

"This is important," Jamie growled. "It's important to me, it's important to the girls, and I swear to—"

I whirled and found him standing *right there*, in my personal space. As if he was trying to trap me. "Do you think," I said coldly, "that it's not important to me?"

A dangerous glint appeared in his eye. "I wouldn't know what's important to you, Carter."

"What's that supposed to mean?"

"Like you don't know." Jamie's lips peeled away from his teeth. "What, exactly, is so important it's distracting you from *music*?" He leaned forwards, so close I could smell the musk of his cologne, and whispered, "Or should I say *who*?"

I reared back, heat flooding my veins in a surge of panic-laced anger. "Shut *up*!"

"Guys…" said Piper.

But Jamie ignored her. His mouth stretched into a mocking grin. "Did I hit a nerve?"

"Back off," I snarled. The fury spread, grew, *boiled* inside me until I feared it would burn me to ash. My hands found Jamie's chest, and I pushed at him. He stepped back but not away, not nearly far enough. I needed him *gone*. "Back *the fuck* off, Jamie!"

"Why should—"

Before he could finish even one more taunt, I did something I had never done in my life.

I threw a punch.

As if from a great distance, I saw my fist fly towards him. It was wide, wild, and since Jamie was taller than me by a good few inches, all the blow did was glance off the edge of his jaw.

But it was enough.

Jamie's head snapped around, and he staggered to one side. I darted past him, abandoning my precious violin on the floor as I tried to hear past the roaring in my ears.

The roaring silenced when I saw the girls. Piper and Paige were gaping at me, their eyes impossibly wide. Stunned.

I didn't wait around. I stormed out of the building without a backwards glance, shock streaming in my wake. Tremors wracked through my body, but I kept walking until they threatened to bring me to my knees.

Then I braced myself against the brick wall of the nearest building and breathed in deeply, harshly, trying to regain some semblance of control.

God.

I'd punched him. Not well, and not particularly hard judging by the way my knuckles barely even tingled, but I had actually *punched* Jamie Ray. I was so angry, so filled with this helpless, frantic rage, and I'd just wanted him to stop. Stop talking, stop pushing, stop prodding at things that were no one's business but my own.

But to punch him...

As my mind cleared, as the anger and shock bled away, remorse came creeping in. Welcoming its bitter sting, I pulled my arms from the wall and stared at my hands. A row of scarlet crescents was etched into the flesh of my palms.

I swallowed thickly. I'd never reacted with violence before. Not like that. Not to another person. The closest I'd ever come was when I flinched away from Remy at Piper's party, but even that paled in comparison to *this*.

"Hey." The word was soft and accompanied by an equally soft touch on my back.

It still made me jump.

"Sorry," Paige muttered. "I didn't mean to startle you."

Reluctantly, I turned to face her. I'd stumbled all the way to the year twelve centre in my daze, and as the sun dipped between the buildings, it silhouetted her, shading her expression so I couldn't read it. "Is Jamie all right?" I asked.

"He's fine."

Something like relief swept through me. "Paige, I—"

"Don't." She inched closer, beyond the reach of the setting sun, and I realised she was grinning. "Before you get all apologetic on me, I'll have you know it was *awesome* seeing you go off at Jamie like that. He was being a dick, and he knows it. Man, you should have seen the look on his face when you left!"

I shook my head. "I shouldn't have hit him."

"He deserved it."

The remnants of my anger winked out, leaving me cold and tired and empty. Brittle, like I was about to crack. Paige wouldn't get it—the guilt. She had an appetite for mischief, just like Jake, who I knew would have paid good money to see me start a fight.

Or end one, as it were.

"Sorry for ruining practice," I said.

Paige scoffed. "Don't be. That's the most fun I've had at practice in ages."

"Jamie was right, though. I did play like shit."

"Carter," she groaned. "*Seriously*. It's fine." Flipping her ponytail over one shoulder, she skewered me with a look. "I'm not worried about *you*. But if Jamie doesn't pull his head in, I might take a shot at him myself."

Maybe you should be worried about me, I thought darkly. I didn't say it, though.

I was glad I hadn't when the nearest door opened, and Katie's head poked around the frame. "I thought I heard you guys out here." She slipped outside, hugging her arms around herself in the unseasonably cool breeze.

Katie looked as tired as I felt. The last few weeks had been rough on both of us, and we'd been up for most of the previous night, dealing with some unexpected developments in our graduation plans. By the time I fell into bed at four a.m., my mind had been too full for sleep.

"What are you still doing here, woman?" Paige asked.

"Working. Is everything okay?"

Paige clicked her tongue. "It's all good out here."

My co-captain smiled wearily and turned her attention to me.

"Carter, we need to finish off that video for the final assembly, and we still haven't started our speech for Friday's graduation dinner."

I throttled back a groan. As much as I wished it were otherwise, that speech wasn't going to write itself. "I can come over tonight after dinner to work on it if you like."

"Thanks, but it'll have to be tomorrow. I'm going over to Spencer's in a bit."

"Katie, you know I work at the soup van on Wednesdays."

Her lips thinned—was that a flash of irritation I saw? I was hyperaware of Paige at my side, her gaze darting between us. "I don't like leaving it until Thursday," Katie said stiffly.

Neither did I, but I bit down on the retort that bubbled to my lips. "Then I'll start work on the speech in my spare periods tomorrow," I countered, "*and* I'll come over to your place on Thursday. Okay?"

"Okay." Her shoulders relaxed, and her smile returned. "Thanks, Carter. You're the best." Satisfied with the solution, she bade us goodnight and stepped back indoors.

Paige turned to me, eyebrows raised. "Dude."

"What?"

"*What*, he says." She threw her arms up in the air. "So, Katie is allowed to go to her boyfriend's place for some aggressive cuddling, but you can't go feed homeless people?"

I coughed. "Aggressive cuddling?"

"Please, this is *Spencer* we're talking about. How else should I describe their sexy times?"

"Um…"

"Don't answer that. *Anyway*," she griped, like this little tangent was my fault, "what I mean is that you should speak up more often.

197

Then maybe you won't need to throw punches."

It struck too close to home. I felt my whole face wobble.

Paige grimaced. "Too soon? Sorry." But she didn't sound that sorry as she glanced in the direction of the music room. "Come on. I'll escort you back to get your violin. Piper will have hustled Jamie out of there by now."

The last of the light died, and the yard plunged into shadow. I let Paige guide me away.

But it wasn't the first two blows that felled me. It was the third. The third blow came when I least expected it…and that was when it all fell apart.

fifteen

Thursday came around more quickly than I could have ever imagined.

Thursday, our penultimate day of high school and the last proper day of classes before we rounded the bend and hit the home stretch: exams. At the finish line lay freedom, but somehow it seemed just as far, just as distant, as it had at the start of the race.

Just as far—and getting further still. Like I was one of those marathon runners who, completely and utterly spent, betrayed by their own body, collapsed with the end in plain sight.

I didn't even have the strength left to crawl.

Remy found me as I emptied the contents of my locker into my schoolbag after last period. I had little use left for the locker, but I needed my books at home for when I started studying on the weekend. I struggled for a moment with the zip, my bag almost full to bursting.

"Looks heavy," said Remy.

"I'll live."

Snorting, he crouched down to help me wrestle the last few inches closed, and his fingers brushed over mine. The touch was feather-light, teasing…and unmistakably deliberate. As was the arresting smile he shot my way. "Come over to my place this afternoon."

The whispered words shivered through me. Not that it mattered in the end. "I can't today, Remy. I have some things I need to get done before the morning, and I'm going to Katie's later to work on our graduation speech."

"Oh." He fought—and failed—to keep the disappointment from his face. "That's okay. Some other time, then." He rose from the floor, shoulders drooping.

If he was a dog, his tail would be between his legs.

I caught his wrist. "Wait."

Remy paused and peered down at me, at the way I knelt on the ground by his feet, his hand clasped tightly in mine. His lips twitched.

I dropped the hand. Stood. Ignored the heat licking up my neck. "Sorry," I muttered. "What I was going to say is…how about you come over to my place instead?"

It wasn't clear who was more surprised by the offer: him or me. I *wanted* to spend time with him, and the way I saw it, if we were at my house, I could get still some work done. But I'd never invited him over before, never even entertained the idea, because—

"What about your mum?" Remy asked.

"She's working late tonight. I'll have to leave for Katie's before she even gets home."

A slow grin spread across his face. "All right. I'd like that."

"Okay." Double-checking my locker was empty, I closed it up and hefted the bulky schoolbag onto my back. "Then let's go."

The wind picked up as we left the school. It was overcast today, clouds stretching across the sky like a lumpy grey-white blanket, but at least there was no sign of rain. Golden sunlight refracted through the clouds and rendered the world in sepia tones. The only splash of colour belonged to the green buds sprouting from the winter-bare trees.

When we got to my house, I squashed down a wave of nerves as I ushered Remy inside. I offered him something to eat or drink, but he shook his head and halted his inspection of the living area. "I want to see your room," he said. "I didn't get to see it properly last time."

Last time—when he came by to confront me the week after Piper's birthday party. It felt like a lifetime ago.

"It's just a room."

"It's *your* room."

So I led him down the short hall and shouldered open my door, dumping my book-laden bag beside the desk. I toed off my shoes, then flopped face down on my bed. The covers muffled my weary sigh.

Remy hummed. "This is nice."

"If you say so." I grimaced and flipped over onto my back, so I could watch him as he explored. I wondered what he made of it.

My room was bland as far as teenage boys' bedrooms went. The desk was black, the bedsheets were grey, and the walls were china white. No posters adorned them, and there weren't any photos either. The only indication that the person who slept here *wasn't* some workaholic middle-aged man was the glow-in-the-dark galaxy scattered across the ceiling.

But the sight of Remy here, in my space, in my inner sanctum, made the whole place…brighter, somehow. More alive.

And it did strange things to my heart.

As if he sensed my attention, Remy turned from where he was examining the contents of my desk drawer. He grinned sheepishly. "I'm not snooping."

"Of course not." I held out a hand. "Come here."

He couldn't move quickly enough. Slamming the drawer shut, he hopped towards me while trying to take off his shoes. He almost managed it, too, but a metre from the bed, he tripped on his laces and collapsed at my side in an ungainly sprawl of limbs.

Holding back the laughter made my throat sting. "Well done."

Remy grumbled something unintelligible and kicked off the offending shoe. "I can't believe it's our last day tomorrow," he said. "The year has gone so fast."

"Hmm."

"Your uncle flies in tomorrow as well, right?"

"That's right." In all the drama of the last few weeks, I'd almost forgotten that Sean was arriving in Melbourne tomorrow evening—and would be here to stay.

Remy huffed. "You're talkative this afternoon."

"I—"

Remy rolled, and suddenly he was lying on top of me. He pressed me down into the mattress, so I could feel every inch of his body where it touched mine. I went still. "One would think," he whispered, nipping the end of my nose, "that you have other things on your mind."

My breath hitched.

His expression was oddly intense. Blue-grey eyes raked over my face like he was searching for some kind of sign. Of what, I couldn't say, but the scrutiny made me feel naked. Exposed. I might have tried to back away, to put some distance between us, were it not for his weight pinning my hips.

Were it not for the silent cries of my own body, begging me to stay.

I'd dreamed of this. In the wee dark hours of the night, I'd dreamed of Remy Montrose and what it might be like to share more than kisses with him. I'd wake, shaking and sweating and *wanting*, and wonder if I would ever be brave enough to try. To ask.

I reached up. Wound my hands into his hair.

Remy's throat bobbed as he swallowed. "You know...I didn't come here for this."

"I know," I said and pulled him down.

He fell onto me with a moan of surrender. His lips found mine, and I gasped his name, and it was a curse and a question and an answer. I moved as he moved, breathed as he breathed, held him and arched up beneath him.

But I needed more of it. More of him. Just *more*.

My hands skimmed down his back, over layers of clothes, and tangled in the hem at his waist. Sensing my intent, Remy ducked his head and giggled as I yanked his jumper off him.

Then I started on the buttons of his shirt. The giggles stopped. He leaned over me with his hands on either side of my neck, pupils blown wide, bottom lip caught between his teeth. Pale gold hair framed his face like a halo. "What do you want, Carter?" he breathed.

"I don't know," I said shakily as I pushed the last of the fabric off his shoulders. "I don't..."

His torso was smooth and lean, the muscles in his stomach prominent from the hours of self-defence classes he still took every week. A dark silver piercing glittered against his chest, and my mouth went dry at the sight of it.

"I didn't know you wore this to school," I murmured. Tentatively, I scraped the ring with my thumb.

Remy swore in English. Then in French.

He was so beautiful. I ran trembling hands along his sides, over skin as warm and soft as silk left to air in the sun. Pangs of longing burst inside me like grenades; I shook with the force of them.

Remy leaned back and perched over my thighs. "Sit up," he said hoarsely.

I was barely upright before he was peeling off my own jumper and divesting me of the long-sleeved shirt underneath. He threw the clothes over the side of the bed, heedless of where they landed. They could have landed on the moon for all I cared.

Remy shifted. He flattened his palms on the bare skin of my back, drawing me closer until we were chest-to-chest. I *groaned* at how good it felt. "You're sure?" he asked.

Nodding, I wrestled back another bout of nerves. "Have you ever…?"

"Some things."

As I processed that, Remy cupped my jaw in his hands. Pressed our foreheads together. "You know you can tell me to stop." It wasn't a question.

He'd always stopped when I told him in the past, but this time… this time… "I don't want you to stop," I whispered. Thrilling, terrifying words.

Remy smiled. "You can still say it. Whenever you want."

Then with a cant of his hips, he pushed me down, and all rational thought flew from my mind. I wound myself around him, as far as

I could go, willing the goodness inside him to blot out the darkness in me.

He was everywhere. His hands. His mouth. All of him, burning against me like a brand.

And I welcomed everything he gave, for I had been his from the very first moment we met.

It was a firm grip on my shoulder that eventually jolted me awake. "Carter, wake up!"

I blinked my heavy eyelids and tried to work through the strange fog clouding my brain. It was dark outside, but my bedroom blinds were still wide open. When I stretched, cotton skated over my bare skin, which was warm and tingly and—

I froze.

I wasn't alone beneath the covers.

"*Carter*," Remy hissed.

It all came back in a flood. The darkness hid the rush of blood to my cheeks, and a surge of heat washed down my chest all the way to my toes. I almost smiled.

But Remy's eyes were wide. "What time were you supposed to be at Katie's?"

I rolled over to look at my clock, and my stomach lurched. Hoping it was a mistake, I rubbed my eyes, but when I looked again, the same green digits glared back at me. "*Shit!*"

"I'm sorry," said Remy. "I didn't mean to fall asleep." He sounded upset, but I didn't have time to comfort him.

It was well after seven; I should have been at Katie's place an hour ago.

I scrambled out of bed and picked up my discarded clothes from the floor. The pants were inside out, the shirt in an impossible snarl, and I fought back a hysterical laugh as I untangled the mess. I slid the clothes back on one garment at a time, but my hands were shaking so hard I couldn't do up the buttons on my shirt. "*Goddamn it*!"

"Here, let me." Remy appeared at my side. I was so out of sorts, he'd managed to get completely dressed—shoes and all—in the time it'd taken me to put on my pants. He grabbed one flap of my open shirt and tugged at it until I turned to face him.

Letting him do up the buttons was oddly…intimate. Somehow, even *more* intimate than what we'd just shared. I watched his deft fingers work, the heat still glowing in my face, and when he reached my waist, I stepped back. "Thanks," I murmured.

Remy smiled, but it didn't reach his eyes.

I turned and crouched by my schoolbag, rifling through the pockets until I found my phone. I tapped on the screen to see if Katie had called me. She had—six times.

She was going to kill me.

A sick feeling slithered through my chest. What was I going to tell her? How would I ever explain? Because I couldn't say that Remy came over and I got distracted when we…

Oh, God. I'd actually…

"I can let myself out," Remy said so quietly I almost didn't hear him.

The sick feeling grew. This was all wrong. Things should be better now, shouldn't they? Things should be good. It shouldn't feel like everything was falling apart.

I pinched the bridge of my nose. "No, it's all right. Come on."

The rest of the house was as dark as my room—a small mercy since it meant Mum still wasn't home. I led Remy through the dimness, but when we reached the front door, he hesitated.

Tension coiled inside me. "What's wrong?"

"Do you regret it?" he whispered. He didn't look at me, and his slim shoulders hunched over as if he was bracing for a blow.

I stared at him. I could never remember him looking so vulnerable, not in all the time I'd known him. Not brave, cheerful, kind-hearted Remy.

But I didn't know if I could give him the words he wanted to hear. Didn't know if the nausea swirling in my belly was regret—or something else. Something worse.

Remy's jaw tightened. He opened the door. "Forget it."

"Hey." Before he could step outside, I gripped his chin and forced him to look at me. His blue-grey eyes were limned with silver tears.

I deserved to burn in hell for all eternity for what I was doing to him.

But still, I bent down and kissed his puffy lips. Remy let out a shuddering sigh and went pliant against me, his hands sliding up to cradle my face.

I didn't stop to wonder why it felt so much like goodbye.

The light switched on. The darkness which shrouded us, *protected* us, fled like shadows before the dawn.

And the gasp that followed marked the end of my world.

I dropped Remy like a hot coal and whirled around. There, standing on the other side of the room, was Mum.

207

I would never, for as long as I lived, forget the look on her face.

I had seen my mother wear many expressions. I had seen her shocked. I had seen her angry. I had seen her sad and disappointed and dismayed.

This was none of those.

This was an expression I had only seen once in my life: in the moment I opened our door to reveal police officers standing on the other side.

This was *fear*.

Panic spiked through me, a bolt of lightning that fried my nerves. "It's not what it looks like!" I tried to say, but the words came out so fast, so frantically, they were incoherent.

Mum's face went blank. "Get out."

My heart stopped. "W-what?"

But Mum wasn't looking at me. She was looking past me—at Remy. "Carter," she growled, "get your *friend* out of my house." Her eyes slid back to mine, cold and unforgiving. "By the time I get back, I want him *gone*."

She turned and stalked out of the room.

I stared dumbly after her, and in the dooming silence that followed, my body started to quake. For one horrifying moment, I'd thought she was talking to me—that she'd told *me* to get out of the house. But she was only talking to Remy.

Okay—that was okay.

"Carter?" Remy said cautiously. "Mon chou, I...I'm so sorry. I don't—"

"You should leave." Cold. Such coldness inside me. In my voice. Like the look in my mother's eyes.

He gulped audibly. "Why don't...why don't you come with me?

208

Give her a chance to calm down, and we can figure out a way to—"

"Just go."

"But…" All he did was touch my hand. Just touch my hand, hanging limply at my side.

I swung around and shoved him out the open door. "*GET OUT!*"

But he missed the doorway. *I* missed the doorway. Caught by surprise, overbalanced by the push, Remy stumbled. Fell. And on the way down, his head smacked against the doorframe. The thud it made, as his skull connected with the timber, was the worst sound I had ever heard.

Bile rose in my throat. *What have I done?*

"Remy?" I dropped to my knees. He was sprawled half on his side, those beautiful eyes dazed—but at least he was conscious. "I'm so sorry. I didn't… Are you okay?" I went to put my hand on his arm.

He shied away. "Don't touch me."

No.

No, no, no, no, no. Anything—anything but this.

"I didn't mean to," I whispered. "I'm sorry." I reached for him again.

"Don't you fucking *touch* me!" Remy slapped my hand away and hauled himself to his feet on the doorframe. Sobs tore from his chest as he scrambled unsteadily back.

He was terrified, I realised. Terrified of me.

"Please," I begged.

He slammed the door shut in my face.

Silence. Such devastating silence, and then—

"Is he gone?" Mum demanded.

Stricken, I stared at the door. "He's gone."

Her face was a thundercloud as she blew across the room to my side. She locked the door like she thought Remy might try to get back in. Or I might try to follow him.

I wouldn't. Not after what I'd done.

"Mum…"

"Save it," she snapped. "I don't want to hear a word of it. Do you think this is easy for me? None of this has ever been easy. *Everything* has been a battle since we lost your father, but at least I thought I could trust you. Clearly, I was mistaken if you've been sneaking around behind my back, doing God only knows what with that boy. And under *my* roof!"

Fury radiated off her in waves. "How long has this been going on?"

"Mum…"

"*How long*, Carter?"

I closed my eyes. Opened them again because I didn't dare look away. "Since March."

I watched her mouth the words, watched the realisation dawn that I'd been lying to her from the start. That I'd never intended to stay away from Remy, even when I promised her I would. "I'm sorry," I croaked.

"Are you?" Mum seethed. "Are you really sorry, or are you just saying that because you think it will placate me?"

There were tears in my eyes. I blinked, and they were streaming down my face. "I couldn't stay away from him, Mum." The truth. The honest, undiluted truth. She deserved that. I owed it to her. "I tried, I swear I did, but I just couldn't stay away. I think I might—"

My head wrenched around to the side.

One moment, I stood before her. The next, I was staring up at her from the ground, a hollow ringing in my ears. Disoriented, I pressed a hand to the patch of fire on my cheek.

Had she just…hit me?

This was a line she had never crossed. No matter how bad things had been in the past, my mother had never raised a hand to me.

Her face was white, her lips trembling; she realised it too. "Whatever you were about to say," she choked out, "don't. Don't you *dare*."

And then she was crying.

My mother, who I had never *seen* shed a tear, not even when Dad and Miles died, was crying. Because of me. Because of what I'd done.

Maybe because of who I was.

I wanted to go to her. I wanted to stand and take her in my arms and tell her I'd do anything she asked of me to make this hurt go away. But I didn't. I didn't move from the floor at her feet as she wept, didn't follow as she fled into her bedroom and closed the door behind her.

I didn't even twitch when she emerged an eternity later, a suitcase clutched in her bloodless hand.

"I'm going away for a few days," she said. Her voice was flat, dead, like all the life had been sucked out of her. Indeed, the only colour on her face was the blotchiness around her eyes; the rest was grey and wan.

I did that. I did that to her.

"When will you be back?" I rasped.

Her gaze darted to my cheek. I wondered if there was a handprint there. "I don't know. Maybe Monday."

Monday.

She would miss my graduation.

"I can't…" She swallowed. "I just can't look at you right now."

Then she was gone.

Gone.

A breath shuddered out of me.

It was hopeless, then. It had all been hopeless—everything I'd done, everything I'd endured and suffered and worked for.

I'd failed.

I'd failed my friends. I'd failed Remy. I'd failed Dad and Miles.

And I'd failed Mum.

Don't you fucking touch me!

I just can't look at you right now.

There was nothing left. Nothing left to fight for. Nothing left to do.

Except one thing.

One last thing to solve all my problems. To fix everything I'd ruined. To make all the wrongs right again.

I knew what I had to do.

I got off the floor. I went to Katie's. We finished the graduation speech.

And, when I got home, I cleaned the house.

sixteen

"Sit down," Katie ordered, gesturing sharply at the rubbish bin in the corner.

I dragged it over and adjusted the lid to make sure it was lying flat, then parked myself atop the corrugated steel. At any other time, this whole thing might have been funny.

But neither of us was laughing.

"Look up."

I tilted my head back and shut my eyes against the harsh glare of the fluorescent lights. Katie squirted some of the tan-coloured liquid onto her hand, and a moment later, gentle fingers smeared it over my cheek. The concealer was cool against my heated skin, but it warmed quickly. Once it was dry, I could barely even tell it was there.

"At least the swelling is gone," Katie murmured as she rubbed the last of the cream into my temple. "Does it hurt?"

"No."

"Liar."

But I wasn't lying. Not about this. I didn't feel any pain on my face.

I didn't feel much of anything at all.

"There. Good as new." Her voice was tight, gruff. "What do you think?"

I opened my eyes and looked at myself in the bathroom mirror.

Katie had been furious when I showed up at her house the night before. She'd ripped her front door open, eyes spitting blue fire as she snarled, "Where the hell have you—"

The demand strangled off. The embers in her eyes winked out. Her mouth opened, shut, opened again as she groped for the right words. "What happened?" she finally managed.

"Nothing."

"Nothing?" Katie echoed. She stared, then seized my arm and dragged me across the threshold. The door had barely closed behind us before she was hauling me through the house to her bedroom and setting me in front of the full-length mirror propped against one wall. "Want to try that again?"

My left cheek was bright red and swollen. I angled my chin, noting the imprint of fingers which extended towards my ear, the thumb-shaped ruby welt beside my eye. I traced the edge of the mark, recalled the crack of her palm on my face; the skin was hot to the touch.

I lowered my hand. "My mum hit me."

Katie inhaled. "What? *Why*?"

"It doesn't matter."

"It doesn't... *Carter*," she protested. "This is not okay."

I ignored that. I didn't even know why I'd told her. Turning away from the mirror, I shoved my hands into my pockets. "Sorry I'm late."

Katie made a small, wounded noise. "Wait here." She slipped out of the room and returned a few minutes later with an icepack wrapped in a tea towel.

I accepted the icepack and pressed it to my cheek.

Katie steered me to her bed and settled down at my side. "We're going to deal with this," she said firmly. "I will help you"—she grimaced—"*conceal* that mark for tomorrow and not a day longer. On Saturday, you are going to come here and tell me what the hell is going on, and we are going to handle it like adults. Understood?"

Her direct, no-nonsense attitude almost made me smile. "Understood."

And that was how we ended up in the girls' bathroom at five o'clock the next morning. It was tradition for the year twelves to gather in the dark on their last day of school and decorate the campus before everyone else arrived. Katie and I had planned to get here first regardless, but now she'd come armed with her concealer as well as a box full of decorations.

I studied her handiwork in the mirror. Despite the water spots staining the reflective surface, I could tell she'd done a good job. The swelling *had* gone down overnight, though the mark was still pink and had yellowed a bit at the edges, but with Katie's help, no one would notice unless they looked closely. Unless they knew what to look for.

"It's perfect," I said.

"Good." Katie still sounded tense, uncertain that she'd done the right thing, but she didn't push the matter further.

"Katie?"

"Yeah?"

"Thank you."

Her shoulders sagged. "You're welcome."

"Not just for this." I stepped closer and met her eyes when she looked up. "For everything. This whole year. I know the last few weeks have been...tough, but I really have loved working with you. You've been awesome."

Katie's smile wobbled. "You're going to make me cry," she said and threw her arms around me. I stumbled back a bit but held onto her. Held her close. "I've loved working with you too, Carter. I'm sorry I've been so bitchy recently. I've been so stressed, but if I'd realised..." She shook her head. "Let's just get through today. Just this one day, and tomorrow we'll talk."

Tomorrow. Right.

"Here." Katie disentangled herself from me and pressed the bottle of concealer into my hand. "Take it with you in case it wears off. I won't be able to sneak you in here once everyone else arrives."

"Thanks." I tucked it into my pocket.

My co-captain rinsed off her hands and squared her shoulders. "You ready, then?"

I summoned a smile. "Let's go decorate this school."

The sun emerged from its hibernation for our final day. Graduation day.

My classmates made the most of the twilight hours, hanging banners of coloured fabric from the balconies and winding striped crepe streamers through the handrails on every set of stairs they could find. Jars of treats were prepositioned at each of the school's gates, while the more artistic students went to work mounting giant painted signs on the walls.

Katie and I dashed around to oversee the progress and ensure all was going to plan—and paused to give Matt Phillips a stern talking-to after he cling-wrapped the entrance to the teachers' carpark.

When the sky brightened with the sunrise, it was clear and unburdened by clouds for the first time in what seemed like months. The light inched up above the buildings, illuminating the decorations in a golden glow that sent cheers bouncing across the main courtyard as the year twelves stood back and rejoiced.

I wondered if anyone noticed that I didn't join in the cheering.

I wondered if anyone noticed my distraction as I walked among them, combing through the masses for a glimpse of a pale blond head. Just a glimpse, that was all I needed. Just a glimpse of his face to know that he was okay.

But every time that platinum hair flashed into the corner of my view, I blinked, and it was gone again, concealed by the ever-growing crowd.

He was avoiding me.

I didn't realise that a tiny flame of hope had flickered in my heart until I felt it gutter and die. There was a moment of sadness as it extinguished, of regret as the dark closed in, but I didn't mourn the flame's loss for long. It never had much of a chance, anyway.

The bell rang.

I turned my face skyward, soaked in the kiss of the sun, the sounds of the younger students laughing and shouting as they scurried off to class.

For so long, I had been drowning, suffocating under an unbearable weight. The turmoil had torn me apart from within, ripped me to shreds until who I was on the inside no longer resembled the boy who wore my skin.

But now, there was only calm. Only peace. Peace like I'd never felt in my life.

I welcomed it.

"Hey, Carter!" Jake's voice. I opened my eyes and found him waving at me, his face alive with glee. "Mate, you coming?"

"Coming," I said.

Time shuddered forwards, and thus the day passed.

The pranks and the games and the indulgent reminders that school wasn't yet over.

The traditions and celebrations and farewells.

The final assembly.

My quartet played, and we played without a glitch. As splendidly and perfectly as always, though Jamie still refused to look my way.

Katie and I presented the film we'd been labouring over, a memento of the last six years that left few dry eyes in the hall.

And then I was walking across the stage to the sound of my name and the roar and applause of the crowd. I didn't even notice Mum's absence. Didn't much care she wasn't there.

Not even later, when most of the school milled about on the oval so families could take all the pictures they liked.

I stood with my arm around Jake, grin fixed to my face as we stared into the lens of his parents' camera—for so long my best friend lost patience. "Mum," he grumbled, "that'll *do*."

Mrs Brenner pouted, but she obliged her son and tucked the camera away. "Where's your mum, Carter? I haven't seen her yet."

I shrugged. "She's not here. She had to work today."

Jake's parents blinked. Exchanged glances. His dad looked like he might say something, but Jake elbowed him in the side and quickly ushered me away. "Sorry about the busybodies," he muttered, glaring at them over his shoulder.

I stopped, school shoes scuffing in the patchy grass. "Thank you," I said.

"Um…for what?"

"For being such a good friend." I held up a hand before he could object. "I mean it. You've always been here for me, and I want you to know…I appreciate it."

Jake's brow wrinkled. "Are you feeling okay?"

"Of course. Today just seems like a good time to say the things I don't say often enough."

Jake studied me, and I almost thought he'd noticed something no one else had seen. But then he made a face. Opened his arms. "Bring it in, you dweeb."

I laughed and hugged him.

He squeezed me tight. "You're my best mate," he murmured. "No thanks are needed."

"That doesn't mean I shouldn't say it. Thank you. Thank you for everything."

"Shit." Jake pushed me back, jabbing a finger at my chest. "Don't you go getting all mushy on me, Cantwell."

"God forbid."

My best friend deliberately avoided my eyes, but I didn't avoid his—I noticed the moment his gaze snagged on something behind me. A wicked grin tugged at his lips. "Oh, look. There's Mr and Mrs Wu. I'm going to go and say hi."

"Why am I not surprised?"

Jake made to push past me, but he paused. "I'll see you at the dinner tonight, yeah?"

"Sure, Jake," I said. "I'll see you later." I watched him melt into the crowd and let the smile linger on my face for a while before I turned away.

It was then that I saw a familiar blond head duck into the nearest breezeway. Alone.

I ran.

For once, not away from—but *towards*.

I burst into the breezeway and hurtled down its length, dashing through the door into the locker room, where I'd seen him disappear. I had to catch him, had to talk to him before it was too late, too late, *too late*—

There he was. A morose figure standing amidst all that flaking metal, the spikes of his hair drooping limp about his face.

"Remy."

His shoulders tensed, but he didn't try to leave. I waited, breathing hard, the damning silence that stretched between us punctuated by the hammer of my heart.

Then Remy turned.

Purple shadows hovered beneath his eyes. Some of them seemed to have leached up *into* his eyes, turning them a murky grey. He surveyed me, stone-faced, his sparkle gone, his beautiful, sunny smile hidden from my sight.

And it was all my fault.

"I'm sorry," I whispered.

Remy remained grave, untouched by the apology. "How mad was your mum?"

Something in my chest collapsed. "Mad enough."

"She didn't…kick you out or anything, did she?"

She left. She hit me, then left.

I didn't say it, though. Couldn't say it, not to him with his accepting, loving family, so I shook my head and hoped it was convincing. "I'm sorry," I repeated.

"I know you are."

"It's…not enough." I wasn't asking him. I was telling.

Remy sighed, and the veil of his indifference peeled back. He fought to hold onto it, but it wavered long enough to expose the brittleness beneath.

Then he rallied, pinned me with that stormy gaze. "I've changed my mind," he said. Slowly. Clearly. Like it was a line he'd been rehearsing all night. "I said I'd tell you if I changed my mind about this—about *us*—and I have. I can't do this anymore."

It was strange. Strange how, even now, with the calm pulsing all around me, those words struck home. Struck hard.

"I know…" Remy swallowed. "I know how difficult it can be to come to terms with who you are. And I'm sympathetic, Carter. I am. But what you did last night was not okay. No matter how much stress you're under or how panicked you were."

He glanced away, jaw working. "I used to get beat up, you know. At my old school. Self-defence classes aside, I've experienced my share of violence. I can't go back to that. I *won't*."

"Remy…" He'd never told me that before. People had *hurt* him, and I'd—

"I'm falling for you."

I blinked. Stared. Scarcely dared to breathe.

"I'm falling for you," Remy's voice broke, "and I know you're sorry, but it's like you said. It's not enough. I could handle stepping back into the closet for you—I don't want you to feel guilty for *that*—but I can't be with someone who makes me worry he'll turn on me the moment he gets scared. I deserve better than that."

He was right. He was absolutely right. It was what I'd known all along, but to hear him say it was like he'd cut the strings on my parachute, abandoning me to the fall. My ending was inevitable now; there was no safe place left to land.

Remy Montrose was the best thing that had ever happened to me, and I'd ruined it.

Like I ruined everything.

Those mournful eyes lifted back to mine. His brows angled down at whatever expression I wore—or perhaps the expression I didn't. "Say something, Carter."

In response, I closed the distance between us. He allowed it, allowed me to back him into his locker in a mimicry of the night that all this started. "You deserve only good things, Remy."

Remy's face crumpled. "For what it's worth, I forgive you. I just…"

I reached for him, splaying my fingers along the sharp line of his jaw. I could see, clear as day, the path that stretched out before me, the one without his light to guide my way.

And I did not have the strength left to walk it. Not anymore.

"It's all right," I told him. "I understand." I leaned in, remembering the previous night, when our bodies pressed so close, I couldn't tell where his ended and mine began. "I've loved every moment I've spent with you."

A heartbroken sound loosed from his throat, and Remy swayed forwards, a magnet drawn to its opposite pole.

I took his face in my hands. "Thank you. For the chance. For showing me what it could have been like."

"What it *can* be like," he whispered, "once you get over your fear."

But it was too late for that. It had been too late before we even began.

Maybe, in another life, he could fix what was broken inside of me.

I laid a kiss on his forehead, then stepped back and looked at him one more time. My eyes devoured every plane and angle of that beloved face, my chest squeezing so tight I couldn't breathe. "Take care, Remy," I said.

Then I turned and walked away.

Walked out of the school, right out the front gate. Glanced back only once—to say goodbye to this place that had made and unmade me.

I dawdled through the streets with a vacant mind and an empty heart. Like I had with Miles all those years ago, I strolled along the cracked footpath with a hand held out to the side. I could feel the ghost of his fingers wound through and tangled with mine.

I squeezed. No one squeezed back.

My hand curled into a fist.

When I got home, I sat down on the front step and let out a deep breath. The sun warmed my hair as it descended, and I watched without thought while the tiny white blossoms of the ornamental pear trees twisted and blew in the wind.

I was content, for a while, to just *be*.

My phone buzzed in my pocket. I dug it out and saw a text from Katie, but it was an earlier message that immediately caught my eye.

SEAN: Hey kiddo, flight just landed. Got a strange voicemail from ur mum. R u ok?

Time-stamped ninety minutes ago.

I could have waited. I'd weighed the pros and cons of enduring just one more day.

But Katie had asked me to talk tomorrow.

My brother never lived past his graduation night.

And there was a good chance my uncle was making for the house at this very moment.

Now, then. Now was the right time. I didn't want to wait any longer.

Life was a burden I was never meant to bear.

Keeping hold of the phone, I hauled myself off the step and went inside. I took my bag to my bedroom and set it down beside the desk. My eyes were drawn to the plastic-wrapped shirt on my wardrobe door. Miles' shirt. The shirt I'd removed from his room two days earlier to wear tonight.

Miles never wore the shirt to his graduation dinner.

I would never wear it either.

I walked down the hall to the bathroom, every footstep lighter than the last. The first thing I did was to take off my shoes. I placed my socks inside them and nudged them under the cabinet with my toe. I did not bother turning on the lights.

Then I took out the packet of razors from where I'd hidden it in the depths of the cabinet. There were eight left. Seven more than I needed.

I remembered it was raining that fateful day. Spring flowers were in bloom and fuzzy green growth sprouted from the trees like hair on a newborn child, but still, the sky wept. It cried for Miles, and for my father.

It wasn't raining now. Not even with what I was about to do. But I didn't expect it to rain. The sky wouldn't cry for me.

In the world beyond the frosted glass, the sun was setting, turning its back on me like everyone did in the end. It cast an eerie scarlet glow across the horizon—the colour of blood.

My grip on the edge of the sink tightened as I looked into the mirror. I didn't recognise the person who stared back. All I saw in my reflection was a shell. A shell filled with so much weakness, so many lies.

How did I become this person? How did I stray so far and get so lost?

I turned away from my shame.

My eyes burned, but my cheeks remained dry. I tasted salt on my face—the memory of all the tears I'd shed—but now there were no more tears. The time for tears had passed.

I'm falling for you, Remy had said, even as he let me go.

I should have told him I'd already fallen. But...but it wasn't yet too late.

I picked up my phone, and for the first time in a long time, my hands didn't shake as I tapped out the words in my heart.

ME: I'm sorry. I love you.

It wasn't enough. It would never be enough. But it was all I had left to give.

My last gift to him.

My Remy.

The sun disappeared. There were no stars tonight. No light, no hope. There was nothing but darkness here for me.

I removed my shirt, my pants, folded them neatly beside the basin. Placed my buzzing phone on top. Cool air caressed my skin, and I marvelled at the goosebumps that rippled along my flesh when I no longer felt anything at all.

Then I took out a razor. Climbed into the bath.

A shadow wound itself around my heart. It ran through my veins and filled my lungs, cutting off my air. I was trapped in a prison of my own making, and now there was only one way out.

I cut through the tethers binding me, and I set myself free.

What do you think it's like to die? Tim asked me.

I reckon it's peaceful, I said. *Like falling asleep.*

It hadn't been a lie in the end. Dying *was* peaceful. Cold—like the distant stars I could no longer see.

But it hurt more than I expected. That shattered sky pressed down, crushing me, pleading with me to hold it up.

But I couldn't. I just couldn't do it anymore. I was so tired.

So I dropped my arms. Let it go.

And the sky fell down around me.

Sorrow

seventeen

An angel sat beside my bed.

His eyes were closed, his hands were clasped, his head bowed forwards in prayer. Fatigue clung to the delicate line of his shoulders, and his porcelain skin was awash with a pallor of grief.

I wondered what he was praying for. I hoped that somebody answered.

The urge to comfort the angel was strong. Difficult to deny. I longed to reach out and touch him, to run my fingers through the dark, shaggy hair curling around his ears. It looked so soft, like a raven's feathers. Shiny, like the iridescent light that dappled the wall at his back.

His wings?

I tried to raise my hands. Tried to reach for him. Couldn't.

Couldn't move. Couldn't feel my body.

I was weightless, falling, and a whimper escaped from my lips.

The angel's head snapped up. "Carter?"

Was that my name? It did not feel as if it were mine.

The angel's eyes were blue: the colour of the sky in summer or the ocean on a clear day. Rich. Vibrant. Even as they spilled over with tears. "Oh, thank God!"

Don't cry, I wanted to tell him. *Don't cry, lovely angel.*

But my mouth didn't work. I had no tongue. No words.

A heaviness was growing in my head. Its dull weight swelled within my mind, crawled across my sight, and I fought desperately against it. Thrashed and screamed and flailed.

I didn't want to leave. I wanted to stay here with the angel.

"Shush," he said softly. There was such care in that voice. Such gentleness. It was like a dream, like a song, and his hand glowed white as it fell upon the crown of my head.

Oh! I felt *that* touch. Felt it tingle all the way down to my toes.

"It's okay," the angel crooned. "Sleep now. You're going to be okay."

That hand felt wonderful, and his words were soothing, so I let the dark tide drag me under once more.

I lay flat on my back, gazing up at a starless sky. There was no sun, no moon, no planets or spiralling galaxies—just a solid black expanse that stretched into infinity.

Directly above me, a crack dissected the heavens. It was a streak of impenetrable darkness, all jagged and askew as if some primordial being had grabbed hold of the sky and *shaken* it so hard it splintered. I wondered if it would fall.

Maybe it already had. Maybe that's what this darkness was.

The end.

But voices were emerging from the gloom. Formless, indistinct, echoing off something nearby. I didn't search out their owners. It was better to stay here, to stay quiet and peaceful and still. Only bad things happened when I opened my mouth.

I wasn't sure how I knew that.

But I did.

"You should stay." A man's voice. He sounded tired. Raw. As if desperation had whittled him down to a single, razor-sharp edge.

"I can't." A woman, this time. Smooth in comparison, but weak. Like she'd already accepted defeat.

"You can."

"No." Eerie silence, then: "I did this."

Did what?

I strained to hear more, to learn more, but their voices faded back into the darkness. Or perhaps the darkness engulfed them. It was a relief, really, to have them gone. It was nice and warm and quiet here, even if I was alone.

It felt...safe.

Had I ever felt safe before? Been safe before?

I didn't know. Couldn't remember.

All I knew was the shattered black sky, the endless dark beneath it. And yet, as I began to drift away again, the woman's words remained.

I did this I did this I did this I did this I did this...

Hearing was the first thing to return.

One moment, hollow silence. The next, an incessant, mechanical beep that tickled my eardrums like gnats. Further out, somewhere beyond me, was the patter of feet, the rustle and hiss of cloth, the muffled hum of chatter that I couldn't quite discern.

My mouth was parched—that was the second thing I noticed. I rolled my swollen tongue around, trying to work up some moisture, but all that did was make the scorching ache in my throat get worse. Water. I needed water.

I cracked my eyes open, and searing, artificial light stabbed into my retinas. A rainbow-tinged haze shimmered across my vision, spinning and lurching in sickening whorls that only slowly receded. Dwindled until all that was left was a faint prismatic glow on the stark white ceiling above.

Stiff, heavy lids shrieked their protests as I opened my eyes the whole way. I took in my surroundings with a sense of detachment: bleached walls, teal-grey linoleum floor, thin cotton sheets tucked tight around my body.

Where was I? Where in the—

"Hey, kiddo."

I flinched. The voice was scratchy but familiar, and with a monumental effort, I managed to turn my head in the direction from which it came.

My uncle looked awful. He hunched in a chair beside the bed, hair protruding from his scalp in greasy, uneven tufts. His eyes were red-rimmed and sunken, and with a sallow cast to his skin, the image he made was ghastly.

Even his smile seemed to fracture across his face. "It's so good to see you awake."

How long had I been asleep? I sensed it was a while.

"Do you know where you are?"

I just stared at him. Waited.

"You're in the hospital, Carter," Sean whispered.

The hospital.

Something dark slithered into my mind. It coiled there, at the fringes of my subconscious, poised and ready to strike.

I looked down.

Both my arms, from palm to elbow, were swathed in a thick layer of bandages. Antiseptic fluid stained my fingers yellow-brown, bleeding saffron into the nailbeds, and an IV line was taped to the back of one hand.

I couldn't feel it. Any of it. Couldn't feel the needle digging into my flesh, the rub or the pressure of the bandages against my skin.

It was as if these arms were no longer my own.

It was as if...

As if...

That dark thing struck.

Between one heartbeat and the next, it sank its teeth deep into my brain, and as its venom fired across my synapses, the memories returned in a rush.

No.

"Carter?"

NO.

I might have screamed it if I had the strength. If I had the will.

I glared at my uncle, and I knew my eyes were blazing. With rage. With despair. Sean recoiled at the bleak fury on my face, but I didn't care.

It was supposed to be over. The guilt. The shame. The constant, unbearable pain. It was supposed to be *over*. It was supposed to be *done*. But it wasn't.

I'd failed. Just like I failed at everything.

Even this.

Tears slid down Sean's cheeks. "We found…we found you in the bath."

You should have left me there.

He'd saved me. Saved me when I didn't want to be saved.

His breaths were harsh, sobbing, and the pain in his features was clear. I wasn't moved. All it did was remind me how good I was at hurting those I loved.

I turned my face away and closed my eyes. Tuned him out as he said my name over and over and over again.

Wished he would just finish what I started and put an end to my misery.

Put an end to *me*.

I was distantly aware of the door opening. Of muted voices, the door clicking shut, then footsteps heading towards me.

A chair creaked, and a puff of exotic perfume wafted into my nose. "Hello, Carter," she said with unflappable calm. "My name is Sophie. I'm a doctor. How are you feeling?"

I didn't move.

"Your uncle has stepped out for a moment. Can you open your eyes and look at me?"

The anger faltered. The sharp teeth eased out of my brain. It left me empty—cold and vacant and numb. But I still didn't open my eyes. Didn't look at her.

"I know you're awake," said Sophie. I could almost hear her smile. "I bet you're thirsty."

I was. My throat ached worse than ever, and my tongue was like a thick, dried-out slug in my mouth. It meant nothing. Maybe if I could bear to deny myself a drink, the abyss would engulf me again.

And it would be done.

Sophie wasn't put off by my silence. "I know it might not feel like it right now," she said gently, "but this is not the end. We know you're in pain, that maybe you have been for a while. But there are people here who love you and care about you very much. They are going to get you through this."

Lies.

There was no *getting through* this.

Not when I wanted to pull at my hair, to slice at my skin until not a drop of my blood remained.

Not when I was chained. Chained to this bed by my damaged arms and chained to this life I no longer wanted any part of.

I wanted to be with my brother. I wanted to be with my dad. And I wanted to be with Tim, who had done so much better than me at this.

I sank into a chasm too shallow to drown out my screams, and Sophie's voice droned on.

The next time I woke, there was yet another stranger waiting by my side.

She was young, perhaps only a few years older than me, and clad in a set of pale blue scrubs that immediately marked her as a nurse. At first, I thought to be startled by her presence, until I realised: they couldn't—wouldn't—leave me alone right now.

Wouldn't give me the chance to try again.

Not that there was anything in this room I could use, anyway. It was virtually empty aside from the furniture, the monitors, and the drip my IV was connected to. Even the tubing was too short to be of any use, and there was nothing to tie the other end around.

I shifted beneath the sheets, alerting the nurse to the fact I was awake. No windows adorned the stark walls, so it was impossible to tell whether it was morning or night, but when she produced a tray of food, its contents suggested it was breakfast time.

Juice and some porridge-like gruel.

My stomach clenched at the sight of it, and a line of fire shot down my throat. My body was hungry. Thirsty.

The traitor.

When the nurse attempted to feed me, I twisted away, refusing to take a single bite, a single sip, no matter how much she prodded or cajoled.

I *refused*.

A light knock on the door interrupted our silent battle of wills. My uncle's head poked into the room, and the nurse couldn't quite hide the relief that stole over her face. She slid the tray onto the narrow table beside the bed and stood to greet him.

I didn't listen to the words they exchanged, but the next thing I knew, the nurse was gone, and Sean was flopping down into the chair she'd just vacated.

He must have got some rest while I slept. And showered, too. His hair was clean and lying flat and smooth, and the patchy fuzz on his jaw was gone. If it wasn't for the puffiness around his eyes or the haunted glimmer within them, I might have said he looked like a new man.

"How are you this morning, kiddo?" he asked softly.

Irritation sparked in the cavernous void. How did he *think* I was?

Sean's face fell a little, but he shrugged off the silence and reached for the juice box on the tray. "The nurse said you won't eat or drink. Won't you at least have a drink?" He put the straw to my lips. "Please?"

I debated spitting it away. Decided I couldn't be bothered.

Sean sighed and put the box back. "Okay. They told me you might be mad when you woke, but I didn't…" He rubbed the back of his neck, huffing out a self-deprecating breath. "Never mind. You don't want to talk to me. I get it. Message received. But *I* am going to talk to *you*, so unless you change your mind, you're just going to have to listen."

He didn't wait for my agreement before he launched right in. "Your friend Remy."

The world tilted. Too far. Too soon. The memories were still too fresh in my mind of Remy in my heart, Remy in my bed, Remy on the ground with agony in his eyes.

Remy telling me it was over and letting me go.

"Hey." Sean's hand cupped my cheek, gently turned my head towards him. "It's *okay*. He showed me the text you sent him."

I'm sorry. I love you.

"That text saved your life, Carter."

No. No, that couldn't be right.

My uncle swallowed, and his hand drifted back from my face, carding lightly through my hair. "Remy knew something wasn't right, so he and his mum came over to your house. They got there about the same time we did, and they'd already called an ambulance and everything. If they hadn't…"

I'd be dead.

He didn't need to say it.

"I don't know what we would have done if it was just us there when we found you."

We. Us. The frown formed before I could stop it.

Sean saw the unspoken question. "Charlie is with me, remember? I told you…" He sat back, let his hand fall to the pillow beside my chin. "I told you about him."

My eyes whipped up to his.

He arched an eyebrow. "That's the thing, isn't it? When I told you about Charlie, you just…*assumed* I was with a woman."

But…but I *knew* he'd had girlfriends in the past. I'd seen pictures. He—

"I'm bisexual, Carter," Sean said. "And I have loved Charlie for every single one of the two years, nine months, and twenty-three days that I've known him."

Never, in all my life, had I ever imagined my uncle saying those words. And yet, it made perfect sense—in a roundabout sort of way.

This explained why my mother didn't like him.

This explained why he'd always appeased her, for fear she'd cut me out of his life.

There was an expression of such anguished hope on my uncle's face, like he'd just ripped out his heart and offered it to me on a platter. All I had to do was reach out, and with a single stroke, I could accept that offered heart—or crush it.

I did neither. Couldn't do either. Not yet.

Because two years, nine months, and twenty-three days…and he hadn't told me.

"You never forget the day someone like that walks into your life," Sean said softly. "There I was in a London café, having my morning coffee, when I saw him. He was one of the baristas, and from the moment I laid eyes on him, I knew. I just knew he was the one for me."

The corners of his eyes crinkled. "So I marched right up to him and asked him out, in front of his colleagues and everything. It could have gone badly, of course, but I decided the risk was worth a possible fist in my face. I've survived worse."

And, with that, he sobered. The tentative joy ebbed away, replaced by a sour bitterness I didn't care for at all. "In some ways," he murmured, "I've been where you are right now."

Sean's hand slid off my pillow, and he rubbed at his chest as if to diffuse an ache lodged there. "I was only eight years old when Ronan moved out and married your mum. Our parents were furious, and they...took it out on me, I suppose. They really cracked down, became super strict. I think they got paranoid I'd end up making my brother's mistakes.

"But it backfired. Their leash chafed. By the time I reached adolescence, I was wild, out of control, and between my ongoing rebellion and frustration over my confounding sexuality, you might say I was completely off the rails.

"Then, when I was sixteen, these punks caught me making out with another guy from my school. Things were different back then, especially in the area I grew up. It was conservative, you know?" Sean shrugged and shot a flat look at the wall. "They attacked us. Pretty badly."

A sliver of emotion wormed its way into my heart. I hadn't heard any of this before. I had *no idea* such a thing had happened, and I was torn between needing to know how the story ended and wishing my uncle would stop. Go away.

"I called your mum afterwards. I knew Ronan would be at work, and I couldn't face my parents, so I called her. We weren't close, but Andrea came straightaway, no questions asked. She took one look at me and decided I needed a hospital. It was lucky she did—I passed out en route. Bastards had broken a few ribs and punctured my lung."

Oh, God…

"When I woke up, my parents were there. I told them what happened, and they were outraged—at me. They said it was my own fault and that I had to swear off boys for good. I refused. They left."

He said it so easily, so calmly. Like he was talking about the weather or the fact he was wearing a dark green shirt. Was he truly so blasé, or was this just a wound that had healed?

"I expected their rejection," Sean went on, "but I wasn't prepared for what it did to me. I fell into this…slump. This dark place. When I was discharged from the hospital, Ronan drove me to my house and told me to pack my things. I spent the next three years living with you."

He dragged his eyes, full of remembered pain, up to my bandaged arms. "I thought about it sometimes," he murmured. "I'd lie awake at night, thinking about dying. About killing myself. I even went as far as planning it all out a time or two, but I'd never been able to keep anything from my brother. Not for long."

The shine in his eyes turned liquid. "Ronan caught me each time I fell. He was my light, my support, my shoulder to cry on. He saved me, Carter. In so many ways. Your dad literally saved my life."

Of course he did. My devoted, self-sacrificing father.

"And now you—" Sean stopped. Pressed his lips tightly together, leaned forwards. Elbows braced on the edge of the bed, he peered down at me with understanding written across every inch of his face.

He knew, I realised. He knew everything there was to know—about Remy and me, at least. He'd probably known back in July when he asked me if I had a boyfriend. He'd been trying to tell me something, like he was trying to tell me something now.

But I couldn't listen. Couldn't go there.

I wasn't sure if I'd ever be brave enough.

Would things have been different if Dad were still alive? Would he have seen the emptiness and pain in my eyes, seen it consume more and more of me each day? Would he have noticed as I hurtled for that precarious edge, caught me when I fell over it?

Would Miles have?

Because we were similar, Sean and I. More similar than I'd ever imagined. The difference was that his brother had saved him.

Mine was already gone.

"I've let him down," my uncle gritted out. "I've let *you* down. I had the chance to return every one of his favours, and instead, I've failed you both. I haven't been here for you, Carter. Not really, and certainly not in the way you needed me."

A deep breath. A watery smile. A hand placed directly in the centre of my chest. "But I am here now." A promise. "I am here, and I'm not going anywhere. We will get you through this dark place and out the other side, and I will be right here beside you every step of the way. I won't bail on you because things get tough. Not again. *Never* again."

Sean's fingers splayed over my heart, and each of them was a spark in the night. A tiny ember, starting to glow anew. "I know you're tired," he said, voice cracking. "I know it hurts. But you can lean on me, Carter. Lean on me until it all gets easier to bear."

With his other hand, he reached for the stand. "I love you."

Retrieved the carboard juice box. "I want you to live."

Touched the straw to my lips once more. "So *drink*. Please, kiddo, for the love of all that is holy, just have a goddamned drink."

I gazed up at him, at the sincerity shining out of his face, and realised I was grateful. Grateful that he was here. Maybe not that I was alive, but at least that I wasn't alone.

So I pulled the straw into my mouth and drank.

eighteen

The numbness in my hands was disconcerting.

Sensation buzzed along the lines of my pinkies all the way to my wrists, but I couldn't feel my palms or the rest of my fingers. Some of the deadness on the backs of my hands had receded since the previous day, but I almost wished it hadn't; the IV itched like crazy.

Not long after Sean convinced me to drink my juice, the doctor Sophie had swept into the room, her long white coat swirling around her legs. "Good morning, Carter," she said brightly. "How are you today?"

I didn't respond. I had no interest in communicating with her.

Unfazed by my reticence, Sophie inspected a chart clipped to the end of my bed. Her eyes darted up when Sean tossed the empty juice box back onto the tray. "I see you've had a drink, at least. That's good."

Yeah. It was just *great*.

The doctor rounded the bed on the opposite side to my uncle

and stopped beside my hip. She ran a few quick tests on my arms, pressing lightly against my palms, the backs of my hands, and each of my fingers, slowly increasing the pressure to assess the extent of sensation.

There wasn't much. I could *see* Sophie touching me, prodding at my skin, but it was as if it was happening to some other person, some other boy. Not to me.

Disconcerting.

Sophie made a few notes on her clipboard and fixed me with a sympathetic smile. "I know it's a bit scary, but don't be too alarmed by the numbness. It's about what we'd expect at this stage. Has your uncle told you anything about what's happened these last few days?"

"We haven't got that far yet," Sean muttered.

I didn't even know what day of the week it was.

"That's all right." Tucking a stray hair behind her ear, Sophie leaned forwards. "You received a blood transfusion when you were first brought in, Carter, and about thirty-six hours ago, you underwent surgery to repair the damage to the muscles and tendons in your arms."

I stared right through her. I heard what she was telling me, but I didn't fully comprehend it. Her words slid through my head like oil through water, touching but never sinking in.

The doctor's voice softened. "You managed to nick your median nerves, which supply most of this part of your hand." She pointed to my thumb and first two fingers. "When that nerve is damaged, it can cause a loss of sensation and might impair your motor skills.

"There's not a lot we can do until the swelling goes down and the wounds have healed up. Once that happens, we'll be able to run more tests so we can assess where you're at and what your treatment options are. Your first operation went very well, so we're optimistic about your chances for recovery."

The numbness spread from my hands to my heart.

They were *optimistic* about my recovery. Right. I wasn't stupid. I knew they wouldn't make me any promises, understood perfectly well how tricky nerves could be. I was the son of a doctor—an aspiring doctor myself.

At least, I had been.

I was nothing now.

I drifted for a time, caught in the ever-tightening spiral of my thoughts. It all felt hopeless, useless. Pointless. And now I was stuck here—trapped, with no way out.

I couldn't use the same escape route twice.

Eventually, the spiralling slowed, ceased, spat me back out into my bleak new reality. Sophie was gone, but Sean still lounged in his chair, ankles crossed as he frowned at something on his phone. Noticing my sudden attention, he straightened. "Hey. You okay?"

I merely blinked at him.

"Still don't want to talk, huh? Fair enough. I've got water for you, though." Sean turned to the stand wedged between his chair and my bed, where the food tray had been replaced by a silicone water jug and a stack of paper cups.

He plucked a cup from the top of the pile and poured some water into it. I didn't resist when he brought it to my lips, drinking greedily and deep.

"Easy. You'll make yourself sick." Sean lowered the cup and placed it back on the table, out of my reach. "You can have some more in a minute."

I bit back a sigh of frustration.

"Carter?"

I rolled my eyes towards him, watched a slight grimace distort his face.

"It's completely up to you, but…Charlie's here." His fingers tightened around his phone. "Do you mind if he comes in?"

Charlie.

My uncle's…boyfriend? Partner?

I wasn't in the mood for visitors. I liked the idea of another stranger in my space even less. But Sean looked rumpled—tired and frightened and miserable—though he was trying to hide it. He looked as if he might fall down if he didn't find someone to hold him up, and Charlie…

Charlie was his family.

Reluctantly, I lifted a shoulder. Inclined my head.

Sean's lips twitched. "Thanks, kiddo," he said and bent back over his phone.

Not even a full minute later, the door opened.

I froze.

A memory danced across my mind. It was faint, murky and flickering at the edges, like a dream half-remembered on waking.

A memory of an angel sitting beside my bed, his head bowed forwards in prayer.

Slender, ethereal frame. Cerulean blue eyes. Hair as black as pitch.

The face of an angel, my uncle had said all those months ago. He wasn't exaggerating.

Charlie was *stunning*.

My gaze followed him as he glided across the room and perched himself on the arm of Sean's chair. I could scarcely believe he was real.

Sean caught my eye, his tentative smirk stretching into a full-blown grin. "I know," he said. "I'm way out of my league, right?"

"Nonsense," Charlie snorted. Even in that one word, his English accent was pronounced. He jabbed an elbow into my uncle's ribs, yet the smile he turned on me was sweet. Bright. Enough like Remy's that it made me ache inside. "Hello, Carter. I'm Charlie. I know this isn't the best of circumstances, but I *am* pleased to finally meet you."

I stared at him. Remembered his tears. Remembered his hand in my hair.

My silence lengthened. Charlie's smile faded.

"Don't take it personally," Sean said, slipping an arm around his waist. "He's not talking to anyone."

"Well, why would he? Clearly, no one's been listening to him."

Anger. That was anger I heard in his voice—anger on my behalf. He didn't even know me.

But he'd known *of* me. Maybe for the entirety of those two years, nine months and twenty-three—twenty-four?—days he'd known my uncle.

Sean read the accusation in my face, and his shoulders drooped. "I've hated keeping this a secret from you, Carter. I've *hated* it. It was bad enough when I was single, but keeping quiet about Charlie…"

He shook his head. "Your mum made it pretty clear what would happen if I spoke to you about my sexuality. She didn't want me to…*influence* you," he spat the words, "in any way. I think she always hoped I'd end up with a woman and the problem would be solved—in her eyes, at least. But when I told her I was seeing a

247

man…well, I had to play by her rules. I couldn't risk her taking you away from me."

I'd guessed correctly, then: he hadn't told me because Mum threatened to cut me out of his life.

To cut *him* out of *mine*.

Charlie remained quiet on his perch. His eyes were fond but sad as they flitted up to my uncle's face, as he traced absent circles on his knee.

Sean placed his hand over Charlie's and threaded their fingers together. "Look," he said. "I don't like badmouthing her in front of you. Andrea came and got me when I called her that day, took me in and fed me and clothed me when I had nowhere else to go. Me—a broken, depressed, sixteen-year-old kid who'd never heard the term 'bisexual' and thought he was going mad.

"I caused her no small amount of grief, Carter. I won't lie about that. When I came to live with you guys, it was the first proper chance your mum had to get to know me, and I was a complete shit. She worried about the impression I would make on her boys. Especially you."

Something bitter and ugly curdled in my stomach.

"Yes, *you*," he confirmed. "You were such a quiet little kid, Carter. She always worried about you more than she worried about Miles."

I closed my eyes. Maybe that was true once. But not anymore.

She didn't love me. Didn't worry. Didn't care.

I just can't look at you right now.

"She was here. Did you know?"

My eyes snapped back open. Narrowed.

Sean's expression was grave. "I have never seen her so distraught, kiddo. *Never.* She didn't leave your side until we knew you were going to make it. She stayed until after your surgery, and the only reason she left…"

He swallowed thickly. "She's not well. I mean, physically she's fine, but she's not well in here"—he tapped his temple—"or in here." He tapped his chest. "She told me some concerning things about what's been happening these last few months, including how much she's been drinking. She told me that she…hit you.

"And this," my uncle waved at my arms, unable to hide his slight tremble, "has been a real wakeup call for her."

At another time, I might have been relieved to hear those words. To hear that my mother had realised how much I was suffering. But now, I couldn't bring myself to care. It was too late.

The damage had been done.

"Tell him the rest," said Charlie.

Sean shot him a glare.

But Charlie set his jaw and crossed his arms. *Stubborn* angel. "He deserves to know, Sean. Waiting won't make it any better."

My uncle sighed. Then, reaching out to toy with the edge of my blanket, he dragged his eyes up to mine. "Carter…your mum has given me guardianship of you."

The world ground to a halt.

What?

"You're still a minor for a few more weeks," Sean explained softly. "Someone has to sign off on decisions regarding your medical treatment, and she…she doesn't think she's fit to make those choices right now. I can't say I entirely disagree with her."

Silence spread throughout me, so profound I could have heard a pin drop.

She really was done with me. She was just…giving me away.

My uncle's smile was watery. "She loves you more than you know, kiddo, but she just needs some help right now. Charlie and I are going to take care of you. We'll be right here with you, and when you get discharged, you're going to come and stay with us for a while."

"We'd love to have you with us," Charlie added. "Our new house has a spare bedroom, and it's all yours. For as long as you need it."

Not only done with me…but kicking me out as well.

Getting rid of me for good.

Oh God. Oh God oh god ohgodohgodohgod—

"Carter?"

I couldn't see, couldn't hear, couldn't think.

"Carter!"

I couldn't *breathe—*

"Shit! Charlie, can you…" His voice faded out. Then back in, its volume deafening. "It's okay, kiddo. Breathe. Just breathe. It's going to be fine."

But I couldn't breathe, couldn't even claw at my throat.

I had no air. No air at all.

Then darkness.

"I am going to ask you a series of personal questions this afternoon," the psychiatrist said. "Whatever you tell me will, for the most part, be confidential. I won't share anything with your family or friends without your consent, but certain details may be given to the medical team assigned to your case."

The psychiatrist, whose nametag read *John*, was a grandfatherly man—or what I imagined a grandfather to be like since neither of mine had ever been interested in me. He had a pleasant voice and a warm, easy expression, accentuated by a mop of salt-and-pepper hair and a pair of full-moon spectacles perched on the bridge of his nose.

My stomach still lurched at the sight of him.

If I had the strength to move, simply the *word* 'psychiatrist' would have had me scrambling from the bed and fleeing down the hall.

"This is what we do when someone is admitted for a suicide attempt"—I flinched a little—"because it helps us put together a picture of your life and health and assists in determining the best treatment options for you. However, if you start to feel anxious or uncomfortable at any time, I want you to tell me. We can take a break whenever you need to."

My eyes floated up to the plain white ceiling. Lodged there.

I sensed John look meaningfully at Sean, whose long body was still folded in the chair by my bed. "As I mentioned, I will be asking you some personal questions. Are you sure you want your uncle to stay?"

It was all I could manage to nod.

I didn't want to be left with the psychiatrist. Couldn't bear to be alone with someone trained to root out my darkest secrets and expose them to the light. When Sean had made to leave earlier, my heart galloped so fast it almost punched right through my ribcage.

Almost launched me straight into another mad panic, and I couldn't endure one more.

Each time I recovered, I felt as if I'd left something behind.

"Very well," said John. "In addition to the interview questions, we have a number of questionnaires to fill out. Normally I would

251

give them to you to complete on your own, but given the current circumstances," he nodded at my limp, bandaged arms, "I will ask you the questions and write down your responses, all right?"

I let my eyes wander back down the far wall to the bump my feet made in the blanket. It was pulled taut over my legs, and if I looked closely enough, looked hard enough, I could see the outline of each of my toes.

If John thought I was going to answer any of his questions, he had another thing coming.

"All right. Let's begin."

He tried—I'd give him that.

He asked specific, probing questions, and when they yielded no response, he attempted a less direct approach. He wanted to know about my sleeping patterns, my weight, my mood, my ability to function on a daily basis. He wanted to know if I experienced tiredness or lethargy, insomnia, a reduced appetite, unexplained anger, or feelings of intense guilt or sadness.

If I'd ever self-harmed before.

But something inside me shut down. Even if I might have said *yes* to all of those things, the words stuck in the back of my throat.

"I don't think he's ready to talk," my uncle said quietly.

"Indeed." John didn't sound mad, and if he was frustrated, he concealed it well. There was only a wry twist to his voice as he put down his pen and said, "Unfortunately, we can't make a diagnosis until he is."

Sean shifted in his seat. "Is it that important—an actual diagnosis?"

"It's important in terms of understanding his mental state and what caused him to try to take his life. Whether we're dealing with mental illness, something more circumstantial, or a combination of the two, may also influence the treatment we pursue."

John glanced down at the notepad on his lap. "From the information we've already gathered, Carter displays some classic signs of depressive and anxiety disorders, but we can't make a formal diagnosis or narrow down which type until he speaks to us."

They fell like bombshells.

Depression.

Anxiety.

"Hey." Sean's hand slid over mine, and he smiled through the sheen in his eyes. I wished I could feel his touch properly; I clung to the sight of it instead. "It's okay. We can deal with this. Whatever it is."

John leaned forwards. "I am going to be frank here, Carter. Refusing to eat or talk are not good signs, and I'm concerned you're at a high risk of making another suicide attempt."

Sean mumbled something under his breath. It sounded like a curse.

"This hospital runs a very good inpatient mental health program for young adults," the psychiatrist went on. "The facility itself is only just down the road, and they have a bed opening up on Wednesday. It is my recommendation to you—to *both* of you"—he nodded at Sean— "that Carter makes use of it."

My uncle bit his lip. "What does this program involve?"

"It requires a twenty-eight-day stay within the facility where he will be closely monitored by professional mental health staff and receive one-on-one therapy from a psychologist. There is also…"

I tuned him out. Let him and Sean decide.

I didn't much care what they did with me.

Then John was standing, peering down at me from above. "This program is entirely voluntary, but I think it will give you the best chance of recovery. It sounds like you've been through a lot, Carter, and all those pressures you've been facing will still be there when you walk out the door of this hospital.

"I want to give you the chance to learn some healthy and effective coping mechanisms before you have to confront them again. The inpatient program allows you to do this by removing all external stressors and responsibilities, so you can focus on yourself and getting better. I do believe this is your best option."

"Thank you," Sean said softly. "We'll think about it."

"I'll be back tomorrow," John replied and left.

I watched my uncle squeeze my fingers. "What do you want, Carter?"

I didn't want anything.

"This program...it's not about locking you up," he persisted, voice tight with emotion. "It's about getting you the help you need, and I think it could be a good thing for you. But I won't force you into anything. You're the one in control here. What do you *want*?"

I didn't want to be the one in control. I was so tired of it—the control.

I wanted, just for once, for someone to take it out of my hands.

"I want..." It was only a hoarse whisper at first, dry and cracked and nearly inaudible. But Sean's eyes snapped to my lips, to the words spilling out of them, torn from the core of my soul. "I want it to stop, Uncle Sean. I can't stand it anymore. I just want it to *stop*."

His face crumpled. "Oh, kiddo..."

"I can't...I *can't*."

"I know," he said. "I know." And then, before I even registered

254

he'd moved, my uncle had climbed onto the bed and pulled me, so very carefully, into his arms.

"You're so strong," he said, even though I was weak.

"You're so brave," he said, even though I was a coward.

"And someday, you're going to believe it."

nineteen

A set of bright pink bunny rabbit slippers adorned my feet.

Long ears protruded from the rabbits' heads, angling upwards and back, so the fuzzy white tips tickled my ankles, and the facial features were stitched in sable thread: whiskers, chevron-shaped nose...sunglasses in place of the eyes.

The slippers had been a gag gift from Jake for my last birthday. They were also the only set of slippers I owned, which was no doubt why they ended up in the meagre collection of clothes I was approved to wear during my stay at the facility. I'd barely taken them off since my arrival...whenever that had been.

I'd lost track of what day it was or how long I'd been here. Days didn't really matter in a place like this; they all blended together into one monotonous stretch of time. Time without meaning. Time without end.

At least the facility was pretty enough. It had a modern vibe, all timber and stone, with large, tinted windows that let in the natural light while offering privacy to those of us inside. Trees and garden beds rimmed the property and formed a living green shield, variegated by colourful bursts of flowers now that winter had finally relinquished its hold.

I yawned so wide my jaw popped and moisture trickled from my eyes. Awkwardly, I lifted my right hand to swipe at the wetness. It was a challenge with so much of the hand still numb, but I managed. My right hand wasn't as bad as the left.

I'd done the left one first.

When my bleary vision cleared, I lowered my arm and saw Misty striding my way. I sighed. I didn't want to move from my chair. I was comfortable, settled, and the sun streaming in through the nearby window was warm against my back.

Why couldn't everyone just leave me be?

Misty smiled. "All right, Carter, it's time for your appointment with David."

I frowned. David—my psychologist. He came in on Mondays, Wednesdays, and Fridays, and I saw him on each of those days. I thought I'd seen him yesterday, but that couldn't be right if I had an appointment this morning. It must have been the day before.

What had happened to yesterday?

"Come on, up you get," said Misty, nudging my shoulder.

With great reluctance, I rose from the chair. I was a bit unsteady on my feet, so Misty took my elbow as she escorted me across the centre to David's office.

I liked Misty well enough—more than any of the other nurses, even if she was the one who'd force-fed me those first few days. I'd been so weak I couldn't resist her efforts, and when I eventually regained some strength, I let her keep feeding me through force of habit alone.

David's door stood open, so we shuffled straight through it, Misty bidding the psychologist good morning as she helped me into the plush seat opposite his desk. Then she patted my knee and sauntered back out the door, shutting it decisively behind her.

Leaving me alone with him.

David was a tall, well-built man. Younger than I'd expected, with laugh lines around his eyes and hair that gleamed like a mass of copper wires beneath the glow of the downlights. He'd set up a cosy little sitting area in one corner of his office, but I preferred our current arrangement: with the desk between us.

With distance between us.

As always, he just launched straight in. "You look confused this morning, Carter."

"I thought I saw you yesterday," I mumbled. My voice felt hoarse, feeble. I couldn't remember if I'd spoken at all since our last appointment.

"No, that was Monday." David nodded at the calendar pinned to the wall beside his window. "Today is Wednesday."

I stared at the calendar. October. Most of the days had been crossed out with a thick black marker, and I followed along until I reached the first clear date. Today's date.

It looked familiar. Why did it look familiar?

"Carter?"

It did not creep up on me. It *slammed* into my chest with the momentum of a freight train, driving the air from my body.

This morning was the year twelve English exam.

This morning was the year twelve English exam—and I was missing it.

I saw my classmates, sitting in the hall as their pens scratched across paper, eyes darting every so often to the empty desk in their midst. *My* desk.

My last chance to prove myself—and it had slipped through my now-useless hands.

Someone called my name, but the world was tilting around me, the ground lurching and buckling beneath my feet. My breath came in wheezing pants, smaller and harsher by the second, lungs shrinking, constricting...

"Carter." A firm voice. A firm hand on the back of my neck. "I want you to recite the periodic table for me."

What?

The hand tightened. Gentle pressure, followed by a command: "Do it. *Now.*"

"Hydrogen..." I gasped, and that single word scraped my whole throat raw. "Helium, lithium, beryllium..." My thoughts were— "boron"—thick and—"carbon"—sluggish but—"nitrogen"—I knew this—"oxygen"—I *knew* this—"fluorine, neon..."

Black spots danced before my eyes, so I squeezed them shut. "...sodium"—I *breathed* and—"magnesium"—*breathed* and— "aluminium"—*breathed* until—"silicon"—finally—"phosphorus"— *finally*—"sulphur"—my pulse slowed.

"Chlorine."

My chest loosened. "Argon."

I opened my eyes—"potassium"—found my vision clear— "calcium"—and took my first—"scandium"—full—"titanium"— *breath.*

The vice around my ribcage eased, and I sucked in the sweet, cool air. "Vanadium, chromium, manganese, iron, cobalt, nickel, copper, zinc—"

"All right, you can stop there," David said softly.

I raised my head and found his face right near mine. I was shivering, and I'd sweated right through my thin tee-shirt, but I could breathe.

I could *breathe.*

David smiled. "You're good at your elements. Don't you only need to memorise the first twenty?"

"I know the first fifty," I rasped.

"Clever boy." He stood back, drumming his fingers against the edge of his desk. "Did you find that helped, reciting the periodic table?"

"It…it stopped."

"*It* was a panic attack, Carter. Have you ever had a panic attack before?"

I thought of the night of Piper's party, when I kissed Remy the first time. I thought of that morning at church with Tim's parents, of the time in Mr Fielding's office, of learning my mother was giving me up back when I was still in the hospital.

Slowly, I nodded.

"Some people find it helpful to focus on mundane things when it comes to dealing with panic attacks. Counting backwards or reciting something, for example. I think we should definitely explore this, see how well it works for you."

David rounded his desk and sank into his chair. "Can you tell me what triggered you just now?"

I glanced again at the calendar. My heart slammed against my ribs once, twice, then slowed. I took a deep breath. "My English exam is today."

"Ah." The psychologist surveyed me for a moment. "Tell me

honestly. Do you think you're in any state, physically or mentally, to sit an exam right now?"

Physically? I couldn't even hold a spoon to feed myself, let alone a pen to write.

Mentally? I could barely recall what day it was, and when I tried to bring my English texts to the forefront of my mind...nothing. I drew a blank.

"Probably not," I admitted.

"I'm pleased to hear you recognise that," said David. "From what I've gathered, you're a high-achieving student, Carter. I know none of this is easy for you. You're not the first year twelve student I've seen in here around exam time, and I'm sure you won't be the last."

"But what about my exams?"

"You don't need to sit your exams. We have liaised with your school and the assessment authorities regarding special consideration for you. You'll be given a derived examination score for all of your subjects."

I stared at the top of the desk. A derived score was based off marks from the school-assessed coursework and indicative grades from each teacher, but it wasn't the same as sitting the exams for real.

It felt a lot like failure. *Another* failure.

"What do you want to do once you've finished school?" David asked.

"I..." Licking my lips, I dragged my eyes back up to the window and gazed out at the belt of green beyond the glass. "I *wanted* to be a doctor."

"And now?"

I didn't respond. He knew very well that I wanted nothing.

But David changed tack. "Why did you want to be a doctor?"

"My dad was a doctor."

"So, would you say you wanted to be a doctor for *him* or for *you*?"

Heat crept up my neck, circling my throat like a collar of flames. I…wasn't sure. I'd spent so long working towards that goal—to honour Dad's memory, to make Mum proud—that I wasn't sure I actually *wanted* to be a doctor. Not for myself.

But I couldn't remember a time when I wanted to be anything else.

David cocked his head as he watched me struggle. "Do you worry a lot, Carter?"

I glared at him.

He tapped his pen on his notebook, sitting atop the pile of questionnaires.

David could be sneaky sometimes. After half a session of silence our first day, I'd broken down and talked to him, but I still refused to complete those stupid forms. So he tried other ways to glean the information—such as setting traps behind questions like these.

"I'm going to take that as a yes," he said pleasantly. "What sorts of things do you normally worry about?"

I sighed. "I don't know. Everything."

"Hmm. Tell me about your brother."

Then he did this—change subjects so fast it gave me whiplash. As if he hoped to catch me off guard, startle me into saying something before I thought it through.

I hated it.

"Tell me about your brother," he repeated.

I eyed him warily. "What about him?"

"That's up to you. I just want to get a feel for what he was like."

262

My chin dropped to my chest, and I studied the threadbare knees of my tracksuit pants. I'd felt so warm before, out in the common area. But now, after the panic attack, with this line of questioning, I was chilled right down to the bone.

Words were inadequate to describe my brother. How could words alone capture the essence of the person who'd been the centre of my world—who was *still* the centre of my world, even if he was no longer here in it with me?

"Miles was special," I said quietly. "He was…he was everything. He was my big brother and my best friend, and he looked out for me and made me feel important. He always had time for me, *made* time for me, even when I'm sure he had better things to do."

My chest ached with the familiar flood of grief. "He was the school captain. He was smart and brave and wanted to be a cop one day. He was athletic and made all the sports teams. He volunteered at the soup van and had a part-time job teaching kids to swim. He was popular and kind and had heaps of friends and a girlfriend who adored him. He was just so…" I let out a shaky breath. "So special."

"He was a lot like you, then," said David.

My brow furrowed. "What? No!"

"You're the school captain," he pointed out. "You're smart and wanted to be a doctor. You make all the sports teams you try out for, *and* you play the violin. You volunteer at the soup van and work part-time at a dog shelter. You have good friends, who I've been told call your uncle every day to ask about you."

David fixed me with a probing look. "Are you not just as special as your brother was?"

"It's not the same."

"Why not?"

I bit my lip, hard enough I tasted blood. "He was genuine. I'm...I'm just a liar."

"What do you lie about?"

"Lots of things." I'd gotten so good at pretending that sometimes even *I* couldn't remember what was real. What was true.

David set down his pen. "How do you know that Miles wasn't lying too?"

I opened my mouth to protest, but—

You were blind to his faults, Megs had said, *and I know he tried to hide them from you anyway.*

"I have to believe it was real," I murmured.

"Why?"

The backs of my eyes burned. "Mum loved him. I know she did. And I thought...I thought if I could be like him, then she would love me too. But it didn't work. I...I'm not like him, and she doesn't love me."

David rubbed a hand across his mouth. "Do you resent Miles?"

"Miles is *dead*," I snapped. The words felt wrong in my mouth.

"I think he's still very much alive to you."

"Well, I don't resent him. I *never* resented him." Even the thought of it made me feel ill. The love I had for my brother was so big, so vast. There was no room for resentment.

David looked thoughtful. "Why do you feel that he was good enough and you aren't? From what you've told me of your family history, Miles was the accident child, not you. You were planned—wanted—and he was a mistake."

"Miles was *not* a mistake!" I said furiously, almost welcoming the anger after all these days of numbness. "Don't *ever* say that!"

264

The psychologist raised his hands, a placating gesture. "Okay. Then explain to me why your mother would love him and not you."

I was on my feet. No memory of how I'd gotten there. "She practically *said* so!" I hissed. "She said I was a *disappointment* and that she couldn't even *look* at me! Miles was the *perfect* son with the *perfect* girlfriend, and I'm the one she caught kissing a *boy*!"

It was the first time I'd said it aloud. Acknowledged it aloud.

Oh God, I'd...

I swayed, nausea churning in my gut.

"Sit down, Carter," David said. He was utterly calm, and I wanted nothing more than to scratch that serene expression off his face.

But I slumped back down into my chair. The despairing rage drained away and took with it whatever was left of my strength. "She saw us," I whispered. "She saw us, and I wanted him to leave, so I pushed him, and he fell. I hurt him. I *hurt* him."

"How do you think Miles would have felt about that?"

I wished the floor would open up, swallow me whole and spit out my remains. "He would have been disappointed in me too."

"Because you kissed a boy, or because you hurt him?"

I spent my ninth birthday cowering in my brother's arms while our parents fought. Miles stroked my hair and held me close, without so much as a hint of complaint as my tears soaked through his shirt.

"*I won't let him turn into a faggot!*" my mother's screech echoed down the hall.

Miles gasped. His embrace became unbearably tight. I didn't understand what Mum was talking about, didn't know what that word meant, but the look on my brother's face—like he'd taken a hit in the solar plexus—told me it was nothing good.

My sobs grew louder.

Miles' eyes glittered with rage—but not at me. "Don't you ever use that word, Carter."

"W-why?" I whimpered, clinging to him like a limpet.

"It's a bad word." My brother brushed the hair from my face and wiped away my tears. "It's what nasty people sometimes call boys who like other boys. Like…as in, to marry. Instead of girls. Does that make sense?"

It didn't. Not really.

Miles saw my confusion and sighed. Hugged me against him once more. "It'll make sense one day. But don't listen to Mum, okay? There's nothing wrong with boys who like other boys. And I don't ever want to hear you use that word."

I promised him I wouldn't. I never had.

I'd never heard my brother use it either.

Miles Cantwell had been no bigot. He…had he guessed? Already? *Then?*

I looked back up at David, feeling oddly shaken. "I don't think he would have cared it was a boy," I said to him. To myself. "But he would have been disappointed I hurt him."

"Would he have forgiven you?"

Miles would have forgiven me anything, just as I would have forgiven him. Hell, even *Remy* had forgiven me for my mistake. That didn't make it any easier to nod.

"Then maybe you can forgive yourself," David suggested.

I wouldn't even know where to begin.

The psychologist leaned forwards, propping his chin in his hands. "Did you receive grief counselling after Miles and your dad died?"

266

"No. Mum said we didn't need it. She said it was a waste of time trying to make someone else understand how we felt."

"The point of seeing a counsellor—any counsellor—is not to make *them* understand how you feel," David explained. "Only *you* truly know how you feel. But a counsellor, or a psychologist such as myself, can help you make sense of your own emotions. They can teach you strategies for how to cope with them so you can move forwards with your life."

The grief struck me again, so hard I could barely breathe. I squeezed my eyes shut. Counted to ten. "I don't want to move forwards without him."

"A part of him will always be with you, Carter," he said gently. "A part of you will always miss him and mourn because that is what it means to lose someone you love. That's *normal*. But you need to learn to get past the sorrow and pain, to remember the good things as well. You need to start *living* again."

I swallowed thickly. "How?"

"You start by letting him go. You start by remembering who *you* are and being true to yourself." David smiled. "It won't be easy, and it won't happen overnight. But it's something I want you to think about, at least."

I did think about it.

I thought about it for the rest of the day and well into the next. I thought about it on Friday and Saturday and was still thinking about it on Sunday afternoon as I lay on my narrow bed and stared aimlessly up at the ceiling. Now that David had put the idea in my head, it seemed I could think about little else.

I didn't know how to let Miles go. I'd held onto him so tightly and for so long that he'd become a part of me, melding into my flesh. Every decision I'd made in the last five years, everything I'd done, had been done with him in mind. With Dad in mind.

I didn't even know who I *was* without them—without the pain of missing them.

Through my open door drifted the first strains of a cello playing.

I stilled. The sound was upbeat, chipper, so unlike the sombre tones I was accustomed to hearing from a cello, especially when it played on its own. I didn't recognise the tune, but it was beautiful. Full of life and light and colour.

Full of hope.

Hope that things really could get better, that a fulfilling life was waiting for me beyond these doors. A life where every second didn't feel like a burden.

The notes of the cello rose and fell like the tides. I may have never heard this melody, but I could imagine what my violin would sound like, looping and weaving through the song. A perfect harmony. The ghost of it echoed in my ears.

I sat up and hugged my bandaged arms to my chest. It would probably take a miracle for me to play my violin again. Even then, it would never be the same. There was a good chance I had lost my music forever.

And it *hurt*. Because I had done this.

I had done this to myself.

For the first time since waking up in that hospital bed…I *wanted*. To go back. To go forwards. To find something better than what I'd had before.

The song ended, but a new one began.

I listened to the cello for a long time. Song after song, every one of them light and carefree and happy. Each transition so smooth and effortless I sometimes missed it when one melody blended into the next.

The song changed again, and I sat up straighter. This tune was softer than the others. Sadder. *Familiar*.

It was the last song I played before I…

A sudden compulsion had me on my feet and slipping from my room. I needed to see. I needed to see for myself who this song and this cello belonged to. Needed to see who was playing the last piece I performed with my string quartet before I walked out of my school and into my house and tried to end my life.

The music wasn't hard to follow. The cellist wasn't hard to find.

He sat on a stool at one end of the common area, near the windows. A small crowd—mainly girls—had gathered around and were watching with rapt attention.

The cellist was dressed entirely in black: black jeans, black combat boots, black tee-shirt ripped around the cuffs. Even his hair was black, thick and wild with the ends falling into his face. Only his skin was white, pale like the moon, marred by a tattoo that spiralled up his left bicep and disappeared beneath his shirt.

Intrigued, I moved closer.

As if he sensed my presence, the cellist looked up. Right into my eyes.

And I realised I should have known. Should have recognised him straight away. The clothes were different, but the way he held himself—the way he played—was the same as it had been for the six years we'd made music together.

The cellist was Jamie Ray.

twenty

His eyes widened, but the song never faltered. Never slowed or skipped a beat.

We stared at each other across the room.

It was hard to believe this was the Jamie Ray I knew—the haughty, self-centred pedant who'd held my secret over my head and taunted me until I snapped. There was little resemblance between that Jamie, always so prim and proper, and this alluring, impassioned young man who was playing music for the mentally ill on a Sunday afternoon.

I couldn't tear my gaze away from him as he played, and played, and played.

When the last note faded and he lifted his bow from the strings, I released a breath I hadn't been aware I was holding. My limbs felt heavy and loose, my mind blissfully blank, and in the icy hollow of my chest, a small kernel of warmth was blooming.

I settled down on a nearby couch while Jamie packed away his cello. He went about the task with his usual single-minded focus, but I knew he knew that I was there.

That I was waiting for him.

My eyes were drawn to his tattoo, a scrolling line of black letters that curled around his arm. I couldn't make out the words those letters spelled, but it seemed so unlike him—a tattoo.

I wondered what it meant. When he got it. Why.

The cello case snapped shut, and moments later, the couch dipped beneath Jamie's added weight. I glanced at him sidelong. He was staring at the ground as if he wasn't sure he could—or should—look at me. His expression, tense but open, held no trace of sarcasm or the bitterness of the last few months.

My eyes dropped to his lap. To the gauze looped around the knuckles of his right hand. "What happened?"

"I punched a wall."

I blinked. "Why?"

Jamie made a strange noise but didn't offer an answer.

"You could have broken your hand." I didn't know why the thought upset me so much. His injury clearly had no impact on his ability to play—unlike mine.

"I wasn't exactly thinking of that at the time," he said gruffly. Dark eyes slid along my bandaged arms to my shoulders, then cautiously up to my face. "The school sent around an email about you. When my mum showed it to me, I...lost it. Broke a vase. Punched a wall."

My mouth fell open.

Jamie blew out a violent breath. "Fucking *hell*, Carter. Do you have any idea how mad I am at everyone? At *myself*? That none of us saw...none of us realised..."

This—the one thing I hadn't let myself contemplate. What the people who knew me would think of me now. What my *friends* would think, how they'd see me differently. There was a reason I'd denied any visitors other than Sean and Charlie.

But now Jamie was here, and it was too late to run and hide.

"It's not your fault," I mumbled.

"Not my…" He reached up and scrubbed his hands through his hair, which was something I'd never seen him do. "I've been a real bastard to you—don't even try to deny it. I just get so…" He stopped himself again. "No. Never mind. It was all my own shit, and I took it out on you. For whatever it's worth…I'm sorry. And I am so *fucking* glad it's not too late to say that."

An apology? To me? From *Jamie Ray*?

Had the isolation finally gotten to me—driven me properly insane?

When I glanced up at him again, our eyes met. I saw the question hovering in his gaze, the question he so desperately wanted to ask but wouldn't.

Why?

"You were right," I told him. "About Remy and me. We were more than just…"

Jamie shifted. "Carter—"

"My mum caught me kissing him." The words spilled out, hung there in the air between us. "She…hit me. Then she left."

Jamie's jaw clenched, but he didn't turn away. "My dad barely talked to me for a month after I was outed," he confessed. "He's come to terms with it now, but it took my mum threatening to divorce him if he didn't get over himself."

I never knew that. All this time, and I never knew. Never even thought to *ask*.

Jamie's hands fisted in his lap. When he spoke, his voice was low enough I nearly missed it. "I still don't know what happened to Lucas."

"Who?"

"Lucas." He said the name reverently, but his smile was a twisted parody of what a smile should be. "No one seems to remember his part in what happened two years ago. I wasn't making out with myself in that supply cupboard, you know."

Realisation dawned, and I felt like a fool. The year twelve boy. The year twelve boy who was dragged out of the closet alongside Jamie—and who never returned to school.

Jamie picked at the edge of his bandage. "You're a lot like him, actually. Quiet. Kind. A little…fragile inside. He had bad anxiety, and his parents were shit about it. He always warned me what would happen if they found out about him, but I didn't…"

He shrugged helplessly. "I was frantic when he didn't come to school the next day. Or the next. Or the next. I squeezed it out of his brother eventually: their dad beat him black and blue and then kicked him out. Lucas ran and didn't look back.

"I was only sixteen," Jamie said thickly, "but I was crazy about him. Not a day goes past that I don't think of him or pray that he's all right. I can't let go of this stupid hope that I'll find him again one day. I…I miss him."

Something inside me fractured. Fractured so permanently, the pieces could never be put back together. Not the way they were.

Never again the same.

"Carter?"

It wasn't fair.

It wasn't fair what the world did to these people. That they were made to hurt, and suffer, and hide for fear of being shamed by those who were supposed to love them—just because they were born a different way.

People like Lucas, like Jamie, like Remy.

People like Sean and Charlie.

People like Tim Halloran.

People like…me.

"I'm gay," I whispered.

Jamie went still.

I wasn't sure what made me say it. Why him, or why now. But the words were out, freed from where they'd been suffocating me, strangling the life from me, for far too long.

They were out, and it was done, and I couldn't take it back.

"Is that the first time you've said it?" Jamie asked quietly.

I nodded. Stared at him, wide-eyed. Aching inside.

"And how does it feel to finally say it out loud?"

The world trembled like I'd shattered its very foundations. Like I'd blown apart the dam holding back the tide. "It hurts," I gasped. "Why does it *hurt*?"

Jamie's smile was sad. "The first light always hurts when you've spent so long in the dark."

They were words only a musician would think to say.

They broke me.

But he caught me as I fell. As I was unmade. Held all the parts of me together so I could be forged anew. "I've got you," he said, and I cried and cried until there was nothing left inside of me.

"I hear you and our visiting cellist made a bit of a scene yesterday afternoon," said David, a teasing glint in his deep green eyes.

Obviously, it was too much to hope that my psychologist *hadn't* been informed of the incident. I'd cried for a long time, but Jamie just held me as I choked out all the poison, until eventually, strung out and worn through, the nurses had led me away.

"He's a good kid," David said. "He's come by to play most Sundays for the last two years."

"Why?"

"Well, he volunteers in our music therapy program. As for what his personal motivations are, I couldn't say. I've never asked."

Two years. I wondered if it had anything to do with Lucas. "We…um…go to school together," I said.

David's eyebrows rose. "You're friends?"

"It's complicated."

"I see." He considered me thoughtfully. "Is having him here going to be a problem?"

I shook my head. Twenty-four hours ago, I might have said yes, but now…no. I didn't think having Jamie here was going to be a problem.

David snatched up his pen from the table and twirled it between his fingers. "Do you mind sharing with me what made you so upset yesterday?"

"I…I told him…" My pulse raced, skating the line between nerves and full-blown panic, and my tongue darted out to moisten my suddenly dry lips. Why was it *harder* to say the second time? Shouldn't it get *easier* each time I said it?

Blood rushing into my cheeks, I looked across at David, swallowed, and blurted, "I told him I'm gay."

The pen-twirling stopped. "I see."

"You see?" I echoed. "That's seriously all you have to say?"

"Should I make a bigger deal out of it?" he asked.

I stared at the psychologist. He was *infuriating*. Right now, he was supposed to be jumping up and down like a kid on Christmas or ripping open his notebook and scribbling all this down or leaning closer to ask me how it made me *feel*.

Wasn't he?

But David simply lounged back in his chair, as calm and unruffled as always. Like my revelation was no more significant than any other I'd made. Like it hadn't taken every skerrick of my courage to make it.

"Carter," he said with endless patience, "I know that was hard for you to say, and I'm very proud of you. Acknowledging who you are—*admitting* it to yourself—is the first and most crucial step to healing."

My eyes stung.

"You've struggled with this, haven't you?"

I bit my lip. Nodded.

"Do you believe your sexuality is a choice?"

The burning in my eyes intensified. "No." But sometimes, I wished it was. Sometimes I wished I did have the choice...and that felt like a betrayal of Remy and everything we'd shared.

"It's biology," David said gently. "It's no more a choice than you choose for your heart to beat. Denying it would be denying you even *have* a heart in the first place. Some people go their entire lives trying to convince themselves of that lie. But, Carter, if you're not honest with yourself about what you want and, more importantly, what you *need*, you'll only succeed at making yourself miserable. That's no way to live."

The first tears trickled down my face. I didn't bother wiping them away, didn't bother hiding the wobble in my voice. "I'm so tired of fighting it. I'm tired of pretending and lying and hiding. I'm tired of being so scared all the time."

"Is that why you pushed the boy you kissed? Because you got scared?"

"Remy." I said his name like Jamie had said 'Lucas.'

David nudged a box of tissues towards me. "How would you describe your relationship with Remy? Would you call him your boyfriend?"

"No." The answer was immediate—automatic and ingrained. But David only waited while I gathered my thoughts and tried again. "He…ended things between us after I hurt him. But even before that, we weren't…open about it. Not with anyone. I couldn't let anyone know, so it was…he was…a secret."

I'd never thought of it as a dirty word before.

David tilted his head. "What did you and Remy do when you spent time together?"

I shrugged, the soft fabric of my tee-shirt pulling across my shoulders. "We talked a lot. Walked home from school together. We studied, sometimes, or watched movies at his house. I took him out to the city, once."

"And you kissed," said David.

I nodded.

"Did you have sex?"

A strangled noise burst from my throat. My entire body flushed hot.

I couldn't look at him—didn't want to see the expression on his face. Didn't want to know what expression was on mine. "What…" I croaked. "What…counts?"

277

"What do *you* think counts?"

My cheeks were on *fire*. I knew they were. How could they not be when I recalled how it felt to press myself against Remy, with nothing between us but our skin? To wake up with him curled around me, sheltered by the covers of my bed?

Groaning, I propped my arms on the edge of the desk and hid my burning face.

David sighed. "Carter, I'm not judging you. You're seventeen, nearly eighteen. It's completely normal to experiment, to explore your sexuality, and it's nothing to be embarrassed about."

That was easy for him to say. And *saying* it certainly didn't take the discomfort away. But I gritted my teeth and mumbled into my arms, "Just the once."

Just the once—the night everything went to hell.

"All right. And how did it make you feel, emotionally speaking?"

I'd fallen asleep after. We both had. Yet in those final moments, before my world splintered into starlight, I'd been so…happy. Euphoric, even.

Free.

Slowly, I sat up. Dark spots marched across my eyes as they readjusted to the brightness of the room. "Remy asked me if I regretted it. What we did. I…I don't think I felt regret. But a part of me did feel…guilty. Ashamed."

"Why?" David's voice was soft, softer than I'd ever heard it.

Why *would* I feel ashamed of what Remy and I had shared that day? It was beautiful and awkward and amazing, and I'd loved every moment of it. I'd loved *him*.

That was no reason to feel ashamed.

"I think," I said slowly, "that I might have started worrying about

278

what other people would think. I was late to a meeting with a friend, and I…I worried about what *she* might think if she found out."

"Ah." David tossed his pen into an empty coffee mug and knotted his hands together. "Does it matter what others think about the things that bring you joy?"

I grimaced. "I know it shouldn't, but it *feels* like it does."

"And that's something we can work on," said David. He seemed pleased. "Had you ever been attracted to a boy before Remy?"

I froze. The room around us vanished. A sunlit bench took its place, and it was another voice saying those words.

"Carter?"

Have you ever been attracted to a boy before? He was looking at my face as he said it, his eyes so big and dark and wide. So lovely.

A part of me had known right then in that moment. Known why that question provoked such terror, known why he was asking it of *me*.

No, I said bluntly and walked away, so I didn't see the hope in those eyes wink out.

He'd been reaching for me. Reaching for me as if I could save him from drowning. But I was too scared to reach back and take his hand—too scared about what everyone else might *think*—so I ignored him while his head sank beneath the waves.

I never got to tell him the truth. I'd lied to him.

And I lied to his parents when they came to me looking for answers.

I was a coward.

David snapped his fingers. "Right there. What was that thought you just had?"

"I'm a coward," I whispered.

His brow furrowed. "How did you come to that conclusion?"

"I didn't tell them."

"Tell who? Tell what?"

I'd stared at my reflection the day I cut my wrists. The person who stared back was so full of secrets, so full of lies. But this—this was the worst of them all.

My greatest shame.

I shut my eyes, longing for it all to go away. "Mr and Mrs Halloran. I didn't tell them why Tim called me the day he killed himself."

David paused. "A...friend of yours?" he asked carefully.

"He went to my church." My voice sounded strange and distant as I fought to detach myself from the pain. It was building, growing, too much, *too fast*—

"Don't do that." David was there, a warm, solid presence at my side. "Don't shut down. Let yourself feel it, even if it hurts. Cry—scream if you have to—but don't keep it trapped inside."

A shudder wracked my frame, and the tears spilled down in a cascade of water and salt. "He killed himself. Two days before last Christmas. He called me before he did it, but I didn't pick up the phone. I didn't want to talk to him."

"Why not?"

"He *liked* me," I wept. "I *knew* he liked me. And I...I...there was...something there. Or there could have been if I wasn't such a fucking *coward*. He was...he was *hinting* at things, and I panicked. Pushed him away."

I sobbed—a harsh, ugly sound. "He called me that day. I told his parents I missed the call. I didn't...I didn't tell them he left a message."

After I learned what Tim had done, I opened the voicemail he left when I let that call ring out. Then I'd fallen to my knees.

I hadn't heard him. I hadn't heard him when he cried out to me for help. I didn't hear him telling me goodbye. Not until it was already too late.

"He called to *thank* me," I choked on the words. "He called to thank me for being his friend. He was so lonely he thought *I* had been a good friend. But I turned my back on him. I left him all alone. He felt like he had nothing left, and he died because of it. Because of *me*."

"Stop," said David, and I clung to the sound of his voice. "Listen to me, Carter. You are not responsible for the choices other people make. I'm very sorry about your friend, but what happened to him was not your fault."

I opened my eyes, blinking through a curtain of tears. "But—"

He held up a hand. "No buts. Maybe there was something there between you and Tim, but *you* weren't ready to acknowledge it. That doesn't make you a coward, and it certainly doesn't make you responsible for his choice to take his life. Do you think your friends should blame themselves for your suicide attempt? Should Remy blame himself?"

I recoiled from the suggestion. "Of course not."

Because it wasn't their fault. It wasn't *Remy's* fault. I'd sent him that message, so he knew the truth in my heart. So he knew that what we'd had was real, even if it hadn't lasted.

But Remy had heard the deeper, darker meaning behind those five short words. He heard me calling for him, crying out to him for help, when I didn't even realise I was asking.

And he came for me. Despite everything I'd done, despite all the hurt I'd caused, Remy still cared enough to come and save me. He *had* saved me.

He'd done for me what I failed to do for Tim.

My tears ebbed, and I slumped forwards, the last of my strength going out of me. Hunched over my knees, staring down at the stupid slippers that were a gift from my best friend, I said to David, "I don't think I want to die anymore. I just want living to stop hurting so much."

"That's why you're here," David replied. "You're here so you can learn how to manage that hurt, so you can learn how to be okay with yourself, with the world." His knees cracked as he stood and plucked a few tissues from the box. He held them out to me.

I accepted them, and as I attempted to dry my face, David settled back into his chair. He looked me straight in the eye. "Do you want me to tell you what I think?"

"O-okay."

"I think you're an incredibly brave, incredibly bright young man who has had a hellish few years," he said. His large hands splayed flat on the surface of the desk, for once not twitching or fidgeting. "I think you're far stronger than you realise, but it's been a very long time since anyone has reminded you of that fact.

"I think you were a shy, twelve-year-old boy, possibly with mild social anxiety, who lost his father and brother in a tragic accident. You didn't receive the help and support you needed to learn how to cope with that loss, and so you developed some unhealthy habits in order to ease the pain.

"You have worked so hard to please everyone around you, *especially* your mother. You have tried to make her proud by emulating your dead brother, and in the process, you've destroyed your sense of self-worth. You've fought and denied your sexuality because it doesn't fit your idea of who you *should* be, and you've forgotten how to love who you *are*.

"I also believe you are a young man living with depressive and anxiety disorders. It's impossible to say if those were triggered by your experiences or if they might have developed regardless, but they've exacerbated the problem. You attempted self-harm to control the worst of your symptoms, and when the hurt became too much to bear, you tried to take your own life. And that is how you've ended up here."

David smiled then—a warm, open, encouraging smile. "Do you disagree?"

I couldn't argue with any of it. He'd cracked me open like an egg and painted my yolk in the sky for all the world to see.

It wasn't as awful as I'd feared.

"I see you, Carter Cantwell," my psychologist said. "I see all of you, and while the road may be long and hard, I can help you live the life you want. I can help you live a life that doesn't hurt so badly. If you'll let me."

The darkness receded. It was still there, lurking beyond my margins, but it was no longer trapped inside. For the first time in years, I could feel the soft, warm glow of hope. The chance for a life worth living.

All I had to do was reach out and take it.

"Please," I said to David. "Show me how."

He shoved the pile of questionnaires at me and grinned. "There's a good place to start."

twenty-one

It felt like a weight had been lifted off my shoulders. A weight which had grown day by day, swelling with every secret I kept and every lie I told. A weight which had, slowly but surely, been driving me into the ground.

Into an early grave.

Now it had eased. I felt like Atlas must have felt when Heracles took the sky from his back: able to stand tall for the first time in eons. Able to stand on my own two feet.

A part of me still held my breath, waiting for the other shoe to drop. Wondering when—not *if*—it would all come crashing down again.

But I tried to ignore that part.

I slept a lot these days. I was tired *all* the time, from the moment I was dragged out of bed in the morning to when I crawled beneath the covers at night. Afternoon naps were now the norm, and when I wasn't fast asleep in my assigned room, I could usually be found dozing on a couch in the common area, in a patch of golden sun.

I cried a lot, too. Small things set me off—a stray thought, a fleeting memory. A kind word. Then sometimes, I devolved into a blubbering mess for no apparent reason at all.

David wasn't concerned. He said it was my body's way of recovering from the ordeal I'd put it through these past few months, of purging all the grief and pain I'd kept bottled up inside. He said it was important to let it all out, or I'd explode like an over-pressurised can.

I wasn't sure whether to believe him—but he hadn't misled me yet.

So I slept when I was tired and cried when I was sad and learned to ignore the voice in my head that warned I was going mad.

Jamie returned on Sunday afternoon. I was huddled in a quiet corner when he arrived, and his roving eyes found me almost instantly. My cheeks heated as I recalled our last encounter, how I'd completely broken down in his arms.

Jamie merely nodded and turned his mind to the task of setting up his cello.

Then he began to play.

I could have listened to him for hours. Piece after piece after piece, Jamie played like it was his last day on earth, his bow blurring the air and his fingers quick and sure on the strings. I'd never heard songs like these before, songs that filled each lonely room with life.

Songs that made my heart soar.

I always knew Jamie was good, but I didn't realise he was *this* good. His was a talent I had rarely encountered, and he possessed a certain flair that Piper, Paige, and I could never hope to match with our own instruments. It made me wonder why he'd wasted his time with us all these years. Why he didn't play solo more often.

But I was starting to understand that there was more to Jamie Ray than met the eye. More than the aloof, disdainful front he chose to present at school, which I'd bought into time and time again.

Now I found myself wanting to dig deeper, to peel back his façade and uncover what lay beneath. To learn the truth of him, as he'd learned the truth of me.

I wasn't surprised when he sauntered my way at the end of his performance. He dropped onto the couch and draped himself over its arm, a sprawl of dark fabric and pale skin.

"How are your exams going?" I said by way of greeting.

Jamie lifted a shoulder. "Okay, I think. I have Music Performance tomorrow."

"And you're here? Shouldn't you be at home studying?"

"I'm ready for it." He picked at the scabbing on his knuckles, remnants from when he'd put his hand through a wall—because of me. "Besides," he added, "it...brings me peace to come here and play. It reminds me of what's important, why music is supposed to be shared."

Another hint. Another peek behind the mask. Another sign of just how badly I'd misjudged him.

Of how badly we'd misjudged each other.

I looked down at my own hands.

I'd lost a lot of weight in the last few weeks—from stress, from the lack of appetite—and without my natural insulation, I felt cold even when radiant warmth spilled in through the windows. My newest bandages were thinner than those I'd left the hospital with, so I could finally fit into a long-sleeved shirt. It pulled taut over the bandages' slight bulk and ended just short of my wrists.

Exposing my long, pale fingers, callused from over a decade with my violin.

"I don't know if I'll ever be able to play again." My voice cracked as I said it. Even Jamie flinched. "I can't..."

I'd tried not to think about it too much. What was done was done, after all, and I couldn't turn back time. But having Jamie here, having heard him play so well, the reminder was acute. Painful. Impossible to ignore. Peering down at my ravaged hands, it was hard to imagine ever holding my violin again.

How long would it be before I forgot what it even felt like?

Jamie leaned forwards, his initial horror morphing into something more pensive. His eyes honed in on my hands, which lay limp and lifeless in my lap. "Nerve damage?" he guessed.

I nodded.

"How bad?"

"We're...not sure yet. We won't know until..." I swallowed, avoided looking directly at his face, "...until the wounds have healed. But the left is worse than the right."

I didn't need to explain. Jamie was a cellist—he'd understand what that meant.

As if on cue, he said, "You're worried about the fingering."

Tears welled up unannounced. They pooled beneath my lashes so fast I didn't have time to blink before they were coursing down my cheeks.

Bowing was essential to controlling the sound of a string instrument, which was why it was done by the dominant hand—the right hand, for most people. Fingering the pitches was the task of the left...and it depended on fine motor skills.

Motor skills I may very well have lost.

"I met this girl once," Jamie said. "A fellow cellist. Her hands were badly burned in a house fire, and the left was worse than the right. She lost a lot of sensation because of the scar tissue. A lot of dexterity, too."

I could feel the steady weight of his gaze. Wondered what, exactly, he was getting at.

"She learned to play left-handed."

Startled, I glanced up.

"It wouldn't be the same," Jamie acknowledged, "not with a weakened bowing hand, and you'd have to get a new violin, but... if it came down to it, you could learn to play left-handed." He hesitated, his lip caught between his teeth. "I could help you."

The offer was so unexpected, the tears came even thicker. "You... you'd do that?"

"Uh, yeah. If you want."

I dropped my eyes back to my lap. "Thank you," I whispered, sounding kind of strangled. "I guess we'll have to wait and see."

But in the meantime, I could hope.

David said it was important to hope.

We lapsed into a comfortable silence. Jamie drummed his fingers on his jean-clad knee, a small furrow between his brows. I was transfixed by the lightning-fast patter of his hand, by the odd contrast it made with my total stillness.

"Jake's coming to visit me tomorrow," I said into the quiet.

I'd thought about it long and hard. I knew that I couldn't hide from my friends forever, though it felt like a valid option while I was safe inside these walls. I didn't intend for any of them to come here, to see me like this.

But Sean said that Jake was all but camping out on his and

Charlie's doorstep and calling them at least twice a day. Like a starving vulture, desperate for whatever scraps of information he could scrounge together from the mess.

My heart squeezed painfully tight. Jake had never been anything but loyal, and I had to trust that now would be no different. "I'm going to tell him about...you know."

Jamie's eyebrows rose. "If you're ready."

"What?" I frowned. "Do you think he won't take it well?"

"Oh, please. Jake Brenner won't give two shits that you're gay." His tone was light, but his expression was dead serious. "I only meant that I know what it's like to be out before you're ready. It's... not ideal."

I almost laughed at the blatant understatement, but something didn't make sense. "Then why were you so angry at me about the formal? About me...not taking Remy?"

Jamie winced. "That was about him, not you. I am in *awe* of people like Remy Montrose, who just put themselves out there and be who they are, consequences be dammed. Do you know how much courage it must—" He cut himself off. Snorted. "Look who I'm talking to. Of course you know how brave he is."

Jamie wasn't wrong.

And yet... "What about Jonah Kennedy? You and Remy baited him, alluded to—"

"Jonah Kennedy isn't gay. Not even the slightest bit. He just hates what we stand for, what we represent."

I didn't understand—not his claim nor the certainty with which he made it. "What on earth are you talking about?"

Jamie eyed me with no small amount of exasperation. "That stupid bastard must be so pleased nobody remembers. Carter, you

289

were the one who got him suspended last year. I always figured he went on that rampage in the change rooms because you'd accidentally seen his bruises. Was I wrong?"

My stomach dropped.

"Yeah, his dad's a sadistic, abusive arsehole who seems to have gotten away with everything short of murder." Jamie's eyes smouldered like embers. "And I'd stake my cello on the fact it's gotten worse since his brother was caught messing around with me in a supply closet, beaten to within an inch of his life, and then booted out of their home."

I blinked.

Kennedy's brother was caught making out with Jamie? But that meant…

"Lucas Kennedy," Jamie said grimly. "Jonah's older brother and probably the only person in the world he cared about." He sighed, all the fight draining out of him. "And being gay took his brother away."

The first time I met Jake Brenner, I was terrified.

Even at five years old, Jake was one of those people who oozed confidence and charm. He was loud and brash and boisterous, and he didn't give a damn what anyone thought of him. He was the kid who always ended up in the naughty corner, and when a scuffle broke out, you could almost guarantee he was involved.

Nine times out of ten, he was the one who started it.

So when Jake marched up to me on our first day of primary school and declared me not only his friend but his *best* friend… yeah, I was intimidated. I didn't get what a boy like him saw in a boy like me. I was the quiet kid, the shy kid, the one who'd never dare to break the rules.

I was Jake's complete opposite in almost every way.

But I didn't argue when he staked his claim, and once I got over my initial fear, Jake and I just…clicked. He'd always had my back. He'd always been there when I needed him.

And I'd told him goodbye. *Sure, Jake. I'll see you later.*

In thirteen years of friendship, I had never been this scared to face him.

I perched on the edge of my favourite couch and waited for Misty to bring Jake through into the facility. My heart was beating so hard I feared it would crack a rib, crack *all* of my ribs and drive their jagged edges into my lungs so I couldn't—

I squeezed my eyes shut, urged the rest of the world to retreat. Rocked back and forth, chanting the periodic table in my head. *Hydrogen, helium, lithium, beryllium—*

"Carter."

—boron, carbon, nitrogen, oxygen—

"Carter?"

I forced my eyes open, and there he was.

His hands were in his pockets, his shoulders slumped, lower lip all chapped from where he'd worried it between his teeth. The dark purple smudges beneath his eyes stood out against the tan of his face.

For the first time, Jake looked just as nervous to see me as I was to see him.

I stood on legs that trembled, on knees that threatened to give way. He tracked my every movement as I swallowed, stepped forwards, and offered him a tremulous smile. "Hi, Jake."

My best friend took a deep, shaky breath—and burst into tears.

I stared at him, agape, as wrenching sobs ripped from his chest. Stood there at a loss for what to do when confronted by his devastation.

Until Jake threw his arms around my neck and held on tight. Refused to let go, like he was afraid I'd vanish if he relinquished his hold for so much as a second.

It hurt, the knowledge of what I'd done to him. Of what my *actions* had done to him.

Carefully, I drew my best friend down onto the couch and slipped my arms around his waist. I hugged him back, my face buried against his shoulder. "I'm sorry," I breathed. "I'm so sorry, Jake."

He shuddered, then withdrew slightly. Arms still draped over my collarbones, hands pressing against my spine, he ran his eyes all over me. I let him look. Let him see the toll the last few weeks had taken; let him see my pasty skin and stick-thin body.

Let him see for himself that I was all in one piece. A muddled, patchwork piece held together by cobwebs and echoes, but one piece all the same.

Jake's arms fell away. "You're really here," he said hoarsely. "You're really okay."

"No," I replied. "I'm not okay."

I told him about the damage to my hands.

I told him about the *major depressive disorder* and *comorbid anxiety disorders*—the outcomes of David's questionnaires.

I told him that the facility's psychiatrist had put me on medication.

Jake looked a bit stunned. "I was kind of expecting you to say you were fine."

"I'm not fine," I admitted, my voice gaining strength the more I said it. "I haven't been fine in a while, but I'm trying to get better now. I don't...it won't happen overnight."

His gaze dropped down to my arms, to the bandages poking out from the sleeves of my hoodie. I sat perfectly still as he brushed his fingertips over the white gauze. "I don't care if you're not fine, Carter," he said tightly. "I just care that you're *alive*."

I fell silent. I could see my best friend wrestling with it—with his guilt and pain and fear and anger and *relief*. I could see, and could read, every emotion which flickered across his face, but I didn't know how to fix it. Didn't know that I *could*.

There wasn't anything I could say to make it better. Not all of it. Not at once.

Especially not with what I had to say next.

"There's something else I have to tell you, Jake. I *need* to tell you, but I'm...scared."

He dabbed at his still-damp eyes. "Why?"

"I don't want you to be angry at me." I looked down at my slippers—the ones he'd given me. "I don't want you to think any less of me. And I don't want things to...change."

Jake let out a noise that was half-laugh and half-sob. "Carter, things have already changed. But whatever. Right now, you could tell me you murdered someone and buried the body in my backyard, and I seriously wouldn't give a flying fuck."

My chest constricted. My mouth had gone bone dry. But I looked directly at my best friend, right into his eyes, and said, "I...I'm..."

I floundered.

"Go on," he said. "Whatever it is, just spit it out."

"Jake...I'm gay."

I watched his eyes widen. Watched the utter blankness steal across his face. Watched his body straighten, untangle from mine. Pull away.

The silence stretched on and on and on.

Nausea churned in my stomach. Blind panic encroached, creeping up my arms from the tips of my fingers and heading right for my heart.

Oh God, I'd *ruined* it again, ruined *everything*, and Jake—

He cocked his head. "Um…" A sheepish grin tugged at his lips. "Is it a cliché to say 'I know'?"

Wait…*what*?

"Well, I suspected," he amended.

I gaped at him. "For how long?"

"A while."

"Jake!"

He crossed his arms. The gesture was almost defensive. "What?"

"How could you… Why did you…"

"Mate. Come on." Jake rolled his eyes. "Are you actually *kidding* me right now? I'm not saying it was obvious or anything, but you're my best friend. I *know* you." His mirth faded a little. When his gaze dropped to my arms, it wasn't hard to tell what he was thinking.

He did know me. But he didn't know it all.

This time, he hadn't known enough.

Jake sighed. "If it makes you feel any better, it took me a while to put things together. It didn't really hit me until Remy walked into the room on the first day of school. Oh my God, the look on your face. I couldn't *believe* no one else noticed."

"You never said anything," I accused.

"Right. And how do you think *that* would have gone?"

Maybe he had a point.

"Carter, you know I don't care, right? Who you're attracted to doesn't make a difference to me. Not even for a second."

Jamie was right. Jake didn't care—had probably *never* cared.

How did he know my best friend better than I did?

Something of my relief must have shown on my face because Jake faltered. "Were you really that worried about what I'd think?" he said quietly. There was a brittleness to his tone that I didn't care for at all.

"It's…not you, exactly," I tried to explain. "It's…I worry a lot about what other people think of me. Everybody. All the time. It's not always rational. In fact, it's usually completely *irrational*, but it's what I feel."

Jake spent a moment processing that. I could see the gears churning in his brain. "Well," he finally said, "thank you for telling me now. For trusting me." He inched closer until our knees touched. "I just wish you'd trusted me sooner."

"Jake…"

My best friend shook his head. "I knew something wasn't right, but when you didn't want to talk, I let it go. I didn't push you when I should have. I just thought you'd come to me when you were ready, but you never did." He let out a breath. "I know we don't really talk about serious stuff all that much, but that's going to change. I'm here for you, okay? I won't let you down again."

It was all I needed to hear.

And then he spoiled it. "So. Remy, huh?"

I groaned.

"Don't be like that." Jake nudged my hip. "Come on, you can

295

tell me. You were, like, *together*, right? I didn't make the whole thing up in my head? I didn't *imagine* your freak-out after Piper's party or that you've hated Jamie's guts since the formal?"

Had I been that obvious? Or was it obvious only to him?

"Remy turned my life upside down." It was a whisper. A breath. But I meant the words wholeheartedly.

Remy Montrose *had* turned my life upside down. In a good way. In a bad way.

He'd changed everything.

"He means so much to me, Jake," I confessed. "But I...hurt him. Badly. And I'm still trying to...come to terms with this part of me. With what I want."

Jake studied me. "Does he make you happy?"

"More than that." I swallowed past the tightness in my throat. "He makes me feel *alive*."

"Then what more could you possibly ask for?"

"I don't know," I conceded.

His brow wrinkled. "We both know how hopeless I am when it comes to romance, but...Carter...that sounds kind of perfect. Remy is kind of perfect for you."

"Yeah," I said weakly. Because while he was perfect for me, that didn't mean *I* was perfect for *him*. "This past year, though...I've just constantly felt like I'm falling."

"Falling is just another way to fly."

I scoffed. "Who said that?"

"I don't know. Some singer, I think." Jake grinned. "It's catchy, right?"

The comment was just so typically *Jake* that I laughed. And laughed, and laughed, and laughed, and then I was crying again.

Weeping so hard I could scarcely breathe, not even with my best friend's arms around me, holding me safe and close.

Together, we weathered the storm until the rains had ceased and the sky had cleared, and a rainbow streaked above our heads. A silent joy I hadn't expected to ever feel again.

"The...the others," I stammered. "How do you think they'll... react to me...coming out?" The term felt strange to say, especially when in reference to myself.

Jake's hand rubbed circles on my shoulder. "Honestly? They might be surprised, but they won't have a problem with it. You've seen how easily they accept Remy." He paused. "Do you want me to tell them?"

I pulled back. Looked at him. "You'd do that?"

"Sure, mate. Whatever you need."

It was tempting. More than tempting.

But I wasn't going to begin my second chance at life by letting someone else do all the work. That had never been my way. It would never be my way.

"Thank you...but no. This is something I need to do myself."

Jake shrugged. "Okay. But the offer stands." He peered at me from beneath his lashes. "You know I'd do anything for you, right? I'd even take the fall for that body you hid in my yard."

I smiled through my tears. "I know."

And I finally let myself believe that everything might turn out all right.

twenty-two

"She wants to see you."

More terrifying words, I had never heard. They stayed with me all day after Sean had spoken them, loitering in my mind and dogging my every step. They plagued me all through the night, their poison-laced talons clinging to the fringes of my dreams.

By the time I collapsed into my seat in David's office the next morning, I felt hunted. Hounded. Beset by some tormented spirit trapped here from beyond the grave.

It didn't take David long to drag my troubles out of me.

"Hmm." He wielded a pencil today, and he tapped its end against his chin. "What did you tell your uncle?"

"I said I'd think about it."

"And?"

"I have."

"*And*?"

Another day, I would have glared at him, but today it took all my effort just to contain the maelstrom inside me. "I don't understand why she wants to see me," I mumbled.

David's expression softened. "She's your mum. Maybe she just needs to see for herself that you're all right."

That was all well and good, but… "What about what *I* need?"

"What *do* you need, Carter?"

There was no straightforward answer.

I had worked so hard to win my mother's approval. So hard, for so long, convincing myself that what I needed didn't matter. A part of me was desperate to hear her out, clutched at the hope now sprouting in my chest—hope that she'd apologise, tell me she was proud of me, that she *did* love me.

But I was also terrified she would destroy what little progress I'd made with a single, careless word. *Ruined. Disappointment.* I couldn't go back to that. I couldn't.

I wouldn't survive it a second time.

"I would like to see her," I admitted.

"But?"

He knew me well.

"*But…*I don't think I can be alone with her."

The humour fled David's face. He looked, all of a sudden, very serious. "We haven't talked a lot about your mother yet. I know she hit you once. If you don't feel safe in her presence—"

"It's not that," I said quickly. "It's… She has this way of just… taking me apart. Eviscerating me. Sometimes she doesn't even need to talk to do it; she just gives me this *look*."

"There's a name for that, you know. It's called emotional abuse."

I flinched. Curled my shoulders in around my ears.

"Look at me."

Jaw working, I obeyed.

David's chair creaked as he shifted his weight forwards. "Thank you for being honest, and thank you for articulating what you need. No one—least of all me—is going to force you to see your mother." He considered me. "But if you want to, we can do it here."

"What?"

"I'm not a family counsellor," he said, "but I have had family members sit in on sessions in the past. If you want, I'm happy to arrange for her to attend one of our appointments. You'll be somewhere you feel comfortable and safe, and I'll be here to step in if matters get out of hand. Is that something you'd be interested in?"

For a moment, I couldn't think of a single thing to say. My words had been engulfed by the fear and gratitude swarming up my throat.

Then I huffed out a breath. Nodded. "Okay. Let's do it."

But I spent the remainder of the week in a state of restless unease. It wouldn't be long now before I was released from the facility into the outside world. Despite how far I'd come, I was scared that I wasn't ready, scared that seeing Mum would set me back.

Scared it would return me to the dark place I'd been trapped in for so long.

And I didn't want to go back. I was ready to go forwards. To move on.

When the day of the scheduled appointment rolled around, I couldn't stomach the thought of breakfast. My queasy insides churned, and my head felt bloodless, too light. As if I was on the verge of fainting or throwing up.

Or both.

Thankfully, Misty didn't force me to eat. She just sat by my side in a silent show of support and walked with me to David's office when the time arrived.

I hadn't been this nauseated since my very first session with the psychologist over three weeks ago now. All my muscles trembled, and my joints were locked up tight, each breath coming fast and shallow and drawing in not nearly enough air.

Was it too late to back out of this? I wanted to back out.

Misty rubbed my arm—a soothing gesture, though it brought me little comfort. "You'll be great, Carter," she said. "And David will be in there with you. It'll be fine. You'll see."

She knocked on the door. My belly flipped.

"Come in!" David's voice called from the other side.

But I couldn't move my feet. Everything below my waist liquefied, and I teetered. Swayed as flesh and bone turned to putty. I could do nothing to resist as Misty nudged me over the threshold and shut the door behind me.

The *click* it made was ominous. Final.

There was no escape.

And, when I glanced up, I came face-to-face with my greatest fear.

My mother.

She was almost unrecognisable. Auburn curls, usually scraped back in a bun, hung loose and dishevelled around her haggard face. Bare of cosmetics, there was nothing to hide the greyish cast to her skin or the lines fanning out from the corners of her eyes, gouging deep furrows along her temples.

She looked as if she'd aged a decade.

My vision spun, scattering her form into a thousand glittering prisms.

"Breathe, Carter," said David.

Because I wasn't breathing—hadn't taken a breath since entering the room. I forced my lungs to contract, to expel the stale air they were hoarding. Then I breathed in.

"That's the way," David encouraged. "Deep breaths. You're safe here."

I didn't feel safe, but I clung to the calm of his voice and *breathed*. In and out. In and out.

"You came," I said flatly. Until that moment, I didn't realise that I thought she wouldn't show.

Mum's lips parted. No sound came out.

"How about we all sit down?" David suggested.

That was a good idea; my legs shook so hard my knees banged together.

At David's prompting, we moved into the sitting area I'd avoided to this point. Mum and I settled down on the two couches, facing each other across a narrow coffee table, while David sank into the upholstered armchair in the corner.

I was vaguely aware of Mum watching me, but I kept my eyes glued to the top of the table. The glazed mahogany wasn't whorled so much as streaked, and I studied the reddish lines with great interest.

David clapped his hands. "Carter, I've just been explaining to your mum that she's here so the two of you can speak in an environment where you don't feel threatened. She's been informed that if at any time I think your wellbeing is at risk, I will have to ask her to leave."

Good—that was good to know.

"Now, who would like to start?"

Crickets. I could almost hear them chirping.

"All right," David said easily. "I'll start. Andrea, can you tell us why you wanted to come and see Carter today?"

Mum fiddled with her wedding ring. I'd never seen her do that before, not in the years since we'd lost Dad. "I had to see...I had to know...why."

"Why? Why what?" I raised my arms. "Why I did *this*?"

I did this I did this I did this I did this I did this...

She rubbed at her face as if it was all too much. "I..."

"You hit me," I whispered. Not the whole answer—but part of it. A small piece of the jigsaw puzzle slotting into place. "I was trying to tell you the truth, and you hit me."

Mum's expression was almost contrite. Then it twisted into something more bitter. "That night, I saw you kissing that boy, and I was so—"

"Disgusted, right? You were disgusted by me. I saw it on your face." My voice cracked. "You said you couldn't even stand to look at me."

"I don't want you to be...*like that*," she said bluntly.

I recoiled. I wasn't surprised to hear her say it—I'd expected it all along—but I was surprised by how much it still hurt. It hurt like she'd poured fuel down my throat and struck a match against my heart.

"*Like that?*" I choked out. "You can't even say it, can you? You can't even say the damn word, and yet you think either of us gets to choose whether or not I'm gay?"

Her cheeks paled. "You're not. You can't be."

I snarled—actually *snarled* at my own mother. "I *am*."

"Carter—"

"No."

"But—"

"*Shut up!*" Violent tremors wracked my body, but no longer due

303

to fear. Fear had morphed to anger, cold dread to searing heat. It flooded my veins, jerking me to my feet until I towered over her. Loomed, like she'd always loomed over me. "Shut up and *listen to me* for once!"

Mum's eyes were wide, glassy, and she glanced nervously at David. He leaned forwards, but made no move to stop me, no move to halt my tirade.

"I didn't *choose* this!" I raged. "This is how I was born, and you have no idea what it's been like. *No idea*. I was barely nine years old the first time I heard you call me a—"

I chomped down on the word. I couldn't say it. I'd promised Miles I wouldn't.

Tears streamed down my face and dripped off the end of my chin. I let them. Let her see what I felt, what I'd suffered for so long. "I've spent years—*years*, Mum—hiding this part of me, pretending it wasn't there. I tried *so hard* to make you proud. I did *everything* right, but nothing was ever good enough for you. It killed me inside. You made me believe there was no hope. You made me hate myself, and I hated myself so much I wanted to *die* rather than—"

"I didn't *mean* to!" she shouted. "I didn't even *realise* what I'd done until I saw you…"

I laughed in disbelief. "How could you *not* realise?"

How did we get to this point?

We were mother and son, but we were broken. Maybe we'd always been broken.

Maybe we always would be.

Mum's lips quivered, and she grabbed a fistful of her hair like she wanted to rip it straight from her scalp. "They died," she rasped. "They *died*, Carter, and suddenly you were the only thing in my life that had any worth. I needed you to be *strong*. I needed you to be not…not *gay*," her face twisted, "because I knew what the world would do to you if I gave it the chance."

Confusion snapped a leash around my rage. My eyebrows angled down. "What are you talking about?"

Mum lurched to her feet across from me, colour spilling into her cheeks like ink. "They nearly killed him!" she shrieked. "They nearly *killed* him for who he is! *I couldn't let that happen to you!*"

It hung there, reverberating through the air, resonating until even the echoes fell silent.

The thoughts were twisted in my mind, hopelessly tangled and sluggish and slow. Only one strand stood out, bright and clear amongst the chaos, and I latched onto it. Realised what she meant. "Uncle Sean."

There were tears in her eyes now. Twin pools of liquid green. "He was just a *boy*," she gasped. "Just a boy, and he was so afraid. You've always been so much like him. I couldn't let you walk his path, couldn't let you be hurt the way he was hurt. I couldn't bear the thought of getting a call like that from you."

"But you got a call anyway, didn't you?" I wished I could hold onto my anger, but her words had knocked the wind right out of my sails. Slumping back onto the couch, I felt only weary. Bleak. "It was just a different type of call than you'd expected. And now you're kicking me out of the house."

Mum blanched. "No. *Never*. I was tossed out onto the street by my own mother, like I was no more than a piece of garbage, and I would *never* do that to you."

"You gave Sean guardianship of me. You're making me go and stay with him and Charlie."

"To *help* you!" she cried. "Because I don't know how to help you through this, Carter. I don't know what to do anymore. And because when I saw you lying there in that hospital bed, clinging to life by a thread, I realised I would much rather have a gay son than another *dead* son!"

I froze. My thundering heart skidded to a halt. "Do you really mean that?"

"*Yes.*" It hissed out of her like gas from a pipe. "I've been a terrible mother," she gritted. "I know that. Motherhood has never come easily to me, not even when your father was alive. Most days, I can't see past my own pain, and it hurts. *So much.* But that doesn't change the fact I haven't done right by you…or Miles."

She scrubbed her hands over her face, and when she lowered her arms, there was grief in her eyes. Old grief, overlain by a new grief so vast it made me catch my breath.

"It's too late for him," she went on, her voice shaking, "but I hope it's not too late for you. I hope that one day we'll be able to… fix things. I don't expect you to forgive me, and I can't promise to come to terms with…all this…overnight. But I'll try. For you, I will try."

Mum swallowed, and the edges of her mouth quirked up. It was almost a smile. "I want you in my life, Carter. I *need* you in my life, in whatever capacity you're comfortable with. You're still my son, my boy, and though I'm poor at showing it…I do love you."

There.

Those words—the ones I'd been waiting for all along. The words I'd suffered for. The words I'd toiled and sacrificed and bled for just to hear her say to me.

And they weren't enough.

Remy was right. Love alone was not enough to heal all wounds—not when it was tainted by so much hurt. Not when it was smothered by the weight of a history that contained more pain than joy.

I looked at my mother, at her tired, desperate face, and considered what she was offering: the chance to be a family. The chance to start again. "Okay," I whispered.

Because maybe love was not enough, and maybe our past was too much to surmount. Maybe this would all end in tragedy, and we'd burn in each other's flames.

But there was one thing I did know for sure: I'd never know unless I tried.

I was released from the facility on a day that dawned cool and clear. The sky was brilliant azure, unmarred by wisps of cloud, and the sun stretched out its golden fingers to wick the morning dew from the grass.

I sat not-so-patiently in the foyer and waited for my uncle. Misty occupied the chair beside me, and I listened with half an ear as she chatted away, recounting the adventures of her rambunctious young niece who'd recently learned to walk.

Excitement and trepidation warred within my ribcage. It was a toxic cocktail of emotions that made my pulse spike every time I thought too hard, but I focused on my breathing, on letting my lungs fill to capacity before releasing the air in smooth, controlled exhales.

Bone-deep exhaustion sapped at my strength, and it was still a continual struggle to keep my eyes open, but after twenty-eight days here, I no longer felt like I was drowning. I was paddling hard, my head just above the water, and I could finally see the shore.

The centre's door opened, scattering light across the polished tiles, and my uncle strode inside. His eyes found me immediately. "Hey, kiddo," he beamed. "You ready to get out of here?"

"I think so," I said. Then I cleared my throat and amended, "Yes."

"Excellent!" Sean bounced on his toes, unable to conceal his excitement as he crossed the foyer to the desk and flashed an equally bright smile at the receptionist. "Where do I sign?"

I watched him scoop up the offered pen and scrawl his name across the paperwork, wondering how I was ever going to repay him for all he'd done.

For the way he'd been here for me, right when I needed him most.

Before I could work myself into a state over it, David slipped through the door leading to the main part of the facility. "Well, Carter, today's the day!" he said with his usual cheer. "How are you feeling?"

"A bit nervous," I confessed.

"That's all right. As long as you take it easy these first few days and remember all the strategies we've talked about, I'm confident you'll be just fine."

David turned to my uncle, and after they shook hands, David handed him a sheaf of papers secured in a plastic pocket. "That's some information for you and your partner, but please don't hesitate to contact my rooms if you have any questions. Carter, you remember that we have an appointment tomorrow morning?"

"Ten o'clock," I confirmed. "I won't forget." On the days he didn't visit the hospital-run facility, David worked out of a health clinic nearby, and he'd agreed to keep seeing me after I was discharged from the program.

I was grateful—the prospect of going through all this again with *another* psychologist did not appeal. I knew David now. I trusted him.

I stood up, my heart in my throat. "Thank you, David," I croaked.

"You're very welcome, Carter," he said. "I'll see you tomorrow.

"Good luck," Misty added.

I pivoted to face the door. Took another deep breath.

It was time.

I didn't need Sean to support me as we exited the facility, not like I had on the way in. I paused on the other side of the threshold, felt the sun upon my skin. Heard the birds chirping in harmony with the purr of motors on the road.

Summer would be here soon, though the world seemed to act as if the spring had just begun.

Once I was buckled safely into the front passenger seat of Sean's car, we zipped out into the traffic. I gazed out the window and watched the world race by, a blur of colour and light that held out a welcoming hand. Beckoned me to come and be a part of it again.

A part of it like I never had been before.

My lips twitched skywards. *Soon*, I promised. *Soon*.

It wasn't a long ride to Sean and Charlie's place. Just under half an hour later, we pulled up outside a single-storey house about the same size as the one I'd lived in my whole life. A small pang rippled through me at the reminder that *that* house was no longer my home.

Swallowing past the melancholy, I climbed out of the car and studied the brick veneer façade. Deep eaves sheltered the white-framed windows, their view partially obstructed by the wild snarl of bushes and a eucalypt whose dangling branches were in dire need of a prune.

"The garden needs some work," Sean acknowledged. "I'll get around to it eventually."

"Not Charlie?"

My uncle snorted. "I'll drop dead the day I see him playing around in the dirt." He gestured towards the front door. "Shall we?"

When we stepped inside, the first thing I noticed was the voices coming from what I assumed to be the kitchen. The *pair* of voices. It sounded like Charlie had company.

Wrestling down my unease, I looked askance at Sean.

He grimaced. "Charlie, we're home!"

There was a muffled oath, followed by something clattering to the floor. Then footsteps headed our way, and I fought the urge to jump behind my uncle and hide. I wasn't in the mood to converse with anyone else. I wasn't ready to—

Charlie rounded the corner with a sheepish smile. His blue eyes were luminous, exuding kindness and warmth. "Sorry!" he said. "We got stuck talking, and then…I might have made coffee?"

"Only you," Sean muttered.

"She's…ah…still in the kitchen."

"I gathered that."

I was about to demand what was going on—and who, exactly, was in their kitchen—when the person in question poked her head into the hall. My eyes widened. "*Megs*? What are you doing here?"

Chagrined, she stepped out from behind the corner. "Well," she drawled, "as it so happens, I was dropping off a present for you."

"A…present?" I echoed.

My uncle threw his arms up in the air. "You may as well show him now since you're still here."

The three of them traded conspiratorial smirks that I did *not* like the look of, and Megs let out a piercing whistle that took ten years off my life.

I heard it, first—the clinking of claws against floorboards. Then movement at the end of the hall caught my eye, and I turned towards it slowly, not daring to believe, not daring to *hope*—

My jaw dropped.

I would have recognised that lumbering gait anywhere.

Shadow yipped when she saw me, and I dropped to my knees just in time for her to plough into my side. Her front paws found purchase against my thighs, and she pressed upwards, pink tongue darting out to lick my chin.

Heart wrenching at the way her whole body quivered with excitement, I peered up at Megs. "I…I don't understand."

"She's yours," Megs said, her eyes overbright. "I think she's always been yours."

"But…" I turned to Charlie and Sean, but they only grinned down at me and shrugged. "But the fees…all the *stuff*…"

Megs shook her head. "Paid for. Everyone at the shelter chipped in."

"Is this real?" I breathed because if this was some kind of practical joke…

"Yes, Carter. Shadow really is yours."

Mine. Shadow was *mine*.

It was a dream come true.

Carefully dislodging the dog from my lap, I leapt to my feet and threw my arms around Megs' neck. "Thank you," I choked. "Thank you thank you thank you thank you thank you."

Megs squished her face against my collarbone and hugged me back, her arms squeezing so hard my diaphragm groaned in protest. "It was our pleasure," she said, voice all rough and thick. "Welcome home."

I held onto her—the love of my brother's life, the sister I'd almost had. Her shoulders were shaking, and the top of my shirt grew damp. "I'm so mad at you right now," she grumbled. "And I'm so happy to see you that I could *kiss* you."

"*Ew.*"

"Yeah, that would be weird." Megs gently pushed me back. Reached up to cup my wet cheek. "Little bro," she murmured. Miles' name for me.

"Megan," I whispered. Miles' name for her.

I glanced behind me and saw that Sean and Charlie had made themselves scarce. "Is it too late," I asked softly, "to take you up on that offer to talk?"

Her hand dropped down to my shoulder. "It's never too late, Carter."

Shadow shifted against my legs, her tail sweeping rapidly across the floor. My lips curled into a smile. "Well, it all started when I met this boy…"

twenty-three

"Twenty bucks on Sean losing a finger," Jake said under his breath.

I shot him a dirty look.

It felt kind of wrong to be spying on my uncle and his partner while they prepared lunch in the kitchen. Not that we were *spying*, per se, and not that it looked like much lunch preparation was actually going on.

The kitchen was in plain view of the lounge room, where Jake and I had been watching movies all morning. Sean stood before a chopping board and was attempting to cut up some salad items— *attempting*, since Charlie was perched on the bench beside him, ankles crossed and a hand on Sean's back. He kept leaning down to whisper in my uncle's ear.

Every time he did it, Sean jumped, then glared. Those glares he aimed at Charlie were becoming increasingly heated—and not from irritation.

"I really don't want to know," I muttered.

Shadow, wedged in between us with her chin resting on my

knee, rolled her one eye up at my tone. I curled my fingers around her ear as far as they could go. It wasn't far—the muscles and joints were stiff from weeks of disuse—but it was something.

Better than nothing.

A shout came from the kitchen as the knife clattered to the floor. "Goddamn it, Charlie!" Sean cried. "I'm going to chop my bloody finger off if you keep that up!"

Jake snickered.

Charlie's laughter tinkled off the walls. "Well, we can't have that." He slithered from the bench and picked up the knife, slamming it down on the chopping board before dragging my uncle in for a kiss.

"They're kind of adorable, aren't they?" said Jake.

"Yeah," I murmured, but I felt a sharp pang in my chest. I often did when I watched Sean and Charlie interact. The love and respect that shone between them, solid and bright like a thread connecting their souls...

I wanted that.

I *had* that, and I'd let it slip through my fingers like sand.

Sean pushed Charlie back with a palm in the centre of his chest. "You're terrible," he growled. "If you want to eat lunch sometime today, get your arse out of here."

Charlie said something too low and too quiet to distinguish, then turned on his heel and flounced out of the kitchen. A wicked smile spread across his features, and as he passed by Jake and me in the lounge room, he glanced our way...and winked.

Jake sucked in a breath. "Fuck me. That smile should be illegal."

I made a strange choking sound.

"What?" he said, with feigned innocence. "Sheesh, mate, you're the gay one here. I mean, I get that Charlie's kind of like an uncle to you now, but if you don't think that *he's* hot, there's something seriously wrong with you."

"Oh my God, Jake," I groaned. He was leaning on the nearest pillow, so I settled for mashing my face against Shadow's coat instead.

My best friend sighed. "So…that's a 'no' to talking with you about guys?"

I peeked at him from behind a furry black shoulder. Jake's face had always been an open book, but I'd rarely seen him *this* open. This sincere, without a hint of a joke. Cautiously, I straightened. "Aren't you…weirded out?"

Jake's brow creased. "Why would I be weirded out? If anyone is weirded out right now, it's *you*." He tilted his head. "I think I'm actually kind of…jealous."

"*Jealous*?"

The shrug he gave was laden with self-deprecation. "I understand guys—I *am* one, after all. But girls, mate? Girls are like another species. I can't for the life of me figure them out."

"Any girl in particular?"

"Oh no," Jake warned, waggling a finger in my face. "Don't try and change the subject. We're still talking about you. On that note…why haven't you spoken to Remy yet?"

Just like that, my levity vanished. Faded into the aether. I raked my fingers down Shadow's neck and nestled them against her belly. "I haven't been ready," I confessed.

It was going to take a whole lot more courage than I currently possessed to face the boy who meant the world to me—and whom I'd hurt so badly.

315

"Are you going to ask him to take you back?"

"No. I'm not."

Jake's shoulders slumped. "Why not?"

Why not? It would be so easy to ask him, to drop to my knees and beg Remy to give me another chance. I *wanted* to, but David had taught me how to see past my wants and figure out what I *needed*.

And, right now, the two were not the same.

"I need to be okay with me before I can be okay with…any of that," I told my best friend. "And Remy deserves more than what I can give him right now."

"I guess that's fair." Jake put his hand beside mine and scratched at Shadow's flank. "You should call him, though. He…he was there when they…found you. You knew that, right?"

I did know. I'd just tried not to think too much about it.

"It…it's done a number on him, Carter. He's been a bit of a mess, really. I've told him you're on the mend now, but I think…I think he needs to hear it from you."

My heart twisted at the reminder of what I'd put Remy through. Of what I'd put *everyone* through. "Okay," I said. "I'll call him."

And I would.

Later.

Later turned out to be the following Saturday afternoon.

At a time when I knew he'd be home after his regular self-defence class, I shut myself in my bedroom and lay down on the bed. Setting my phone on the pillow by my ear, I switched on the speaker so I could talk to him hands-free.

My heart hammered in my chest.

The dial tone went on forever.

Then—

"Hello?"

I shut my eyes as his voice washed over me, a wave of comfort and warmth and everything that was good in the world.

"Hello? Who is it?"

He mustn't have checked the caller ID before he answered. I could picture him, darting around his room with the phone tucked between his ear and shoulder as he prepared to take a shower. The image was vivid and clear—the opposite of a dream.

I swallowed. "Remy."

A sharp intake of breath from the other end of the line, then silence. He was quiet for so long I wondered if the call had dropped out. "…Carter?"

"It's me."

I heard his bed squeak, imagined him sinking down upon it. "It's…it's so good to hear from you. For a while there, I thought I wouldn't get to…I thought…"

I'm falling for you, he'd said.

And I'd almost taken myself away from him for good.

"I'm here," I said softly. "I'm alive. And Remy?"

"Yeah?"

"I'm gay." Another silence. Another pause. This one even heavier than the last. "After everything," I forged on, "you deserve to hear me say it. But you knew, didn't you? You knew I was only lying to myself."

When he spoke, Remy's voice was so very gentle. "We all lie to ourselves sometimes, mon chou." That nickname, once hated, now sent a shudder through my bones. "But yes. I knew."

My eyes burned. "I wasn't ready for you. I'm sorry."

"You don't need to be sorry. Not for that."

"I *do*," I insisted. "Because I hurt you. I know you kept reminding me it was your idea, but I made you hide who you are, and when I got scared, I physically *hurt* you. You were right to tell me that it wasn't okay. It's *not* okay."

Remy clicked his tongue. "I was hurt, yes. But…I don't know if I'll ever forgive myself for not realising how much you were hurting too."

"It's not your fault. I fooled everyone."

Even myself.

I fooled myself into believing that I could have this forever.

"I just want you to know," I continued, "I'm getting help now. I'm going to be okay." Maybe not quite yet, but someday.

Someday I would be okay.

"I'm glad," Remy said.

I stared up at the ceiling, devoid of my moons and planets and stars. I missed them, for they were a reminder that, though the universe was vast, I was not in it alone.

"You're the best thing that has ever happened to me, Remy," I told him, gulping back the sob that longed to escape, "but I think we shouldn't see each other for a while."

There was a rustle down the line as if Remy had scrunched his bedsheets in his fist. "How long are we talking about here?"

"I don't know," I said honestly. "However long it takes to get my life together."

"If that's what you want."

I almost laughed. "It's not what I *want*. But it's what I need."

"Okay," Remy whispered.

"I need to be sure."

318

"Of what?"

My cheeks were wet. My throat was aching. "Of who I am. Of what I want. I need to be sure that, the next time I see you, I won't be scared to hold your hand. If that's still something you want. I know I had my chance, and I don't expect you to wait for me."

"Oh, Carter," Remy croaked. His voice was thick with tears.

I was destroying us. Again. But this time, at least, it was for the right reasons.

I only wished I could see his face one last time. "The text message I sent you…that night. Do you remember what it said?"

I love you.

His breath caught. "I remember."

"I mean it. I want you to know that I mean every word."

Remy was sobbing now. I couldn't bear the sound of it.

"Goodbye, Remy."

I ended the call and watched the screen go dark.

I had to do it. I had to set him free. Remy Montrose wasn't mine to keep.

But it *hurt*. The grief welled up inside me, thick and black and noxious as it ripped through my chest and screamed from my lips in a cry of anguished despair. I hurled my phone across the room, hard enough to crack the plaster, choking on the taste of my pain.

Then there were arms around me. My uncle's voice in my ear.

It wasn't enough to drown out the sound of my breaking heart.

"Are you sure about this?" Charlie asked.

"I'm sure."

Judging by his death grip on the steering wheel, he wasn't

convinced. "Well, okay. But you know you can call me at any time, right? *Any time*, and I'll come straight over to get you."

I knew he would. Charlie was like a mother bear and I his cub, snarling at all those who'd harm me. We spent most of our time together these days, and while he claimed he was looking for work, he hadn't gone to a single interview yet.

"Thanks," I said, "but I'll be fine."

Which of us I was trying to reassure was anybody's guess.

I sat in the safety of the car for a moment longer, then steeled my nerve and climbed out. The door made a *thunk* as it fell shut behind me, but I didn't look back. With a deep breath and a half-hearted wave at Charlie, I started up the path to the house I'd called home for the first eighteen years of my life.

It no longer felt right to just walk straight in. I didn't live here anymore—hadn't lived here for weeks. But before I could raise a hand to ring the bell, the door swung open to reveal Mum standing on the other side.

As if she'd been waiting for me.

"Thank you for coming," she said.

"Thank you for asking me over."

She stepped aside so I could enter the house, and I followed her into the living area—where I promptly screeched to a halt.

My eyes bulged within their sockets. "What…what's all this?"

"It's for you," Mum said quietly.

Every horizontal surface was crammed full of cards and hampers and drooping flowers. The tables. The mantlepiece. The bookshelf. Even the floor was covered.

"For me?" I breathed.

She nodded. "A lot of people came by with gifts when they…

320

heard what happened. People from church, from your work, from the soup van. Your principal and that Mr Fielding brought some things from the school community."

I gazed out at all the gifts, completely overwhelmed.

"Sean thought it best I keep everything here until you were ready," Mum said, brushing her fingers over the wilting petals of a bluish-purple hydrangea. "I wanted to make sure you saw it all before I got rid of anything."

Got rid of anything—because it had clearly been here for weeks. The air was saturated with the cloying perfume of dying flowers and brown petals littered the ground, sprinkling all those hampers we couldn't possibly have any use for.

Anna would know what to do with them.

The cards, though…there were so many, but I would keep every last one of them. A reminder of all the lives it seemed I'd touched. Of all the people who cared.

It made me feel grateful I'd failed that day.

It made me grateful to be alive.

I turned to face Mum and found her staring at me. No, staring at my arms.

The weather had finally warmed with the onset of summer, and today I wore a tee-shirt. With the last of my bandages removed, my forearms were left bare, exposing the ugly, jagged scars running from my elbows to wrists.

My cheeks heated. "Um…"

"Sorry," she muttered, and her eyes darted back to my face. She looked vaguely ill. "Your arms…how are they?"

"They're weak. Still a bit numb in places. I've started rehab, and I'll probably have more surgery in the new year."

"I'm so sorry, Carter," she said.

I shrugged with far more nonchalance than I felt. "There's no undoing the past."

There was only now—only the future, stretching out before me. I kept my violin at the foot of my bed as a reminder of what I was striving for.

Mum cleared her throat and rubbed her palms against the front of her pants. "Well, would you like anything to eat or drink?"

I almost declined. Almost asked if we could just get on with it. Get this over with.

But then I recalled why I came. Not to help, like she'd asked, but to *heal*.

I licked my lips. "May I have some tea?"

Five minutes later, we'd cleared a space on the dining table and sat nursing our steaming cups. I had to be careful with mine—had to make sure I didn't scald my numb fingers on the hot ceramic—but there was an odd sort of comfort to be found in something as ordinary as having morning tea with my mother.

"I've been seeing a counsellor," Mum said out of the blue. She stared at a spot on the table, her knuckles white around her mug. "I should have done it years ago, but I was...afraid."

I set my own teacup down. "Of what?"

"That they would find something wrong with me." Her jaw clenched. "That they would take you away."

My chest tightened at the admission. Her fear was irrational, perhaps, but I knew all about irrational fears...and their insidious effects. "It's good that you're talking to someone, Mum."

"That night," she went on as if I hadn't spoken, "I didn't leave because of you. I left because of *me*. Because I hit you. I couldn't look at you because all I could see was you sprawled on the ground. I hurt you like those people hurt your uncle."

"It's fine," I mumbled, even though I knew it wasn't. I'd said as much to Remy.

Mum pushed her tea away and met my eyes. "It's not fine, Carter. There is no excuse for what I did. For any of it. But I can't take it back. All I can do is to try to make amends."

"Is that what today is about?"

"In part." Tension crawled down her neck and settled in her shoulders. "It's also because...I can't do this alone."

I nodded. "Shall we get started then?"

I was shocked when I learned that Mum was selling the house. The thought of auctioning off the home that Dad had worked so hard to provide for us—of never again walking through its rooms and soaking in the imprints of those we'd lost—was an ache that was difficult to bear.

But I knew, deep down, that it was for the best. The house was too big for Mum alone, and it was filled with too many ghosts.

So I'd accepted her offer to help pack our things away, and that was how I found myself standing beside her on the threshold of Miles' room, both of us hesitating to take that first step.

The first step was always the hardest. The first step hurt the most.

We started with his clothes. The majority we folded into garbage bags to donate, but some we put aside to keep. His school blazer, with all his accolades embroidered on the breast pocket. His favourite tee-shirt, which Megs had given him for Valentine's Day. His football uniform, still smeared with grass stains that Mum had never been able to wash out.

When the wardrobe and dresser stood empty, we moved on to

the rest: the books, the photos, the knickknacks on his shelves, lined up in perfect rows.

I considered each item at length. Those to keep went into one box, those to donate into another. I yearned to keep it all, so every time I placed an item in the box to give away, the weight in my chest grew heavier.

I tried to breathe through the pain, but it was becoming harder by the minute. Miles' life was melting off these walls, and it felt *wrong*.

It felt like letting go.

I paused when I reached his desk. A pair of wooden picture frames sat in one corner, angled towards the centre so he could see them while he worked. The first was the picture of Miles and Megs—the one I'd snapped at Katie for touching all those months ago.

The second picture, beside it, was of the two of us.

Christmas Eve had been sweltering that year, hot enough that neither of us was able to sleep. We snuck out into the lounge room in nothing but our underwear and switched on the TV, keeping the volume low, so we didn't wake our parents.

Eventually we'd drifted off, my head on Miles' shoulder and his head on top of mine. That was how Mum and Dad found us on Christmas morning. That was the photo they took.

It was the last Christmas we had together.

I picked up the frame and stared at my brother's sleeping face.

Letting go, I realised, wasn't the same as forgetting. I could never forget Miles, could never forget all the good times we'd shared. I could never forget how much I loved him—how much I would always love him.

And I would never *want* to forget.

I would carry this piece of him with me forever, safe inside my heart, and I would let it be enough. It *had* to be enough because that was all there was.

The memories.

"It was my fault," Mum whispered.

I whirled around to find her at my shoulder. "What was?"

Her expression was stricken as she gazed at the photo in my hand. "If I hadn't forgotten to buy those Pringles, then they would still be alive."

I fought to keep the shock off my face.

Never—not once—had I thought about it like that. Dad and Miles had been out fetching the Pringles that Mum forgot to buy when they were struck by the car that killed them, but I'd never blamed *her* for the accident.

It had never crossed my mind that she might blame herself.

We were so alike in so many ways. Ashamed and blaming ourselves for things outside our control. Suffering and struggling to cope with the pain that festered within. Lost and unable to find our way forwards.

But, maybe, we could find our way forwards together.

I placed the frame back down on the desk and hugged her.

Mum stiffened at first. She'd never been one for close contact, not even before our lives took their turn, but I held her close and held her still until she relaxed and hugged me back.

"I miss them too," I said into her ear. "So much that sometimes I can't breathe. But Mum...what happened to them wasn't your fault."

Her arms tightened. Then she let me go.

It would take more than my words to convince her.

We went back to our task in silence, but it was an easy silence now. Lighter, as if we'd finally come to realise that we weren't ruined, weren't alone.

Not while we still had each other.

When we were done, we stacked the boxes and bags up against one wall and stood back to examine our handiwork. The sudden starkness of the room was confronting, almost horrifying, but there was something kind of hopeful about it too.

An empty room. A blank canvas.

A clean slate.

My bedroom was next on the list. There wasn't much in there since Sean and Charlie had moved most of my things to their place while I was in the facility. It took all of twenty minutes to pack up the last few bits and pieces.

Then there was only one thing left.

I looked up at the glow-in-the-dark galaxy spread across my ceiling.

Mum followed my gaze. "I'll get the ladder," she said.

I was still staring up at it—at all those suns and moons and planets and stars—when she returned. "Do you remember where they came from?" she asked quietly.

I shook my head.

"Miles won the first set at the school fair." Her voice was fond and soft. "You were so jealous and kept hinting that he was too old at twelve to fully appreciate them. So he gave them to you."

Of course he did.

"He used his own pocket money to buy more of them, until the whole ceiling was covered. You didn't stop talking about it for months."

The galaxy blurred before my eyes. "I want to take them home with me."

No—letting go did not mean forgetting. And I wanted to always remember this.

"Okay," my mother said.

And together, we set up the ladder.

Together, we tore down the stars.

Surrender

I can't forget the last words my brother said to me.

You know I'll always be here for you, right?

They bounce around in my skull like an echo off the walls of a steel drum, only the sound never fades. Never. It's like he's cradled there, in a vacuum, so the echoes will last forever.

No matter what happens next year, I'll be here.

But Miles didn't see the next year.

I always knew he would leave me one day, just not like that. Never like that. I've learned the universe can be cruel, even to someone like my brother.

I'll always be here for you. I promise.

It was the first time he'd ever lied to me. It was the last time he ever had the chance. He and Dad walked out the door, and they never came home again.

Miles never meant to lie. He never meant to leave me. Fate would have dragged him screaming from this world and, wherever he is now, I know there's a piece of him that's missing.

Because it lives on inside of me.

I sit by the pond and breathe in. Breathe deep. The sun beats down in a shower of golden light, and the water shimmers as a faint breeze ripples across its surface.

I love it here. Love watching the fish dart in and out of the reeds. It's the perfect place to sit and work on the exercises that should strengthen my arms—that *will* strengthen my arms.

I *will* play my violin again.

"Carter."

My heart starts beating like crazy, and I lower my hands to my lap. I don't have to turn to know it's him.

I turn anyway.

He wears cargo shorts and a tight black tee-shirt. Azure streaks mottle his pale blond hair, and his piercings glint like diamonds as the light strikes his equally pale skin.

For a moment, I can't breathe.

Remy Montrose is even more beautiful than I remember in my dreams.

"May I sit down?" he asks.

I shuffle over to make room for him at the water's edge.

He sits. He's looking at me. He's looking at my scars.

"They're ugly, aren't they?" My voice is hoarse.

But Remy shakes his head, and he does not look away. "Nothing about you is ugly, Carter." Then he does something that no one has done before: he reaches out and touches them.

I watch as his fingers skate across the shiny skin. There's no sensation in the scar tissue, but I still *feel* his touch. In my heart. Shivering down my neck. Pooling at the base of my spine.

When he's finished mapping out the wounds of my past, he

drops his hands and skewers me with those eyes I've missed so much. "How are you?"

It's a loaded question, but I tell him I'm well. It's not a lie.

"I've missed you," Remy says.

"I've missed you too."

Not a day has gone by when I haven't thought of him. Staying away these past few months has been one of the hardest things I've ever had to endure.

But it was the right thing.

I have grown in our time apart. I imagine so has he.

"I want to know," Remy says quietly, "whether there's any hope for us." His fingers clench in the grass like he wants to yank the soft green blades out by their roots, but he doesn't. He holds perfectly still, awaiting my response.

If my heart beats any faster, I think I might pass out. "You're willing to give me a second chance?"

"Yes." No hesitation. No doubt.

Until this moment, I haven't let myself believe he wants this as much as I do.

"I'm not all magically cured," I warn him because he needs to know what he's getting into. I will not lead him into the dark again. "I'm on medication now, but sometimes there are still bad days."

"Jake told me." He unwinds his fists from the grass. Inches closer. Bites the lip that I want to taste for myself. "I know there will be challenges, but I want to try. You're worth it, mon chou."

I can't stop the smile from blooming. I don't think I have ever smiled this wide. "In that case…will you let me take you to dinner tonight?"

Remy ducks his head and peers up at me through his lashes. It's a coy look—a teasing look. "So soon? What will everyone think?"

"They'll think I'm crazy about you."

There's a twinkle in his eye. "All right," he says. "But you're paying."

"Deal." I lean a little closer. Hear his breath catch.

And when Remy takes my hand, I don't pull away.

It's a promise.

A vow that I'll keep holding up the sky.

If you—or anyone you know—are affected by any of the issues portrayed in *Holding Up the Sky*, you are not alone. There are many organisations out there who can help you.

IN AUSTRALIA, THESE INCLUDE:

Suicide Call Back Service (crisis support)
1300 659 467 • suicidecallbackservice.org.au

Lifeline (suicide prevention)
13 11 14 • lifeline.org.au

Kids Helpline (youth counselling)
1800 551 800 • kidshelpline.com.au

Beyond Blue (mental health support)
1300 224 636 • beyondblue.org.au

QLife (support for LGBTQI+ Australians)
1800 184 527 • qlife.org.au

Griefline (grief and loss support)
1300 845 745 • griefline.org.au

If there is an emergency where someone's life is in danger or at immediate risk of harm, you should call emergency services. In Australia, this number is **000**.

Acknowledgements

I can't tell you how many times I've imagined this moment. The one where I sit before my trusty laptop—my closest companion these last few years—and write the acknowledgements for my first published book. Now that the moment is here, a part of me doesn't know what to say.

What words can possibly capture what it's like to fulfil your longest-held dream?

Of course, the *other* part of me is an author, so not knowing what to say is generally a temporary problem.

The idea for *Holding Up the Sky* came to me all the way back in 2014, when I was a young university student just starting to find her way in the world. Since then, this story has undergone multiple drafts and dozens of read-throughs, occupying so much of my time and so many of my thoughts that it feels surreal to finally be…done.

The first person I need to thank is you. Yes, *you*: my reader. At this very moment, you are holding my dream in your hands, and I can't express how grateful I am that you gave my book a chance. So, whether you enjoyed it or not, thank you from the bottom of my heart.

Publishing a book is my no means a solitary experience, and I would not have reached this point without my beta readers Lorraine Ambers, Adina Denner, and D. Allyson Howlett. You were the first "strangers" I ever let read my work, and your constructive advice and words of encouragement gave me the confidence I needed to follow this path to its end. And I think it's safe to say we're no longer strangers, either!

To my editor, Charlie Knight: thank you for your frank and fearless feedback, for fixing my commas and em-dashes, and the lovely comments that banished the last of my doubts.

To Franziska Stern: thank you for this stunning book cover! I am in awe of the way you turned my mess of ideas into such a perfect concept, and you were an absolute delight to work with.

I also appreciate the support I've received from the online writing community. From my first tentative steps into the world of blogging in 2017, to the incredible social media discussions in the lead-up to this book's release, and everything else in between, I have learned so much from you all and treasure every moment you've given me.

But none of this would have been possible without my family and friends.

The Dream Team (you know who you are) have had a front-row seat to a large portion of my writing journey, and I wouldn't have it any other way. Thanks, guys, for your friendship, for reading that million-word saga I wrote in high school, and for not minding when I disappear down the writing rabbit hole for months and months on end.

As for my parents and brother...well, this is where the words dry up again. I'm very lucky to have grown up with so much love and the support to follow wherever my dreams might lead. They've taken me to some interesting places so far, but without your guidance—and your patience—I don't know where I'd be. I honestly could not ask for a better family.

And, finally, to my nanna. I will never forget that I wrote my first "novel" at your kitchen table, that you always had pencils and a stack of paper ready for me when I came around, that you were the first to brag about what I was doing, whether it was writing-related or not. I wish you could have read this book, but I know you would have been proud.

For you, Nanna, I vow that I'll keep holding up the sky.

About the Author

Rebecca Alasdair lives in Melbourne, Australia and has been writing from the moment she learned to hold a pencil. Public sector worker by day, teller of stories by night, she loves dogs, coffee, and researching everything under the sun.

When she's not carving out time for her authorly pursuits, she can be found reading until the dawn light peeks through the curtains, reorganising her rainbow-coloured bookshelves, or tending to her many, many plant children.

rebeccaalasdair.com

CPSIA information can be obtained
at www.ICGtesting.com
Printed in the USA
LVHW042220311022
732007LV00002B/179